THE BEAST TALE SCROLLS

Raising Kings

Book 2

JOAN WALSH

CONTENTS

RAISING KINGS

He changes the time and the season; He removes kings and raises up kings; He gives wisdom to the wise and knowledge to those who have understanding. He reveals deep and secret things. He knows what is in the darkness, and light dwells with him. Daniel 2: 21

FOR

GRANDMA ANNA THORESON

AND

ANN HANCOCK

WHO ALWAYS WALKED IN THE LIGHT

CHAPTER 1
RUMORS OF WAR AND HUMORS OF WAR

As was his custom, Khoa was on the rise above the valley of the Wilds making his rounds. It had been the practice of the white wolf to come to the topmost hill every morning. From here he could survey the valley below. Most mornings he would wait until the sun had risen high enough to burn off the mist from the lakes and the valley before heading back down.

Today Khoa paced back and forth over the rise. There was something that disquieted him. He looked again in back of where he stood, back to where the forest lay. Nothing was stirring but the wind, which now and then rustled the leaves into piles about the forest floor, and then dispersed them again. It was nature breathing in and out. There had not been enough rain this spring to mat the leaves to the ground. In the intermittent gusts of wind, the rustling leaves created a watchful eeriness in the wolf.

Khoa turned to look again at the Wilds below and out over the lake. He stood facing into the wind. Only the mist rose up. All seemed quiet, too quiet, but it spoke loudly to him. Khoa kept searching over the lake. Something was out of place, but what was it? Then it came to him. There were no birds hovering over the lake, skimming gracefully over its surface, and seizing their prey almost as if in a single motion. Nothing stirred. It was like every animal, every creature was holding its breath.

Were they waiting, too, for the return of Tor? It worried Khoa that Tor and his army were weeks late in arriving from their patrol to the north in the Blackstone Mountains. There had been reports of clashes with dark wolves who had begun to take over towns from the white and mixed wolves. Some of these animals had managed to escape, and now lived among them in the Wilds. They were pouring in faster than the town could absorb them. Tor and the warriors had gone to verify the rumors.

Khoa ran through the refuges stories in his mind as he watched them in their settlements on the edges of the Wilds. Their stories were similar. Mixed and dark wolves had begun to move into their towns. The newcomers had lived peacefully at first and accepted the rules. Little by little, these foreigners had demanded that they have rights just like all the other animals.

"We animals thought that the newcomers were making ant hills into mole hills. We didn't know what they were talking about because they were not kept from doing anything in our towns, but we agreed that they should have whatever rights they wanted. It was a way to keep peace," one wolf had told them.

"They wanted their spots on the school tribunal, the city tribunal, and the worship tribunals. One by one, issues came up," Bayer continued. "On the school tribunal, they claimed that teaching the Way in text books was distressing for those students who didn't practice it and wanted all mention of it taken out. Over the years any mention of the Way was removed from all books and now can only be spoken of in the cathedrals, not among the diverse population."

The animals were all in agreement. "Yes, and in the city tribunals the newcomers said the mixed wolves weren't being treated equally. Then, and this still seems strange to me, within a few days a wolf, who was of a mixed breed, was arrested for stealing. He was let go after agreeing to repay the beavers for the fish and clams he had taken, but within hours the leaders of the 'Raiders,' as they called themselves, were rioting in the streets claiming that he had been beaten almost to death by vigilante citizens."

The others nodded their agreement with someone saying, "We had never known any animal among us to attack anyone and we just couldn't see why it would happen of a sudden."

"Tell them what you know, Leap," Bayer encouraged the deer, who was standing beside him, to step forward and tell his story.

"Next, it was the fact that the only worship available was the Way. They wanted their religion, 'All Ways' to be accepted and honored. They told the town that it was a fairer religion and didn't brag about being the only one that had answers, but gave freedom to any form of worship. They carried banners that proclaimed 'Many gods, Not one," and 'All gods or No gods."

"It sounds like things became fair to all except those who practiced the Way," Tor said.

They animals nodded their agreement.

"One day they brought up the fact that the town was not safe, that the city militia wasn't doing its job. We regular town's animals couldn't see their reasoning, but before we could settle the matter our cubs and babies began to disappear. The wolves went on a rampage, telling the town that what they had claimed about it not being a safe place to live was true. The old way of protection needed to be thrown out and their way adopted, they said. They claimed to have talked with the enemy factions of wolves in secret to bargain a peace treaty and keep our babies safe. It was war or peace, they said. We could keep peace if we let them change our laws to fit their model of fairness, or we could fight them. They claimed those who practiced the Way were bigots and sought to oppress all others," the deer explained.

Bayer took up where he left off and added, "The town wanted peace at any price by this time, and told them to make their deal. The next morning an army of dark troops lined our streets. Shops, offices and even the worship center had signs that said, 'Closed for your protection.' No one was allowed on the streets. Those of us who still had our children, left before they could be stolen."

A gust of wind roused him from his thoughts. What had Tor said about the strategy used by the wolves in making the towns submit to them without a fight? Create a crisis and solve it. Create another crisis and solve it, and then another and another.

This had a snowball effect on the public and created a sense of desperation in them Tor had told the assembly. The only cost had been that the animals had given their freedoms away an inch at a time during each faked crisis by letting the dark wolves solve the crisis under the guise of protecting them. This cycle actually got animals to be willing participants in helping the new regime take over; gave power to them unanimously without a struggle.

The dark wolves were again at their door step. They just had a new method. The new strategy used peaceful, covert means instead of open acts of hostility, which made it difficult to tell they were actually waging war. Instead, it made them look like pacemakers, but only at the onset. By the time the town's animals realized what was happening, it was too late; the dark wolves were in power. Like Tor had said, "They've gotten smarter."

Khoa turned once again to look behind him, to look northward. No warriors of the white wolves could be seen returning home. What could be keeping them? Somewhere in the distance were the Blackstone Mountains. Is that what the wind was telling him, warning him about? Yes, it was speaking to him about things that no animal, wolf, or otherwise could stop.

So what was it telling him he was supposed to do if he couldn't stop it? He sensed there were impossible odds assembling, coming together somewhere in the distance. Khoa looked up into the sky. The sun was still low in its arc, having just risen in the east. Yes, what he was feeling moved by a force like the path set by the sun, and it was just as immutable.

That morning Pieces was up early and just coming over the rise when he saw Khoa standing on the summit. For a moment the rabbit was startled by an odd feeling of familiarity that seeing the lone wolf brought to him. Why was it so disturbing this morning? The uneasiness of the thought kept him from moving a muscle one way or the other. He felt paralyzed. What was it? Then it came to him. It was the stories his mother had told him about Khoas' father, and their life before the Great War and before their sudden departure from the Wilds. A fear gnawed at the old rabbit. He had not moved from his spot, but Khoa had sensed him immediately and acknowledged his presence.

"Pieces, you're up early."

Although the rabbit heard his friend, it took a while for him to respond. "I didn't sleep well last night."

"You're moving a little slow this morning," Khoa agreed.

"Yeppers," Pieces said trying to shake off his feelings of uneasiness. "How about you? You're up earlier than usual, too."

"I thought it best to do my pacing up here away from Ani."

"Ah." The rabbits voice was distant, low, and quite unlike him.

When Khoa didn't answer, the rabbit continued. "Seems more like fall than early spring, doesn't it?" he asked, looking up at his favorite tree. "No buds out yet, either."

Khoa stared at his friend. "Are you sure you're alright? I mean, anything in particular bothering you?"

Pieces shook his head. "Just a queasiness in my stomach is all." He looked briefly at Khoa and then away. He didn't want to worry him. An expectant father didn't need to hear the alarms that ran through an old rabbits mind.

"Bad clover?" Khoa laughed.

"Let's hope so. That's why I came all the way up here. I need some of the sweet stuff that grows underneath this oak, but it doesn't look like there's any to be had."

Pieces couldn't take his eyes off the wolf's face. They stood looking at each other.

"Somethings up. You're staring at me."

"Sorry, Khoa. It's just that when I saw you standing alone here I couldn't help but think back to all the stories my mother had told me about your father. He used to stand just where you are now."

Khoa looked away from the rabbit and back out over the lake below them.

The rabbit shivered. "I wish this fog would hurry and lift."

Khoa wished so, too. A slight wind blew against him. It was colder than it had been the moment before. It spoke of war, of change, of things he thought he would never face again. He looked back at Pieces and he knew what the rabbit had not said out loud to him.

"This is where my father stood that morning before the Great Fire and the Great War began, isn't it?"

"Yes," was all Pieces answered, still looking into the distance where the wolf looked. Remembering that story deepened the feelings of dread he already felt.

"That was the day the world changed, fell apart," Pieces answered, nodding. "Your father felt that change coming. He just didn't know what it meant. At least that is what my mother and the others who told the story related to us."

"Yes, change. I feel it today. I'm not sure I'm ready to become a parent. Ani is. She takes everything in stride. I need to learn that from her."

The wind blew against him. 'No, listen,' it said. 'There is something more.' The voice had caught him off guard. It hadn't spoken to him this insistently for quite some time. He felt it had something to do with an idea he had read in the Book.

He turned to Pieces. "You've helped me to begin to understand something I read in the book that I didn't grasp all the way."

"I have?" the old rabbit asked more than a little surprised.

"What?"

"One of the truths in the Book says, 'watch for a sign in nature for it will repeat itself in the spirit.'

"That's beyond me."

"No, Pieces. You of all animals should understand it."

"How so?"

"Remember when the clouds covered us and ran ahead and you were scared of its shadow?"

"Yeppers. It turned me cold inside."

"Well, that's the first part, the part the Alpha reveals in nature. The warning, the omen."

He waited for the rabbit to nod.

"Then remember what happened after that?"

"Yeppers. The Venger came."

"That's the event that took place, that repeated itself in the spirit."

"Hmm. I see, but I don't."

"Let me put it this way, Pieces. The first was an omen of something bad, the shadow of the great bird that took away the light of the sun. It was tangible. You could see it in nature, but nothing happened that day."

Pieces waited quietly for the wolf to go on.

"The second happening was that shadow in its repeating form, its real form. Venger. He tried to take the light out of all animals in their spirit, their heart for real."

"I can see it afterward, but how do you tell before?"

"That's part of the mystery I'm trying to unravel. Like the Book says, 'the Great Wolf gives mysteries and it is the work of animals to divine them.' "

"Divine?"

"Understand, figure them out."

"Can I practice with you?"

"You have a knack for it, Pieces."

"I do?"

"Yes, you sense things."

"Is feeling the same as seeing?"

"In a way I think it is, but remember, it speaks to you quickly and only once. Mostly when you're not ready for it."

"I felt like that this morning when I came up here. Is that what you mean? Is that why we miss it?"

Before Khoa could answer the rabbit, he heard Zen, who was acting as midwife, calling to him from the cave. As he turned towards Pieces, the rabbit noted a pleading in his eyes. He could see the wolf was torn between answering his question and fulfilling his duty to Ani. "It's time Pieces. The cubs are coming. "

"Go on. You have a higher calling than to answer the questions of a foolish old rabbit. We'll talk another time," but the feeling that something was about to happen wouldn't let go of him.

As Pieces watched Khoa bound off the rise, he caught a glimpse of something dark overhead and stepped back. Talk about shadows, he thought, and looked skyward to see a family of owls coming in to land in front of where he stood. They seemed to be watching after Khoa and staring towards the crowd that had gathered at the entrance of the cave.

"You'd think these cubs were the only babies to be born in the Wilds, or in the world for that matter," the old mother owl commented as she tramped up and down in front of her brood. The owl family seemed to take no notice of Pieces under the tree even though they were within touching distance of him.

Pieces recognized the old owl. It was Oh-Oh, who had made the comment. They had come, like so many others, seeking refuge from the war being waged by the dark wolves. They had come, too, to see what all the hub bub was about. Was there a king or wasn't there? The old owls name was really Who-Who, but she was a nosy sort of a flyer and every animal that saw her soaring above them would turn to warn others who were nearby by saying, "Oh, oh," and the name just sort of stuck. She wasn't one of Pieces' favorite newcomers in the Wilds.

Pieces was irritated and angered by the owl's comments. Deciding to set the record straight he said, "Of course they aren't the only babies to be born in the Wilds. It's spring. There were many white wolves born this spring. Tor and Zen had four cubs, Scout and Sara had their trio of girls, Fisher and his new bride, KT, had six." Pieces hopped a little closer to the owl, who continued to look at him with popping eyes. "Hmmmm," she hooted.

"Yeppers. Almost fifty new wolves. A hundred or more babies if you count all the other species in the Wilds," he boasted.

Oh-Oh ignored Pieces' census of the new births and turned back to her owlets and husband as one of her babies said, "There must be hundreds of gifts piled outside that cave, mama."

"Thousands," his brother hooted.

"Can we go down and see them?" one of the other owlets asked, which seemed to agitate the mother owl further.

"I've never have seen such a fuss made about a few wolves coming into the world."

What Oh-Oh was referring to was the fact that everyone in the Wilds had come by the little cave and brought gifts which were stacked two mountains high. They had all made a personal call on the wolf family.

"Never have seen such a fuss," the owl repeated in her mocking tone.

"He let you stay here didn't he? Build your homes here,

didn't he?" Pieces asked her.

The owl kept her silence. Pieces hopped around to see her face. "Enough said. You wouldn't have stayed in the Wilds if you didn't think Khoa could protect you. You might be tolerant of our customs here and Khoa."

"He's the king, you know," her mate, Swoop, reminded her, but he knew it didn't carry much weight with her.

Oh-Oh turned away from the old rabbit and motioned to Swoop and he took flight, seizing Pieces in his talons.

"Why does everything happen to me?" the rabbit asked in a low voice.

"I'm just giving you a ride down to where all the excitement is. I mean you no harm," Swoop said, looking down at him.

"Such a fuss over some animals come into the world," Pieces heard mother Oh-Oh repeating behind them.

"It's her way. Try not to pay her too much mind," Swoop said.

"He made you and all the others welcome here, didn't he? He fed you and helped you build your homes, didn't he?" Pieces called back to Oh-Oh.

The owl still didn't answer and Pieces looked up at Swoop and directed, "Put me down right there where Khoa is."

"The white wolf king?" Swoop asked.

"Yeppers, the king." At least Swoop had respect for their customs.

Directly after Pieces was set loose on the ground, he hopped over by Khoa and began walking back and forth with him to show his support and prove to the owl family that he was a friend of the kings. The pair tramped up and down for some time before Serious called out, "Sit down, Khoa. You're wearing a hole in the earth."

"Yes, I'm out of breath," puffed Pieces, pacing alongside of Khoa, turning when Khoa turned, stopping when Khoa stopped.

"You sit down, too, Pieces. You're not the father."

"No, but I'm the grandfather."

"How long is this going to take? We've been waiting all night," Khoa said aloud. He was thinking so hard that the sound of his own voice startled him.

"Yeppers," Pieces said, turning to Serious. He walked over to him and stood directly in front of his friend. "You're the teacher. You're supposed to know these things. You know everything else. Why don't you know this?" he demanded.

"Yes, come on. I'd like to hear this myself," said Washer, bursting in through the crowd that was gathered around the cave. He was dragging a line of fish with him.

"Well," Serious paused and then continued with a shrug. "It takes as long as it takes."

The raccoon was shaking his head in disgust. "That's no answer. We're paying you too much if that's the best you can come up with."

"Nature has her own ideas. Some things don't have a definite answer."

Then Serious, noticing the look of disbelief on the raccoon's face, added, "Just take my word for it. After all, I am the teacher." It was a proclamation in partial defense of himself.

"Yes, and you know everything," Washer said, irritated, and waved back at him without looking, "until someone asks you a question."

Washer stood facing the throng of animals. "I brought supper for everyone," he announced, dropping the line of fish by the crowd. He turned and pulled a few fish off the line and threw one over to Serious. "You better eat this."

Serious picked up the fish and threw it back at Washer. "I'm a rabbit. Keep your brack'n'snaffle, brack'n'fraffle fish. I need greens. Carrots. Crunch cruncher stuff."

"It used to be good enough for you."

"That was in hard times. You eat what you have to. I ate enough fish to last a lifetime. You need to be considerate of us animals who don't eat fish. You need to be considerate of me as a teacher. You're not. Never have been."

It took everything inside the young rabbit not to begin stomping his hind leg. He was getting into that tone, that cadence of short words. He was determined not to let the raccoon know he had gotten the best of him by thumping.

"I am telling you right now that birth doesn't happen on a time schedule. You can't say, Oh, by the way, the little cubs will arrive at 9:15. Nature doesn't have a time schedule for such things," the rabbit continued. By now he was holding his back leg still with his paw. "I shouldn't have to explain such things."

"I wasn't asking for an exact time. I know they don't come at some exact time like 9:15. I was just asking for a general idea about how long it usually takes," Washer answered, picking the fish up and hurling it back towards his friend.

"There is no timetable for such things, general or otherwise," Serious yelled back. By now he was almost spitting the words out. Just as he finished talking, the fish struck him in the stomach. He hadn't seen it coming.

"At least you're not thumping," Washer complimented him. "You've risen above it."

"That does it!" the rabbit warned and Serious was on the raccoon in an instant, slapping him about his head and body with the fish. Scales and small pieces of flesh littered the air. Serious hit him over and over until the fish slipped out of his paws, and then he began pounding at the raccoon with his back kickers. "You eat it," he was screaming. "You inconsiderate…. ignorant….. black faced…. black hearted….black footed….." Here the rabbit paused for an instant, unable to find another word to describe his friend, and then just blurted, "rascal."

Someone in the crowd yelled, "He doesn't want fish, Washer," which sent the gathering into roars of laughter.

Another animal called out, "Let him thump, next time. It's safer."

Everyone had read the sign above the entrance to the schoolhouse and knew Washer was the one who had placed it there, though Pieces had been blamed for it at first. It had since been taken down, but a new sign had been placed a few days ago, which had reinvigorated the tenseness between them.

Washer was so dumbfounded by the rabbits' antics that he was unable to move. He was completely defenseless. Finally, Bigger came and picked up Serious and carried him away still kicking and yelling. The bear held him away from his body so the rabbit couldn't hurt him.

"He's just all nerves what with the cubs being born and all," the bear called back to the crowd.

There were chuckles and titters all around.

Washer stared down at the fish lying at his feet. "No one can eat this fish, now," he said quietly, picking the fish scales out of his fur and brushing them off in downward motions. "It hasn't even been washed."

Just then the old stork, Sticks, appeared in the entrance to the cave. His irritated manner and self-important air was apparent to all. Sticks had arrived with an attitude of scoffing and it hadn't changed. When he had first alit by the small cave he had said, "I was told that these were offspring of the king. I must be lost. Where's the palace?"

When no one answered him, the great bird looked around at the crowd, raised up higher on his legs, and began flapping at them.

Springer, the deer, came forward. "There is no palace, but this is the right cave. The king lives here."

Sticks at first had refused to help deliver the cubs because he was the chief stork and these cubs were ordinary and not the king's as he had been led to believe. It was Zen's teeth snapping around the small of his neck that made him change his mind.

It was nearly five hours later when the great stork reappeared. His manner was more arrogant and abrupt than before, having been forced to deliver the cubs by Zen against his will.

"How many?" came the cries.

"Is Ani alright?"

"Can we see them?"

Sticks wiped his brow and then flapped his wings at the approaching crowd. He clearly was not paying heed to any of their questions. "Back off. I don't want any of your germs to get on me."

When the throng crowded in closer, Sticks ran forward,

making a great motion and noise with his wings. "Get back, I said. Father only. Where's the father? I don't even see a wolf here. I need a wolf father for these five new cubs."

"Khoa!" everyone began calling.

"Where is he?" the animals began asking.

"Someone went to get him hours ago."

From the back of the crowd Khoa heard his name, and felt Pieces pushing him from behind.

"Five," he kept saying over and over, and looking behind at his friend.

"Yeppers, five. Now get going," came Pieces' winded voice.

"Make way. Move," the rabbit scolded, waving at the mob.

Slowly the crowd parted, and Khoa made his way through them. His steps were slow and tentative. The wolf was aware enough to sense the animals were staring at him with their mouths hung open. He couldn't help his plodding movements. His feet felt like they weighed a thousand pounds each. It took a tremendous effort on his part to struggle forward. Everything seemed to be happening in slow motion.

"Here I am," Khoa managed, his voice cracking with each word. With that said, he fainted dead away.

The stork moved up to the wolf, and looked down over him. "First timer, huh?"

Everyone nodded, and Pieces exclaimed, "Yeppers. You can see, can't you?"

"I thought he was the king," said Sticks. The bird stood on one leg and shook it, and then stretched his wings leaving his wide mouth open. It was clear that this stork meant to do things in his own time and on his own terms. He closed his beak, shook his head and muttered condescendingly, "Not very kingly, if you ask me. He's filthy."

"That's because he's been pacing back and forth in the mud wait'in for you," Pieces said, stepping up to the stork.

After the gasps from the crowd quieted, the bird asked, "Any smelling salts around?" Sticks looked matter of factly at the crowd, and blatantly over the head of Pieces. The rabbit was not about to let the storks snubbing of him go unchallenged. Pieces had had enough of this bird, and he waved back at the raccoon and motioned for him to look down at his feet. Washer did so and smiled knowingly.

In a second, an object flew through the air and landed at the stork's feet. It was the battered fish.

"Try this," a voice called out. It was Washer.

"I see others don't respect this so called wolf king, either," the stork said, looking straight into the old rabbit's eyes.

"Oh, we respect our king. The dead fish is for you. It's yours. Payment in full," Pieces replied and the other animals in the crowd rushed in on the stork as he struggled to take flight.

"Let him go," called Zen from the cave entrance.

Once he was safely in the air, the bird called down, "I won't be back. No stork will deliver here. I can assure you of that."

"Yes, and make sure you tell them that roasted stork tastes like duck, too," Washer yelled back.

The great stork dove down over them as they tended to Khoa. "King? Look at him lying in a heap. Why, that wolf is no more of a king than I am."

"What would you know of kings?" Pieces yelled up at him. "He has a good heart."

Washer came up alongside of Pieces and put his arm around him. "You amaze me sometimes, old rabbit."

The rabbit just shook his head and said worriedly, "This doesn't bode well. That's two bad omens in a day. What's next? They come in three's, you know."

"Only if you can count," the raccoon said.

CHAPTER 2
PIERCING THE LIGHT

It was just into early summer and the meadows were full in bloom. Khoa looked at the litheness of the purple and white columbines as they waved among the slender light green grasses in the wind and the daintiness of the yellow and blue violets that sprouted amid them. The colors were light and airy shades, and the blue in the violets matched the color of Ani's eyes. Honey comb butterflies and Indian paintbrush flowers added a stark splash of red that caught his eye. Sand dune sunflowers with their red heads and daisy like petals gave a vibrant yellow to the mix. It was a startling array of colors that stretched clear to the base of the foothills in the distance. He loved to lie in the midst of the field. It brought a sense of reverence to his being. It was quiet, and when the wind breathed gently through the field of flowers, they tippled ever so slightly forward; bowing as if they sensed the Great Wolf was passing by.

Today the white wolf found that even the meadow with its brightness failed to raise the veil which haunted his spirits. He had been given to dreams in the weeks since Tor was gone which carried over into his waking life; taking the lightness and the joy out of his fatherhood.

A voice spoke within him, reassuring him. 'It is not the time, Khoa. The sun will set as usual. Your life will go on as it has. Things will be as they have been.' It struck him that these were strange thoughts, not like his usual ones, not his own voice. It was familiar, yet something about it had left him off balance. He was trying to discern what that odd feeling was when he saw Ani, Zen, and the cubs coming out of the trees below the ridge. The voice and the thoughts vanished as if he had never heard them.

When Tor left, it had been arranged that Zen and the cubs would stay in the cave with Khoa's family. They all shared in the cub's development. Khoa showed them how to challenge one another in play by nipping at their heels; teasing them to chase him. When they caught him, he would turn suddenly, and facing them, he would pounce towards them until they pounced back. Ani and Zen showed them how and where to fish and what the names of the flowers in the meadows were. At night he and his brother had taught them about the stories in the skies and about the Great Wolf who gives all life. Before Tor had left they had spent each night together by the cave and Khoa had watched his brother raise his cubs so he would know what to do when his time came. He now carried on what he had seen Tor do.

In the eighth week they took the cubs to the water fall and christened them. All five cubs, Tristian, Arro, Savor, Anna, and Jen were pledged to follow the Way just as Tor had committed his four cubs before he left. Zen and her cubs had come for the witnessing as Khoa and Ani had come to witness Challenger, TJ (Tor Jr.), Hunter, and Ginny's' pledges the month before.

As his cubs stood in the water, Khoa read: "Now count your spirits among the lions in the House of Alexander, whose teeth are sharp as swords and whose word is truth. You have given oath to the Great Wolf. Know he walks on the mountains and in the tall grasses, in the shadows of the valleys, and in the dry lands. Trust in his heart, trust in his power, trust in his love."

That night Khoa toured the perimeters of the Wilds until he was tired enough to sleep. There was too much happening all at once and he couldn't seem to get a hold of it. The voice kept whispering, 'Dark days are ahead. Prepare. You have let them come. You have not listened.' The more insistent the voice became, the more he seemed to resist it. This was supposed to be a time of joy and celebration and happiness, yet everything was falling apart. Ani was steady and unwavering and seemed to be able to push the unimportant issues into the background. He was trying, but having Tor gone and the nine cubs to look after was more responsibility than he felt ready for. There were many everyday details which demanded his attention. Everything that went on seemed to be out of his hands. Nothing was under his control. What to do with all the new arrivals, the tiff between Washer and Serious seemed to grow wider as the weeks passed, and whether or not to send a unit after Tor. Why had Tor not sent a runner back? It had been months. Whenever he thought about Tor, a feeling of inaction paralyzed him with fear. He had to do something, anything that was action. It's time, he told himself. In the morning he would send a runner or go himself even if he had promised Tor not to risk coming after him. With that resolved, he trotted back home to sleep.

It was cold in the predawn when Khoa awoke again. He felt an acute pain in his right side. The dream had been so vivid he could actually feel it. *Had something attacked him in his sleep?* He opened his eyes and looked around. No, it was a dream and nothing more, he said to himself, but the pain in his flank was real and he turned to lick at it.

Noticing his sleeping cubs and Ani, he rose quietly and walked out. Ani felt him stir and woke as well.

"What's the matter, Khoa? You're limping," she whispered over the cubs.

"My dream. I can't get over how real it was. I can still feel it. It's as if the dragon in my dream actually attacked me."

Ani moved from the cubs. "Let's go outside."

"Show me where the dragon touched you."

Khoa pointed to his left flank. Ani went to him and searched over him a long time before telling him, "I don't see anything. Does it still hurt?"

"It's fading, but I still feel its sting."

"Tell me about the dream," said Ani.

"We were all in the meadow. The cubs were chasing each other, and then I saw this tiny box sitting among the flowers. I knew it was for me so I went up to it. I wasn't afraid because I already knew what was in the box. I knew, but I didn't know," he said, pausing to look at his mate. "That sounds like I'm off center doesn't it?"

Ani shook her head. "I know what you mean. You just don't remember it until it happens."

"Yes," agreed Khoa. "That's it. It was like reading a story over and over, but not remembering the ending until you heard it again. I barely touched the box when a huge dragon appeared all at once. It didn't frighten me because I already knew there was a dragon in the box. I kept asking myself how it was possible for this gigantic dragon to fit into such a tiny box. I was more concerned about the size of the dragon than the fact that it was a dragon." Here Khoa paused and shook his head.

"Anyway, the next thing I realized, I was running, but I knew I had always been running just like I knew everything in the dream. No matter where I went the dragon was right behind me. There was a sentry wolf standing on the wall calling, 'The dragon has pierced the light.' That's when I woke feeling the pain in my flank. Even after I opened my eyes, I could hear the sentinel calling out his words like they were some final lot of judgement passed that could not be altered. The light had been pierced. It was as if he was in the room with me. I knew there was a dragon in the box, I knew I would run, and I knew what the sentinel was going to say, but I couldn't stop it."

He looked up to see Ani studying him pensively. "What light did the dragon pierce?" she asked.

"I don't know. I didn't see it, I just felt it," he said, and twisted around to look at his flank again.

Ani looked over her mates flank another time. "There isn't any visible mark or blood," she said before coming over to place her head across Khoa's back. It was a habit of hers Khoa loved and he marveled at how she knew the times he needed her comfort most. They had so little time alone since the arrival of the cubs and even less now that Zen lived with them. Nine little cubs prancing about kept him busy.

Just as he thought that, Zen came out with her cubs and Ani lifted her head from Khoa's back to look at her.

"I didn't mean to disturb you, but the cubs needed out," Zen said, emphasizing the word out.

"Me, too," she added laughing. She sat with Khoa and Ani and watched the cubs. Ani howled to her own cubs and waited for them to come out.

As the cubs bounded away Zen turned to them. "You're up early."

"Khoa didn't sleep well."

"I haven't slept well since Tor has been gone," said Zen looking at Khoa.

Khoa walked closer to Zen and put his paw on her. "I know. He's been on my mind, too. I decided in the middle of the night I was going out to find him. I have to do something. It doesn't make any sense to keep waiting."

"Thank you, Khoa. I know something has happened. Not because Tor hasn't sent word, but I just have a feeling. I can't explain it," she said, turning away from both of them.

Khoa knew she was crying, but thought it best to let her have her privacy and kept his distance. Her words left him cold and he couldn't get them out of his mind.

Zen still did not turn to face them. "I better see to the cubs," she said and bounded after them.

Ani moved around to look at her mate. "There's something else isn't there?"

Khoa nodded and explained about discovering a secret he had started unraveling about how the Alpha used patterns that repeated in nature and spirit to warn animals about things which were to come.

"I'm sure this dream is an omen, but what? It is telling me directly that the light has been pierced. But what light? Is it something that has already happened, about to happen, or is it way off in the future?"

Ani began to walk around in small circles. "Yes, I see what the dilemma is. Look at it for what it is, not what it will be. It seems to me to be simpler that way."

Khoa nodded, but Ani was sure he hadn't heard her. He was already half way down the path to the training ground. There was one thought on his mind now and that was Tor. He was on everyone's mind.

As he ran, the voice intruded on his thoughts again. 'You know what you thought you didn't. Listen, Khoa. You let the dragon grow.' The time for listening was over, he said to himself.

It was months ago that Tor and his army had left for the Blackstone territories. The first part of their journey had been over easy terrain so Tor and his army had loped effortlessly until they saw the dark pines of the Blackstone Mountains ahead. They were still in the lowlands and the spring migration of birds was at its peak. When Tor and his warriors approached the marshlands to drink, tremendous flocks of swifts, swallows, and warblers took to the air. The sky was black with them. Being small birds, they rose quickly, noiselessly. The only sound was their song, which when heard from a single bird was faint, but now, heard in unison from thousands, became a crescendo. The wolves stopped to watch them as they took formation. A single bird would fly point, then directly behind it two birds fell in line, then three birds, then four, until a giant V took shape. In seconds, out of the seemingly panicked and scattered take off, thousands of birds were all in formation. All birds were accounted for in their specified place.

"That's precision drilling," Winter commented.

"Nature's best disciplined army," Tor added. "We could learn something from that."

"If we could fly."

"No, from the way they signal. Silently."

"How about learning that their noise hides an advancing army?" a loud and unknown voice called out to them.

Tor and Winter turned to face the voice. A dark wolf stood looking at them and they could see they were surrounded by dark wolves. Tor estimated there were hundreds of dark wolves. His patrol of fifty was no match against them. It was not the time to fight.

"So the hunters find that they are the hunted," the dark wolf taunted.

They had planned the ambush well, Tor thought. *They had been watching us and they had counted on us coming to drink at the marsh.*

"What is your name white wolf?"

Tor remained silent. "No matter. You are one of two white wolves. Twins? Am I right?" he said, pushing Winter and Tor forward through the shallow water.

"I am Warrior. I fought against you five summers ago, or rather I fought against the avalanche your horn created." Warrior was looking directly at Tor as he spoke. "I see my name means nothing to you. So looking you over, you are not Khoa, but the twin."

When Tor didn't speak, Warrior said, "My father was Deuce."

Tor felt the dark wolf push him again. "I knew of him."

Another dark wolf came up beside them. "I have a brother as well. This is Snuffer. Another one your avalanche failed to kill. So now it shall be brothers against brothers. Interesting, wouldn't you say?"

As Warrior spoke, they were being herded across the waters of the marsh and its tall cover of reedy grasses. Soon they had crossed it and come onto dry land. They seemed to be headed for the base of the mountain directly ahead of them. When they drew closer to the mountain, Tor could see an opening like an entrance to a cave. What looked like a pile of boulders jutting out from mountain suddenly began to move apart. It was like an apparition before his eyes and startled him until he realized what was opening were two great doors. There was no cave behind the rock like doors, but a great embattlement with open sky above. He could see the inside had been carefully constructed as a military compound. The two giant doors were made to look like rock boulders when closed and part of the mountain itself. No one would guess those boulders were doors and hid a fortress behind them. It was the best piece of camouflaging he had ever seen.

Inside, and at the opposite edge from the entrance, was the real face of the mountain which afforded maximum protection from behind and rose nearly a mile straight up. With the use of their fake boulder walls, they had extended the front of the mountain some four to five hundred yards beyond the natural one. It was a spectacular feat of construction, thought Tor. You couldn't tell the fake boulders from the real ones.

"Take these two to the hole," Warrior said, pointing at Tor and Winter. "Put the others to work until tonight," he ordered and walked off with Snuffer and two other officers.

Tor watched as his army was led away to help finish the new sides of the mountain, which were still being built for they were only a foot or so high. The front, with its magnificent boulder like doors, was finished; closing the fortress away from the outside world. It was obvious that they had taken all manner of animals captive to be used as workers in this project.

He quickly took stock of everything around him. Barracks lined the interior of the fort for six to eight hundred wolves. There was a storehouse of food and water. Weapons were stacked in neat tripods, ready to grab at a moments' notice.

The black wolves prodded him and Winter to the back of the compound where there was a number of holes in the ground covered by open metal grates. They were told to stop at the second metal grate and wait as the guard wolves removed the covering over the holes.

"Home, sweet, home," one of the black wolves said, shoving Tor over the edge.

It was dark inside and Tor could not judge how far it was to the bottom, but he hit the ground in seconds. An instant later he heard Winter land beside him. "Must be about six feet," Tor said.

"Or less," Winter said sarcastically.

Tor moved over closer to Winter and whispered, "We need a runner to get back to the Wilds. Unless they were looking for this fort, they would never find it."

"Taylor's still out there," Winter said. "He was on scout this morning."

"Then there's a chance we will be rescued when he reports back to the Wilds. Still, let's check things out for a weakness we can…"

Before Tor could finish his sentence, he heard heavy iron being moved, and turned to see a small black door being opened behind them. In the light, he could see Warrior standing with three other wolves beside him. "Bring the big one to me," he said.

So it went week after week and month after month. The door would open and Tor would be brought in and questioned. Tor noticed habits of Warriors he used to his benefit. The less Tor spoke, the angrier the dark wolf became, and talked more himself. He also became angry when Tor answered his question with a question. Seeing the scowl on the dark wolfs face, it would be a good strategy to employ today. Warrior walked around and around the wolf. "So do you still favor war, or are you willing to negotiate with peace in mind?"

"Peace? Is that what you want?"

"Yes." Warrior stopped and looked intently at Tor. "I can't tell if you asked that seriously, or you are making fun of me, white wolf."

"I never joke about war."

"But we were talking about peace," the dark wolf said, continuing to circle his prisoner.

"Sorry, but when you talk about peace, I think about war."

"My father, Deuce, use to call your brother a devil dog. I see why," Warrior said, slowly turning to face the white wolf.

"You think yourself a superior wolf, don't you?"

"In what way?"

"Intelligence," the dark wolf yelled at him.

He turned to Snuffer. "Is he more intelligent than we are?"

"No."

"Tell him why, Snuf."

"Because we have him, he doesn't have us."

The whip that Warrior was wielding zipped across Tor's face and back like sudden lightening and knocked him off his feet.

"Put him back in his cell, Snuffer."

As the dark wolf escorted him back towards the cell door, Warrior said, "Your intelligence just earned you no food and water again."

The questioning of Tor had gone on for weeks, but he had not agreed to surrender his homeland to them without a fight. He was questioned two or three times a day, bitten and beaten, and then returned to his cell. He was thankful for Winter, and the two of them passed the time making plans for an escape, but tonight he had other things on his mind.   "What do you think is keeping Khoa and the others? Surely, Taylor should have made it to the Wilds and told them by now."

"Unless he was caught as well," Winter offered. "I'm sure they found Taylor. That's why Khoa hasn't come."

Tor turned to look at his friend. "Either way, those left in the Wilds need to be warned of this camouflaged mountain and the invasion that's coming."

Suddenly a sword clanged on the metal grate above them. "Quiet down there or we'll muzzle you."

An hour or so later a guard rapped on the metal grating again and called, "Anyone dead down there?"

"No," Tor called back.

"Too bad, king," the guard said and snickered.

They could hear the dark wolves above moving away, and then stop again and call out at the next cell. "Got any meat to haul up?"

No answer came and the same voice said, "Open it up and drop the ladder. I'll have to go down and tie them on so we can haul them up." They heard the grate being removed and the wolf who had been talking said, "Better give me a mask. They've been there awhile."

Winter turned to Tor. "How many do you think we've lost?"

Tor only shook his head and listened intently as the guards removed the bodies next to them. They sat in silence as the wolves moved down the row of grated cells, shouting out, "Dead call," and waiting to hear the answer, "Alive down here."

Finally, Winter got up to pace in the small cell and whispered, "There's only one way out."

"Shh," Tor whispered. "Someone's still up there. I heard feet padding up and stop right above us."

Overhead, one of the wolves said, "I hate this job."

"With you there. I'm glad you came up with the idea of just hauling the bodies into the forest and letting the animals carry 'em away."

"Yeah, they gotta eat too, don't they?"

"Better than breaking our backs digging holes every night."

"And we got to spend time with the girls sipping sweet cider rum," the other wolf laughed.

Tor and Winter could hear as the dead wolves were being loaded on carts somewhere in the distance. A voice called out to the wolves standing above them. "Last one. Come and get 'em."

"Time to get to work," one of the guards snickered.

When Tor could no longer hear the wolves or the cart rattling, he turned to Winter. "Hearing those wolves gave me the idea of how to get out of here."

The look on Winter's face showed his eagerness even though his voice didn't. "How?"

"By playing dead."

"In a few days that will be a fact."

"It's a risky plan, but it's the best odds we've got. These lazy wolves aren't burying the dead any longer, just leaving them as carrion for the forest animals. All you have to do is get carried out, wait for them to leave, and head for the Wilds."

"Me? It's more important that you escape. You're the twin king. The trainer of warriors."

"Listen!" Tor said sharply. "Warrior would insist on looking me over closely and probably keep my hide for a trophy. No, you've got the better chance."

"Yes, I see your reasoning."

"Let me see you stiffen your legs."

"What?"

"You have to make them believe you're dead, don't you? Dead wolves are stiff."

Over the next few days Winter practiced playing dead. Khoa had found some stones that were lying in the corner of the cell and placed them on top of Winter to bring down his temperature. As they practiced Tor said, "Let Khoa know that Warrior and Snuffer survived the avalanche. Since he once knew them, maybe it will provide him with an advantage."

"Anything else?"

"Yes. There's another encampment in the East somewhere. I heard Warrior order some troops there. Let's guess there are about the same number of wolves stationed there as here."

Winter poked at Tor lightly. "I meant anyone else. It was Zen I was thinking about."

"Tell her I'm alive."

"Stay that way, Tor," Winter answered. He understood that his friend could not speak of his family and did not want them to know of his torment.

The next day a great feast was laid out in the room when Tor was brought in.

"You don't look so kingly now," Warrior said in contempt. "You're dirty and smell like a half rotted corpse."

Tor refused to watch the dark wolves eat and closed his eyes. He lay with his back turned to them and thought of Zen and his cubs. The smell of the food roused a painful hunger in him.

"All this food," Warrior said, waving his paw across the table, "for a simple yes. Will you give the order that all white wolves must surrender the Wilds back to the black wolves?"

He waited for an answer, and then began to bang on the table. "We are the rightful inheritors. Admit that and live."

When Tor remained silent, Warrior placed a bowl of water before him. "Water then?" the dark wolf asked.

When Tor still didn't answer, Warrior kicked the bowl away from him. "You think you are making things difficult for me by not surrendering your animals, but you are making it harder on them. We will kill them all now and take back the land you stole from my father."

"It is not your land. It has been the home of the white wolves since Grey Dawn brought them there after the Twenty Year Wars."

"Where do you get such nonsense stubborn, white wolf? Oh yes, from the Book. Fairytales. Lies. Well, you will die for them now."

"Dying for the promises in the Book makes them true."

Warrior laughed in contempt. "No, it makes you stupid and dead."

"Not one white wolf will cede the Wilds. Many of you dark wolves will die also."

"I have wasted months on trying to arrange peace among us, fallen king. I will do what my father couldn't."

The two wolves stared at each other. "Tell me, condemned wolf, if you are the one who is right, and the one who has a historic right to the Wilds, why is it that I hold the power of life and death over you?"

"Now, the tide of evil swells on the shore, as you say, but like all tides it must ebb again into the sea and drown in its backwash. Nothing holds the tides. Not even you, black wolf."

"Are you prophesying now? Cursing us to lose? Words meant to threaten, but they make no sense."

"Let me put it plainly then. You think you win against the white wolves and that our land is yours, but you lie to yourself. The Great Wolf will raise up the white wolves to come against you."

"You won't live to see it."

"I don't need to. I know it will be. It is promised."

"There is no Great Wolf, who created all life. It formed on its own over eons. Admit it and live."

"If life is just a hodgepodge as you black wolves believe, and came about by chance, then why does it follow laws of nature and physics that we know exist? Why is it a logically ordered universe?"

"No Great Wolf designed all this. I have heard it said that you of the Way believe he used math to design this world. That he was some sort of great mathematician. Pfffff! It evolved over eons and eons of time."

"Math gives us a transcendent truth. The rules of math apply even if you naturalists do not believe in them. They still hold true. They work in this world. You can't account for the truth math gives us, so you ignore it. The laws of math were discovered, not invented. That means they already existed. "

"Words you can't prove."

"But I just told you that math proves it. The laws of nature are constant through time. If the laws of nature were to suddenly change and rearrange themselves, science would not be possible. Past experiments could no longer be relied upon and would tell us nothing about the future. Just because you don't believe in their constancy doesn't erase them. The laws of physics and chemistry existed and the world used them long before you were born, and they will continue to work long after we are all gone. Explain that."

"It is a simple philosophy. We came from the same cell and all life divided itself from it. It's proven we have common DNA."

"If life was just random, why does it repeat itself in creating the same life forms over and over? Why doesn't it just keep changing and adapting? Why did it stop putting cells together to form other things? Where is the evolution you speak about?"

"It takes time, white wolf, eons for all to evolve. That's what you can't see. Your mind is too limited."

"And just what are we going to evolve into?"

"A higher species, of course. One that is able to understand and control the universe on our own terms."

"Then you, not the Great Wolf, would be in charge. You trust yourselves, you who create war and kill, more than you trust in a divine Wolf to rule over you?"

"There is no Great Wolf. There are only wolves. It is easy to see all life evolved into what it is today. First, a single grand explosion and the universe came to be and then a second spontaneous event that created all life."

"What about the law of biogenesis that shows that life only comes from life? Siuol Teurpas proved that molecules from nonliving chemicals can't create life. From his time it has been seen as a universal truth that only life begets life. There are no exceptions."

"You lack imagination, Tor. You can't see what the world could be."

"I see the world as the truth it shows to all. From observance, it is easy to see that all things move towards entropy and not evolution."

"Your truth is stupidly dull."

"You have no truth. You make yours up. There are no fossil records to show how things evolved, so you drew them in the textbooks. It's art work and wishful thinking. You deny that all things decay and die. Your body dies, Warrior. Rivers dry up. Houses that man built fall to nothing. Even the leaves fall to the earth. Nature shows us the pattern."

"That is the cycle of life as it is now. We will one day change it. I thought all those books that gave credence to the

Great Wolf had been destroyed. I will make a note of that. And also the fact that white wolves shouldn't be allowed to read. Your arguments are stolen from those who came before you. You are not intelligent, you merely echo the same rhetoric we secularists have proven to be illogical. I'm done toying with you, wolf."

"You and your naturalists set yourselves up to be kings instead of the Great Wolf. You deny that you are only a mortal wolf."

"I'll make a mortal wolf of you, Tor. Tomorrow."

The contempt Warrior felt for the white wolf had changed into rage. He turned to the dark wolf behind him. "We kill him at daylight. His companion, too."

Hearing the orders of the black wolf brought renewed hope to Tor. It was the opportunity he had been waiting for. It couldn't have been better timing.

"He's already dead," Tor said quietly, hoping that Winter was listening by the door as usual. He needed to give his friend time to get ready and attacked the wolves nearest him. It was a short struggle, for eight more wolves were on him instantly.

"Muzzle him," Snuffer ordered.

When the tussle ended, Warrior motioned for the wolf closest to the cell door to go in and check on Winter. The dark wolf came back and reported, "Cold meat, alright."

Tor's fight with his enemies had taken the rest of his strength. He could barely raise his head as they tied the rope around his jaws.

"Get rid of the dead hide," Warrior spat. "Put this one back until tomorrow's execution. We start to even the score, Tor. You will pay for my father, and Khoa will pay for Staver. All the white wolves will die now."

His captors dragged him by the tail and placed him back in the cell. His body ached from weeks of beatings and torture. The coldness of the stone floor helped ease the pain and settled his stomach from its churning. A thought struck him. The cold stone walls and floors that had once kept him from getting warm, and had once been his enemy, now aided and gave comfort to his tortured body.

Tor watched in the half-light of the cell as the wolves placed Winter on the tarp and dragged him away.

"No food for you tonight, but you won't be hungry long. You die in the morning," his guard laughed.

As the door closed, Tor was alone in the darkness. Through the grates, he could see the sky. Clouds covered the moon and there was no light. He lay prone in the humbling position and spoke silently to the Great Alpha. 'Guide Winter home. Let your strength be his legs.'

The white wolf forced himself to stay awake in the darkness to hear if any word came about a wolf rising from the dead. No alarms were sounded in the next hour. Tor was hurting on the side that lay next to the floor and he wanted to turn over. It took great effort for the wolf to move. The coldness of the floor had entered his bones and stiffened his body to the point of numbness. He felt better once he shifted positions, and he lay awake listening. Two hours passed, then three, then four, and no alarm had been sounded. Winter was on his way home. Tor let himself drift into sleep by concentrating his thoughts on the Alpha. 'It has come down to me and you, Great Wolf, as it comes down to all animals in the end. Many will see it as irony that you have given me hope by way of death. Give them wisdom to unravel the mystery in that. It is great and profound.'

It was the sound of the grate being removed above that woke him. There was the haze of first blue light in the sky before the sun comes up and deepens it. He felt his heart drop for it reminded him of the Wilds when he had stood on the shore of the lake watching the dawn break. He would never see it again. He would not let himself think of Zen and the cubs.

A strong wind blew on him and the cold crispness of it stung his nostrils. He wasn't fully awake and he felt immobilized by the stiffness in his body. Suddenly a lasso tightened around his neck, and he was being hauled upward by the rope in jerking motions. He lifted his paws to pull the rope away from his throat to keep from strangling. When he touched solid ground, gasping noises escaped from him his throat. The cold air entered his lungs and filled them with a raw and burning sensation. The black wolf yanked on the rope again. "If it was up to me, I'd finished you now. Hanging's an ugly way to die."

Tor growled and lunged forward. The guard smiled knowingly. "Go ahead. I'll kick you back down and let you swing, king."

Tor looked away from the guard and beyond him. Lines of wolves, six rows deep, stood on either side of him forming a path and hemming him in. A sudden terror seized him and he wanted to bolt. Where could he go? He felt his legs move, but was not sure how. The stares of the dark wolves on either side of him were humiliating. He decided to look straight ahead. At the end of the path he saw a post and the black wolf lead him to it and tethered him.

"Look at the king quivering and shaking!" the dark wolves called out.

"White wolves are only thieves. They stole our land and killed our leaders. They deserve to die."

He tried to steady his legs, but every muscle in his body seemed to betray him. He was weak from no food, and the cold wind stung his open wounds. It wasn't fear, it was physical exhaustion, he thought. He was not a coward. He had fought many a foe, but that was different. He had been in fighting shape and well fed; not tethered to a post, starved and muzzled. It was the weakness he felt in his own body that panicked him. The will and strength to live was gone.

'If I can't fight and die like a warrior wolf,' he pleaded silently to the Great Wolf, 'Then give me courage.'

Gasps came from the ranks, and some of the dark wolves broke from their formations as Tor lay in the humbling position.

Snuffer rose and shouted at his wolves, "You cower at a gesture to a wolf god who doesn't exist. Let him pray to his god."

His words stopped those who had begun to run. "Does his wolf god seem to be around to rescue him?" Snuffer asked, trotting over in front of the frightened wolves.

"No," he continued, answering his own question. "It is we that have the power to destroy. I ask you, where is his god?"

Shouts rose from the ranks again, and Warrior, sensing that his army had regained its composure, went back to his place by his brother. He held up the decree and waved it where all could see. Then roars came from the wolves. When they quieted down, Warrior read the decree loudly and with anger in his voice, "Tor, you have been found guilty of:

1) Being a self-proclaimed king.

2) Murdering the ruler of free wolves everywhere, Deuce, and his son, Staver.

3) Stealing the first kingdom of the black wolves called the Wilds.

Our true king, Deuce, and his son, my brother, gave their lives to end the tyranny of the white wolves. Today justice has begun to be restored. Be assured, we will not rest until justice reigns on all the free territories of the dark wolves and until the Wilds are restored to its rightful owners. Let your death be a warning to all that this is the price of treason and treachery."

Great shouts went up in the ranks. When the cheers subsided, Snuffer waved his hand and ten wolves stepped forward from the ranks, swords in their paws.

Tor padded around the post to get a better look at them, which only made his leash shorter, so he abruptly reversed his path to give him more play in the rope. *Keep on the long end of the rope. Don't pace back around the post. You need to be able to dodge their swords.*

"On the command," Snuffer called and the execution squad came to attention.

"On the ready." Tor watched as the squad stepped forward.

"Strike!" came the order.

The black wolves ran at Tor, each stabbing at him in passing. Seeing death was eminent he did not fight, and with the third strike fell.

The earth trembled as he hit the ground.

Warrior took it as a good sign and turned to Snuffer. "We have struck a valiant blow against the white wolves today. The king is dead. Khoa is greatly weakened. I feel it."

The sky grew dark and the wind rose up violently.

"Look it has become night," one of the dark wolves in the execution squad shouted.

"The earth is taking revenge against us for the white wolf's death," another wolf shouted.

The shaking beneath them became more violent and the partially built walls that surrounded the compound began to topple. The massive front walls and the great stone doors fell outward and the black wolves broke rank and fled over the fallen walls and the opened gates.

"I fear it is we who have been weakened, Warrior," Snuffer said running. Warrior, seeing he was left alone, ran after him.

What was left of the company of white wolves, which had been assembled to watch their kings death saw the chaos, and began to break ranks as well, but Traveler ran up and down in front of them shouting, "The earth will not harm us. Stand fast. Follow me!" he said running towards the post where their king was tied. The warriors of the Wilds followed at his heels. They looked down at his body. His fur was matted with blood, dirt, and grasses; his flesh torn and exposed on his left flank.

"I do not know who I look upon," one white wolf said.

"Untie him. We will take his body with us," Traveler said, looking around for something to place Tor's body on. "Quick, fetch that tarp over there."

As soon as the white wolves touched Tor's body to pick it up, the rumbling lessened a bit. Once the body had been put on the tarp, Traveler yelled, "Now, let's out the left side. Most of the dark wolves have gone out the front."

As they ran across the compound where the pits were dug, Traveler said, "Free the other wolves." Dutifully his warriors worked quickly and opened the grates to the pits. There were ladders by each pit and they put them in place. A mass of prisoners streamed out and began running with them. One of the wolves let free was Scout, and once he was outside the compound, he took command from Traveler.

"We can't go by way of the marsh. They would be expecting that," he said and looked up at the great Blackstone range. They others looked up, too. "We have no choice but to go up and over."

"That's weeks out of the way," one of the white wolves said.

"If we go by way of the marsh, we will have to fight. Anyone here strong enough to make a stand?" Scout asked, glancing at the wolves' faces. Most hung their heads.

"We will come back," he shouted. "We will take back our honor. We will avenge Tor's death and finish what the Great Wolf started." Hearing his words, the wolves gave a cry of renewed hope, picked up the tarp on which Tor lay, and began the long climb upwards past the scrub pines and into the barren terrain of the Blackstone Mountains.

CHAPTER 3
THROUGH A GLASS DARKLY

Summer was well into its season and the cubs were just beginning to lose their wooly appearance. At five months old, their fur was taking on the more coarse texture of maturing wolves. As the cubs legs had become stronger, the afternoon treks stretched to cover greater distances. Both Khoa and Ani could now see clearly the unique characters forming in each of their five offspring. Zen's cubs, being almost a month older, challenged the younger ones to keep up with them. Khoa and the she wolves decided that the cubs were old enough now for Khoa to leave and find Tor.

Khoa had spent the week getting his army ready. He found the cubs asleep as he entered the room where Ani was and she rose to meet him. He wanted to spend the rest of the night alone with Ani and asked Winter to get Pieces and Washer to watch over the sleeping cubs.

The two wolves padded along the lake, listening to the waves lap, lap, lapping rhythm slap against the sand. Light from the moon lit up the small cresting ripples of water like some luminous sun; making a moving pathway through the dark water and seeming to bring it to life.

The two wolves talked about everything and nothing until light began to replace the darkness along the horizon. The higher the sun rose, and the bluer the sky became, the more the moon's substance faded. It had become smaller and transparent enough to see through; losing the look of heavy fullness that had weighted it in the night sky. Now the sun was behind it in the east, seeming to chase it from the sky.

"It's rare that you see the moon and the sun together, but it's beautiful," Ani said.

"So are you," he whispered into her ear. He looked at her as if it would be the last time. That was the way Khoa wanted to remember her; in that moment, in that light, with that look of tenderness in her eyes that softened his heart.

A short time later Khoa stood at the entrance to the cave. Looking at Ani and Zen made it all the more difficult to start the journey. "I've made the rounds. Everything is in order so there is no immediate danger, but I will post sentries around the farthest perimeters as we travel towards the Blackstone's. Send a runner out if you need help." The cubs jumped on him and nipped lightly at the fur on his flanks entreating him to chase them.

"Cubs, listen to your mothers. Protect them, too." The cubs playfulness left them as they watched Khoa kiss the she wolves and bound away. They had never heard the low wailing of a wolf in mourning and stopped their play to look at their mothers.

"I'll run that fast one day," Tristian said.

"Let's hope you don't have to," answered Ani.

"He'll come back won't he, mother?" asked TJ, which was short for Tor Jr.

"Yes, and your father with him," Zen said.

Khoa stood on the knoll and took his last look at the Wilds. He had not traversed more than twenty miles from the Wilds since settling in with Ani. Now he had to leave her and the cubs and the beauty that surrounded him. He thought of last night and her head resting on his back. He loved that Ani would find him standing on the hill, or by the stream and come to him of a sudden, quietly, and just place her head across the small of his back.

He and his army had gotten a late start. As he moved off the ridge with the warriors behind him, he thought about the past few years. They had been nurturing days, healing, and soothing days. There was an unearthly feel to things in the Wilds, he thought. How far the west was from the life he had been born to in the east. It was not merely distance that made his current life so unique, but it was the fact that he had been born as a white wolf, the least of all wolves and yet here, in this western land, he had been allowed to mate, carry on his lineage, and be called a twin king. He had moved into a destiny that was called into being by an unseen force he had once not believed in at all. It was that force that moved within him now, that told him he must defend all that he loved. An uneasiness settled on him as he moved further from his home. The voice whispered, 'You've waited too long. Like the moon biding its time in the sky until it becomes a hollow specter in the face of the sun.' Khoa silenced the voice. There was no other way, and he pushed the thought away, and his army towards the Blackstone range. There was one thing in his mind now. He needed to find Tor.

Khoa had been traveling for nearly two weeks and this night found him and his wolves still running. It was the easy paced, loping gait that wolves used to travel long distances. The terrain was hills and grasslands and presented few obstacles to slow their journey. Overhead, a quarter moon lay tipped on its side, which provided little light, but the sky itself was clear, and the stars guided their way.

In the distance Khoa could see a wolf running towards him. A scout had been sent out and was reporting back. A dead body of a wolf had been found in the hills below. It was quite a distance to the site and the wolves changed their pace to a gallop. When the party of wolves drew close to the targeted area, they spread out over the landscape seeking any hint of trouble. If dark wolves were present, they would be in a position to close in and attack. Khoa trotted head down; nose close to the land to pick up any scent of the enemy. He was about a mile out when he caught the first scent that was foreign to his nostrils. Since the flesh had decomposed, it was hard to tell who the scent belonged to.

Suddenly Khoa lifted his head and sprinted down the rise. He knew what he needed to know. There were others wolves present. Khoa signaled for his units to move forward as he saw a wolf dart into the cover of the trees. They weren't all dead down there, he thought. The unit spread out in a circle, the way wolves do to entrap their prey. With heads low, and bodies slightly crouched, they moved the rest of the way down the hill. If there was any animal left hidden, they would bring it down.

Less than a minute passed before they had surrounded the lone wolf. He was dirty, bloody, and half starved. He was in no shape to attack. The smells that came off the wolf were like none Khoa had inhaled before. He wanted to turn away.

"Khoa!" the voice was raspy and barely audible. "It's me, Winter."

Khoa moved closer to the wolf.

"Winter?"

The wolf nodded and lay down.

"Healer wolf up here," Khoa yelled, turning from his friend.

"We're going to get you fixed up," he said, looking at Winter.

"Bring up water and food, too."

When the healer came, Khoa said, "Clean him up."

While Winter was being treated, Khoa went to look at the body of the other wolf. A shallow grave had been started near the body.

"Winter must have been trying to bury him when we came along," Khoa said.

"Giving his last ounce," Justice said.

Khoa nodded and reflected briefly on the first time he had met Winter. It had been on the battlefield and the wolf had asked him for water. He had lain wounded under a hot sun, unable to move and yet had no bitterness in him. He was an honorable wolf.

"That means the dead wolf is one of ours, but where are Tor and the others?" asked Justice.

"Winter will have to tell us that," Khoa answered and turned around to his sergeant. "Finish burying Taylor."

He watched Winter drinking water in gulps until the healer wolf said, "Wait awhile before you take in anymore."

"Give me some food then."

"Can you eat?" the healer wolf asked, applying another bandage.

"Yes," Winter said. "All you have with you and then some."

Khoa laughed and then took a closer look at Winter. "You must have lost about thirty pounds."

The two remained silent while Winter ate.

"Can you tell us what happened?" Khoa asked.

The wolf nodded.

"Start with who you were burying here."

"Taylor," he said glancing over to where the body lay. "He wasn't with us when we were ambushed. He had been sent to scout the terrain on our left early that morning. We had hoped that he had seen our capture and the location of the fort and reported back to you." He still looked past Khoa to where they were burying his friend.

He paused for a moment before continuing, "The black wolves must have seen Taylor, followed him this far." Here Winter turned towards the healer wolf. "Can I have some more water?"

"Okay, but take it slow. You want to keep it all down," the healer advised.

Winter nodded, took a long drink, and began to tell the story. Khoa listened while the battered wolf told him everything that had happened to him and Tor and about the great fortress with its deceiving entrance.

After Winter finished talking, Khoa said, "We'll need a full army to attack that fortress and a raid that will succeed the first time. We won't get another chance. That'll take some time to prepare."

"Khoa," Winter said touching the wolf, "I wanted Tor to be the one to go."

"Thank you, Winter. I know that's the kind of wolf you are. It's enough to know that he is still alive."

Khoa rose from where he had been sitting and called to his sergeant, "Justice, tell the men we camp here, and head back to the Wilds at first light."

Khoa's words made Winter freeze. *First light. Tor was to die at first light, yesterday.*

"Khoa," Winter called out urgently. "There's something else you need to hear. I don't know how to say this to you."

He studied the face of his friend as he told him about the orders to execute Tor the day before. He could see Khoa was troubled, but the king remained silent.

"I'm sorry to have torn your heart out," Winter said in a voice broken with tears.

Khoa got up and started away, and Winter called to him, "I can offer you this hope. There was a giant shaking of the earth at dawn. I felt it nearly twenty miles away. Maybe that stopped the dark wolves from carrying out their plans."

Khoa had no words to say to his friend. He was numb. *There was the answer to his dream. His brother was the light that was pierced. It would be a long journey home. Pieces had put it succinctly, 'How did you tell what or who it was before it happened?'*

The whole army caught his mood. Tor's death removed the hope they had set out with some weeks before. The wolves traveled at a quickened pace and in silence, their eyes fixed on their king.

Khoa's mind could not erase its single thought. Tor was gone. There it was again, this void, this erasing of something that would never be again. He could feel the absence. He let this cycle of emotions chase him until he knew it by heart, but a sudden epiphany came to him. The Book said the spirit departed at death. It was the spirit that held the essence of you; that carried your real life force, and the spirit never died. It went to the great kingdom of the One True Wolf. That's why he could no longer sense Tor's essence on this earthly realm because it wasn't here; it was in the great kingdom. That made sense, he thought. Tor's spirit lived, just not here. Remember that, he told himself. Here, pain lived and the journey was unknown. Here, was learning how he could possibly replace Tor, who was the warrior, the gallant one. Tor had taught him everything. Here, Tor was gone. The voice had been right, he had waited too long.

The old rabbit had a similar feeling of doom. He just couldn't shake the feeling that something had happened or was about to happen. Pieces had been feeling under the weather. The old rabbit hadn't slept well since Khoa and the hundreds had pulled out two weeks before. To compound matters, Serious remained on the warpath. Everything bothered the old rabbit during the last few weeks, even that silliness, which he usually let slide. Ani, Zen, and the cubs were under great stress and he took that to heart. The old rabbit felt his Wilds were changing into a place he didn't know. The new citizens were sometimes more than his old bones could handle, and the peace that had once settled on the Wilds was vanishing. There was nothing he could do about it, and it was that fact which disturbed him the most.

Today he was up early to pay a visit to the raccoon. When he reached Washer's place, he hopped on top of the hollowed out section of a tree which had toppled in the spring storm. Washer had taken over the site from a family of squirrels who had moved on to safer and higher ground. Like most raccoons, Washer was partial to an already made habitat, and being opportunistic, once the squirrels moved out, he dashed in. This was roomier than his last den and offered not only the knot hole opening on the side, but another door at the broken end of the tree where it had split off; affording two avenues of escape.

Inside, Washer felt Pieces trouncing. "Get off my roof. You're shaking all sorts of dirt down on me."

"Sorry, I was just pacing and not aware."

Pieces immediately jumped off the log and knocked by the knot hole opening with his back kicker.

"I know you're there, now," Washer yelled as he came out of the bottom end of his log.

"For Pete's sake, what are you so grousey about this morning?"

Pieces could see he was holding a piece of paper in the air.

"This has been a day to end all days," the raccoon said, waving the paper back and forth.

Coming up to his friend, he shoved it right under the rabbit's nose for him to read.

While Pieces was reading, Washer continued, "One letter in two years, and it's bad news. It makes me want to end my mail service."

"It doesn't sound like bad news. All it says is that your nephew, Stasher, is coming to visit."

"He's the bad news," Washer said, walking in circles around Pieces. "This is not a good time. We have those growing wolves to tend to, and Khoa gone and Tor."

"Yeppers. Say, how old is Stasher?" Pieces asked, scratching his chin. "Is he close to the same age as the cubs?"

Here the raccoon stopped pacing and said, "Yes, the difficult stage… birth to death."

"How can you say you want to help all those wolf cubs, and not even want to help your own species?"

"I'm a bachelor. I'm used to doing things my own way."

"Selfish, you mean. He might want one of those blackberries you hoard away."

Washer reached down for the empty bag on the ground. "Now there's an idea. Let's get breakfast. Fish and berries. Nothin' can top it."

As they headed for their favorite breakfast spot, the old rabbit just couldn't shake the uneasiness he felt. It was a beautiful morning. The sky couldn't get any bluer, he thought.

The sweet scents from the flowers in the meadows came on the cool breezes off the lake. Everything was perfect.

While they walked, Pieces asked, "How long do you think Khoa will be gone?

The raccoon shrugged and Pieces continued talking. "It's rather lonely around here with almost all the troops gone. It makes me cold."

Washer looked at the rabbit and could see that his brows were furrowed and his friend was deep in thought. "Everything's fine. The cubs were born and they're fine, aren't they?"

Pieces nodded, relieved that nothing out of the ordinary had happened in the Wilds itself. Experience had taught the old rabbit to listen to his feelings, but even he had to agree with Washer this time. Everything seemed fine, like the raccoon had just reminded him. Maybe he was worrying more about things than he should. Even when the great wind came, it had only gathered strength over the Wilds as it passed through. Not much damage had occurred to them. The storm had delivered its force on other parts of the land to the east of the Wilds.

"If there were anything to your feelings," Washer said. "Don't you think that something would have happened by now? I mean you've been feeling this way since the cubs were born."

"I'm worried about Tor and Khoa."

"They're fine. They'll be back any day now. You'll see."

The rabbit wasn't going to commit to an answer one way or another. There were only a few soldiers left in the Wilds right now. Mostly there were young ones and women, so Washer and Pieces had spent their days under the big elm that overlooked the school house. A big patch of berry bushes grew nearby and the clover was sweeter than sweet under the shade of the giant elm. Pieces munched on green clover and the raccoon was particularly fond of the blackberries. He stuffed a big bag full of them every day and took them back down to the lake where he could wash them.

Pieces had just finished eating, and was leaning against the old elm with his hands behind his head. He was feeling satisfied and a little sleepy. In front of him, he could see the entire back of the Wilds for he was on the side of the tree that faced away from the town itself. Rolling hills went on for miles, and they were green and shining in the sun. Pieces liked the scene; the unendingness of it. It made him feel as big as the world itself, that he could go anywhere and do anything; that life stretched out before him.

He saw something standing on the second or third hill over. It looked like a wolf. Though he could not see its color or markings, its dark shape was distinctly wolfish. "Look," he said to Washer, who was still busy picking berries, "there's a wolf over on the ridge."

Washer stopped gleaning the berries from the bushes and turned to look where his friend was pointing. He too, could see clearly that it was a wolf. "Maybe they're back early."

Pieces was about to agree with him when the wolf vanished from sight. "That's strange. The wolf went back down the hill the other way, not toward us."

Pieces was fully awake now. He fixed his gaze on the hill, expecting to see hundreds of warriors being led by Khoa and Tor pouring over the top of the rise any second.

"I'll bring these berries to Ani. I bet she'll make a pie, or cobbler, or tarts," the raccoon said, tying up his sack and walking over to where Pieces sat watching. He sat down and watched with him.

After what seemed a long while, Pieces asked, "Where are they?"

"Should we go see?"

"No!" came the rabbit's quick reply. Something told him there was danger. Now the hills lost their warm appearance. They lay silent, but their stillness echoed a warning.

"Let's get back down to town," Pieces said, grabbing onto Washer's front paw and pulling him from his spot.

The raccoon could hear the trepidation in the rabbit's voice. "Okay," he said, letting his friend pull him along, "but you'll see. Khoa and everyone will come pouring over the rise any minute now."

"No," Pieces said emphatically.

The rabbit's voice made the raccoon halt in his tracks. "Stop it, Pieces. Stop saying it like you knew for sure that there was something dangerous out there."

"I do."

"How can you possibly know who it was? You can't see that far. Shoot, I can't see that far."

"Instinct. You're an animal. You have instinct. Use it."

"Well, my radar says its Khoa and the patrol coming home early."

"That's your feelings, your top layer. Instinct is deeper inside. It's the part that whispers stuff to you."

"Whispers? Whispers what?" the raccoon said becoming irritated.

"Danger, Washer, my friend. Danger."

CHAPTER 4
WOLVES AT THE DOOR

It was after midnight when the small band of wolves entered the Wilds boundaries. There was nothing quiet about their arrival. Pieces was a light sleeper, and the first one to awaken. He poked his head out of the nest he had made in a natural furrow below a fallen log. They were shouting so he could hear their cries quite plainly.

"Help us please."

"Give us shelter."

"We are not intruders."

"We are citizens of Fen. We mean you no harm."

When no one came out to greet them, they grew quiet.

"This city seems to be empty, too."

Pieces peered intently at the group. He noticed that the wolf who had just spoken was a mixed wolf. He thought for a moment and then decided he better get Washer and a few others before venturing out to meet the new arrivals. He would go the back way. There was less chance of him being seen if he hopped under cover of the persimmon bushes and the wild out cropping of prairie grasses along the creek. The grass was cold and wet with dew and snapped him awake. He could still hear them talking.

"Maybe the raider wolves have been here already," another of the wolves said.

"Ras, look for a shelter where we can build a barricade." It was the leader, Connor, who spoke to his son.

"You'll touch nothing in the Wilds," came a clear, strong voice, and Pieces recognized it at once as Zen's. Pieces stopped and turned back towards the group. He couldn't see any of them now, but began his way back. Once he had made it back to his burrow, he could see that some of the others who were left in the Wilds had lit torches and stood in a ring around the newcomers.

"We're being pursued by a pack of raider wolves. We came here for protection."

"Why come to the Wilds for protection?" Zen demanded.

"We heard that Khoa of the Way lived here. That it was he, his brother, Tor, and their band of warrior wolves who ended the reign of the black wolves some years ago," answered Connor.

"You are mixed wolves, and your offspring more dark than you." It was Ani who spoke as ten warrior wolves with torches encircled the small band of travelers. There was a male and female with two older cubs and another mated pair with tiny cubs who stood in the flickering light.

"Who are these raider wolves you spoke of?" asked Fischer.

"You haven't heard of them?" asked Connor turning to his mate.

"They are called that because they come into a town and steal whatever they can. Even cubs." It was Connor's mate, Trin, who spoke, and she looked at Zen and Ani hoping to garner support among the she wolves.

Those in the Wilds were well aware of what was going on, but this band was different. It was two families and the wolves were mixed, almost dark. Most of the others had come in large groups.

"We have no armies in the outlying areas. That's why we fled and sought refuge here."

"If you will permit us to camp by the lake shore this night, we will leave in the morning," Connor said in a subdued manner.

The youngest animal began to complain. "I'm hungry and tired."

"I'm thirsty Mama. Ask them if we can have a drink from the lake."

While Fisher, Zen, and Ani discussed the new arrivals a few feet away, Pieces took it upon himself to begin his own appraisal of the band of animals. When he saw their condition and the young among them his heart softened. As far as he could tell, they weren't black wolves fully, but mixed. They looked tired and weak. The dirt was visible on their fur and made them appear darker than they probably were.

He turned to Washer and the others and asked, "Do they remind you of anybody?"

"Like who?" Washer demanded.

"Like us a few years ago."

"Yes, but, best not be too hasty," Serious warned the group.

"They don't look like they are in any shape to fight or attack us. They're just two families of wolves," Washer scoffed.

"Mixed wolves whose cubs look darker than them. Those two cubs must be a year or more old," Pieces shot back at the raccoon. "I don't like their eyes."

Fisher came back and announced their decision to the travelers. "We have decided that since there are so few of you that you may stay among us if the rest of the citizens agree." He turned towards the crowd. "Any among you have objections to the new wolves staying?"

Washer stepped forward. Immediately he felt awkward and noticed that everyone was focused on him. He looked at Connor and then quickly away. "I don't have an objection, but a question for our arrivals. May I ask it of you?" he said going up to Connor.

"I hope I can answer it for you."

"Were you on the ridge to the north within the last few days?"

Connor paused for a long while, looked at his mate as if to ask permission to answer. The she wolf gave her consent and Connor answered in a hesitating fashion, fully aware of the intense stare from the old rabbit. "Yes. We had found your town and I had scouted all around to see what inhabitants were here. I didn't want to lead my family into a settlement of dark wolves."

"What he says is truth. I saw him yesterday on the ridge," the raccoon answered. "I have no further objections."

"Anybody else have concerns?" Fisher asked the crowd.

When no one said anything, he added, "You may stay."

"May we camp by the lake?"

"You have access to it," Zen added.

After the family had departed, Washer, the rabbit, and the others stayed where they were. They watched the family plod forward to the lake. Other animals began to shuffle back to their homes quietly.

"There's something about those wolf's eyes that spook me. It's like seeing a ghost, I tell you," the old rabbit said, rubbing his arms to warm himself.

"You had your chance to speak up and didn't," Washer upbraided him. "Go back to bed. It's the middle of the night."

"A couple of questions isn't a rigorous enough test to allow strangers in our midst. Maybe Pieces is right," Serious said, but turned to leave.

"There's a hundred new animals among us and have been for months. Why make a big deal about a few more?" Washer said as he and Pieces followed behind Serious.

"I don't like it. Two minor questions isn't a good enough test. It just isn't," Serious continued, his voice trailing off into the distance.

"Officious rabbit," the raccoon said under his breath, but Pieces heard it and chuckled. "And he call calls me a rascal. A black hearted rascal."

"What?" the young rabbit called back. "I heard that."

"Then why did you ask?"

"I wanted to see if you would own up to it," Serious said, stopping and turning to face the two animals behind him. "You won't side with my objections even if it means putting the whole Wilds in jeopardy. You are a black faced, black footed, black hearted rascal," Serious said.

"Good night," the raccoon called out in a disgusted tone to Serious, who was running ahead of them.

"At least he's talking to you, Washer," Pieces said, stopping to watch Serious run off into the distance.

"I'll see you home, old rabbit."

About a week later Ani and Zen had arranged to hold the summer retreat in the absence of Khoa and Tor and the warrior wolves. They decided that First Training of the wolves was too sacred not be honored. Though generally lead by the males, those families whose fathers were on patrol were given over to the mothers to train. The Way required that all young be taught about the Great Wolf and how to know his spirit. At the end of the retreat, all newly born lives were consecrated and each animal pledged his heart to the Great Alpha for himself. In the Christening the parents pledged for their young, now the young were expected to give their own oath. It was the first step in the process of the Way. All animals who wished to initiate their young were free to come.

Today, the last day of the retreat, Ani and Zen had taken the cubs and were headed for the steep ridges above the stream. They had been learning about how the Alpha reveals himself all week. The two she wolves had raced ahead of the cubs and were standing at the top watching the cubs make it up the slope after them.

"It's remarkable how much little Tristian looks like Khoa's grandfather," Ani commented.

"They're all perfect, Ani," Zen said as they watched the cubs running up the slopes. "They learn so fast from you. You're a natural mother. A natural leader."

"You give me too much credit, Zen. It is the teachings of the Way that is easy and natural to follow, not me."

Hearing a high pitched yelp from below, Ani called out, "Tristian! Ease up a bit."

"He's always biting too hard," Arro yelled back, and then turned to nip harder at his brother.

Ani started to run down the slope, but before she could reach the cubs, Savor had come between his two brothers.

Zen touched Ani to get her attention. "Watch. Savor's a leader, too. The others follow what he directs them to do."

Ani looked towards him. "Yes, I think Tristian is a little jealous of Savor. There might be a contest there someday."

"Ah, Tristian does things with force, but don't worry. He has a good heart," Zen said.

"Challenger, keep track of them," she called out to her son. The pup immediately corralled his brothers, CJ and Hunter, with his cousins Savor, Tristian, and Arro, but the girls hung back and would not come into his circle. After barking at them, he heard his mother, Zen, say, "We'll watch your sisters and Ani's girls, Jen and Anna. Stay close."

"Challenger is a natural leader. He will be king one day," Ani said, looking at Zen.

"Well, he acts older than he is."

"He is Tor's shadow to be sure. When he is grown, it will be hard pressed to tell the difference. You can be proud."

"We better follow them," Ani said to Zen, and the two she wolves bounded down the slope after the cubs. Ahead of them, the young wolves chased each other, nipping as they ran, while the three females walked daintily behind, stopping to pick flowers.

To the left, Zen noticed Trin's two cubs standing and watching them and she stopped.

"Would you like to join them?" Ani asked the cubs.

"We can't. We were told not to," Ras said, turning to his brother and motioning for him to follow as he walked away.

"That family sure keeps to itself," Zen said.

"They have been through a lot seeing all their people killed," Ani said, thinking of what they had learned about their flight from the dark wolves, and the takeover of Fen.

"They didn't seem to know much about the city, though. They don't seem to know much about the practice of the Way, either," Zen said.

"Yes, we must change that. Those cubs look to be almost a year old, and darker than most mixed wolves."

"Well, at least they're here, but watching from a distance isn't the same as learning with the others."

"Some of it has got to rub off."

"Yes, distance," Zen said, looking northward towards the Blackstone's. "Both Tor and Khoa have missed out on giving the cubs their First Training."

The she wolves sat silently and watched their cubs until Ani broke their silence, "Time to end their break."

Immediately the mothers gathered up their cubs and gave them their assignment with a warning to stay close. As they watched their cubs separate and head out alone Zen said, "I wish the Way didn't specify that each cub had to seek out the Alpha alone. I would feel much better if they could travel together."

"Let's ask the Great Wolf to protect them," Ani said, and the wolves humbled themselves in the meadow.

Savor was standing with his body stretched to his full height. His ears were forward and his eyes alert and intent. The wind blew the fur on his face and neck back into him. Was this the Great Alpha? he wondered. Just then he felt Tristian nip his flank playfully and dodge away, taunting him. He would answer that challenge, and bounded after him. He caught him and the two cubs tumbled over each other in the grass. Before they were able to get to their feet, Hunter and Arro were tangled in with them.

Challenger galloped up the steep slope after them. "Enough chasing, now. Seek your paths. Alone." The cubs listened to Challenger and without a word they went their ways.

Savor walked across the part of the mountain that was flat and leveled off. Large patches of grass grew where there were no rocks to stop it. Suddenly he became aware of the warmth from the sun on his back. He looked up. Jen, who was a short distance from him, noticed him and looked up, too. Had the sky spoken to Savor? she wondered. She stood absolutely still. Maybe he would speak to her. Soon all the pups were staring upwards. Savor noticed them and moved on across the flat, open section of grass. He liked the feel of the wind. It opened up his heart. The green summer grasses were beginning to fade to brown, and they no longer smelled sweet, but more like the straw that was in the stables back home.

A gopher darted up from his hole, but upon spying the wolf, darted back in. Savor decided not to chase him. The gopher was frightened enough, and he was on a mission. He hadn't found anything yet. He wondered how his brothers and the others were faring. He wanted to be able to tell everyone tonight that he had met the Great Wolf.

Tristian was standing under a tree looking up at a red bird who was clacking noisily down at him. "Looking for something?"

"Yes," the cub answered.

"What?"

"The One True Alpha." That should quiet him, the cub thought, but it didn't. Instead, it made the red bird chirp and rock with cackling sounds. "I know of him. I know of him."

"You do? Do you know where he is?"

"I sure do," the bird said smugly.

Now he was getting somewhere. This was going to be a cinch. He hadn't been out an hour and he was going to find the Alpha straight off.

"He's in me."

Tristian could hardly believe what he had just heard. He went over to the tree and began scratching against its rough bark with his front claws. "You ate him?"

"No, silly coyote. He's in every animal. Why, he's even in you."

"I'm not a coyote. I'm a wolf. A white wolf."

The bird cut him off. "You don't look white. You're painted. You are a white wolf who the Alpha painted black spots on. That's the correct way to describe yourself. You may once have been a white wolf, but now you're painted."

Tristian stopped scratching his paws upon the trunk of the tree. The bird had him there. He had often wondered about that very thing himself. His father had said they were called white because of their species, and because their dominant color was white. He would get no real answers from the red bird and turned away. This bird, red or not, did not even know the difference between a coyote and a wolf. How could he know about anything as grand as the Alpha? The cardinal, watching Tristian walk away with his head down, chirped, "Don't feel bad because you're painted. There are lots of animals who are painted. Me, I'm all red, so I can say that I am red."

When the cub didn't turn back around to acknowledge him the bird said, "Suit yourself. I haven't got time to argue," and he took flight.

Tristian continued onward. What had his father told them? The Great Wolf speaks to all. He is in the leaves, the trees, the wind. He is in all things. Listen. He will come to you. The young cub looked at everything about him. Yes, he had accepted that the Alpha 'speaks to all things,' but was he in them as well? Could it be possible? The sound of splashing water reached his ears. Hearing the water made him realize he was thirsty, and he bounded in the direction of the splashing. Before he reached the stream he saw all the other cubs there except for Savor and Anna. It looked to him as if they were having a pretty good time. He pounced in the stream to join them, but his approach sent them scattering in every direction. "Don't tell mother," Arro called back. Hunter was side by side with Arro; matching him stride for stride. They ran almost as if they were one.

Soon the sound of their footfalls disappeared. He was alone again. He was standing in the icy water and lowered his head to drink. He could feel the heat of the sun on his back. It seemed to penetrate into him; making him nauseous. Tristian decided a roll in the coolness of the water would feel good. The water in the stream was only a few inches deep this time of year. There was not much run off, like in the spring when the snows melted and rushed off the mountains, swelling the streams. This part of the stream was far from the source that fed it. There had not been much rain that summer to deepen it, either.

Rolling in the water had been the right thing to do. It had brought relief to the hotness in his back and refreshed him. He stood up and shook himself off. He looked up at the sun. It glared so brightly he could not look directly into it like he had that morning. Its brilliance seemed to add a deepness to the blue. He had never seen that particular shade of blue before, and he knew it was special. He had seen many blue skies in his few months alive, but not like this one. This was a perfect blue. It was like he had been let into a secret. Who else was aware of this perfect blue that looked so deep, yet let you see beyond it into forever at the same time? The Alpha probably knew of this color. Yes, that's what he would call this color; the Great Wolf's Blue for he was the one that made it.

He bent down for one last drink and noticed the trees mirrored in the water. He could also see the suns reflection in the water and his own. He studied himself. He searched his eyes, his face. Was there anything else in there behind all those features? Was the Alpha somewhere in there? How did one tell?

Just then a monarch lit upon the water for an instant before flitting upwards again. It seemed to float on the wind, yet follow a pathway just the way the water in the stream did; like it knew where it was going. Did that butterfly have the spirit of the Alpha in it as well? If the spirit fit into a creature that small, just what size was this spirit? Tristian felt disheartened. If the spirit was that small he would never find it. He could never see it. A thought came to him. That's why father said you couldn't see it! It's too small!

Just then he caught the reflection of two larger wolves in the water. They were directly behind him. Before he could see who it was, a bag was fitted over his head and a noose cinched securely around the dark and smelly cloth.

It was an unusually warm day even for early fall. This year the leaves on the trees stayed green longer. There had been no cold, or wind, or rain to dry them or shake them loose. The only way to tell the season was by the shortness of the days themselves. The trees around the Wilds looked beautiful in their green garb with a few shadings of reds, oranges, and bright yellows at the tops to signal the turning of the year. The wind was gentle and light.

Pieces and Washer had spent the morning at the community garden patch. The raccoon often pulled the root vegetables up for the rabbits so they could store them in a cellar before they froze in the ground. In exchange for his muscle, the rabbits provided him with some of the green tops, which added a soft cushion for lining his nest. The raccoon found them to be aromatic to his nose. He liked their sweet smell mixed with a few sprigs of pine tied together, which he hung on the insides of his tree stump. The raccoon ate vegetables in the winter as well. A small section was planted in corn, which the raccoons and squirrels shared.

"A good mornings work," Pieces said, looking at the crop of rutabagas, carrots, fennel, corn and broccoli that lay strewn about.

"Let's bag it up and call it quits," Washer said to the rabbit as he pulled the last carrot out of the loose soil with his front paws. "We've still got to haul it home and about to some of the others." He looked up at the sky.

"I hope the weather holds so we can get some more fishing in this week."

A loud voice broke in on them. "Washer! There you are!"

Both animals turned to see Mr. Nipper, the wolverine, waving a letter in the air. "I didn't want to leave this on your stump. It's got to have a reply and your print that says you received it. It's going back air mail."

"Whoa, who do you know that would spring for all that?" Pieces asked.

"Sounds like trouble to me. Maybe I don't want it. Where's it from?" he asked, eyeing the wolverine.

"Same place the other letter I delivered here last month came from. Fienix Forest, Northwestern Section."

"Climber. I bet he's telling me why my nephew hasn't come."

"You read it and write your answer on the back," Nipper said, picking up his sack. "I'll be back to get it after the other deliveries. Mind you keep it to thirty words. That's what's paid for."

"Thirty words! I can answer it with one. Good!" Washer said, opening the letter.

The raccoon began to shake his head as he read. "He's yelling at me," he said to Pieces, "for not writing to him about how Stasher and I are getting along."

"You must not be reading it right. Let me see it," the rabbit said, taking the letter.

"Hmm. Not so good language there in parts. Bleep, bleep brother of mine. You've bleep, bleep," and the rabbit looked up from reading at his friend who was pacing back and forth in front of him. "Oh, that's a zinger. I never heard that one before," he exclaimed before looking back down at the letter. "We've been bleep, bleep worried." Here the rabbit scanned the rest of the note quickly and began picking out words here and there, "inconsiderate, bleep, irresponsible," then continued, "so you better bleep, bleep write back and let us know how Stasher is faring. Love, Climber and Family."

They both stared at each other in disbelief. "How are you going to tell your brother you've lost his son?"

"Lost him? Lost him? What do you mean, lost him? I never had him to lose," Washer ranted, pulling on his tail.

"Of course. Of course. How can you lose something you've never had? But what are you going to tell him?"

"I don't know. I don't know. That I died."

Pieces was shaking his head. "He sounds like the type to want to dig up your body and hang your hide on his shed." They sat quiet. "Does he have one?" the rabbit asked. The raccoon only turned to look at him.

Just then the bell in the school began to clang over the early evening meadow. It generally rang four times to signal the start of the school day, but it was summer. Other than the commencement of school, it was used to alert the town of danger. Both the rabbit and the raccoon jumped to their feet and ran down the hill towards the school.

By the time they reached the schoolyard, almost all of the citizenry was there. Serious was coming out of the schoolhouse and down the steps calling out, "Tristian is missing. Challenger, too."

Pieces and Washer had just caught up to him. "How? What happened?" Washer asked him.

Serious ignored him and spoke to Tru. "When will you be ready?"

"Ten minutes is all I need to assemble the search party."

"What's to be done, Serious?" Washer asked as the younger rabbit passed by him.

When no answer came, the raccoon turned to his friend and said, "I can't believe it, Pieces. He still won't speak to me."

"Always splitting hairs," Washer called, loud enough for the young rabbit to hear and chased after him.

"Yeppers, and at times of utmost peril," Pieces quipped, running beside Washer.

"I'm not speaking to you, Washer," Serious said with an emphasis on the raccoons' name.

The raccoon stopped in his tracks, "Well, whoever you were speaking to, my ears heard it, too. They don't know any better."

CHAPTER 5
A PARABLE OF NATURE AND SPIRIT

Washer and Pieces followed Fisher to the cave. They needed to tell everyone about Stashers disappearance. Ani and Zen sat quiet as Fisher related his plans for the search. In the fading light of early dusk the two mothers looked more subdued than ever. Pieces noticed that the marvelous light which usually came from Ani's eyes was gone. When it seemed that all the plans for the search had been finalized, Washer stepped forward. "May I have you search for someone one else as well, Fisher?"

"Yes, of course, Washer. Who?"

"My nephew, Stasher."

"He wasn't here, though." Ani said. "How did he go missing?"

"Been missing for a long time. I just got a letter from my brother who thought he was here and had been for over a month. He was supposed to have come on the Burro to Burrow line over a month ago and he never arrived."

"That means all the passengers must have been taken as well," Fisher said.

Ani looked at the two little animals. They were grief stricken. "You better stay with us tonight. It'll be safer. Fisher and Scout are asking everyone to double up on housing arrangements for a while."

The two friends nodded and followed Ani to their room.

The faint first light of dawn came over the Wilds. The sun had set the night before and rose now, as it always did, ignorant to the news of the missing. Brilliant pinks and oranges painted streaks across the sky above the mountain tops to the north. Tru and Fisher were busy assembling the search party and posting guards around the perimeter of the city and the rest were busy with breakfast. "Look, there's birds flying in from the east," Fisher said.

It was true, but in the dim light of dawn all they could see was black moving objects. Soon the birds were overhead. "Oh-Oh," Washer groaned and everyone laughed.

The laughter died away instantly as the birds landed.

"We heard that the cub kings had been taken. Is it true?" Oh-Oh remarked, taking in all the faces of the group. She immediately noticed the look on the she wolves' faces.

"Khoa and the other king wolf still gone?"

Immediately Pieces, Washer, and the others looked sheepishly at the ground and then at their guests.

When no one volunteered a single word to the bird, she said in her no nonsense manner, "We need to get word to him."

Oh-Oh quickly took stock of the animals around her. Yes, they were all small and older or women or too young.

"Hmmm. This all that's left?" Without waiting for an answer she said, "Looks like it's up to Swoop and me."

"I'm ready for a stretch of the wings," Swoop said.

"Little owls of mine, you stay put until we return. Mind the old rabbit here."

The pair was in the air just as the sun rose fully in the sky. As Pieces looked after them, he noticed just how amazingly blue and clear the morning was. It did not belie any of the events in the world below, he thought.

"You're leaving me in charge!" Pieces grimaced up at her. "I'm too old," he called out after her.

"Not old, wiser. You sit for the King, don't you?" Oh-Oh shouted back.

"She might have asked," he said to Washer as he walked towards the owls.

"It's not in her nature," Swoop J commented.

"Hmmm," the rabbit retorted.

Pieces stood looking at the three owls with a scowl. "Okay, get in line. Follow me. Don't do anything unless I tell you to. We have many things to attend to."

"He sounds just like Mom," one of the girls whispered. The rabbit, hearing her voice, turned back around to look at them. All got quiet and their little peepers blinked at him.

He moved forward to where the others were gathered before heading on with his charges. Fisher and the other wolves had been discussing the arrangements for all the strangers they now had among them. "They will have to be watched now," he was saying.

"Possibly asked to leave," Tru said.

"It was Conner, Trin, Brusher, and his mate that took the cubs. We know that because they're gone. The others have been here for months," Zen said.

"That doesn't mean we know them and what they're up to."

After much discussion about the resettlement camp, Ani said, "Let them stay."

Fisher called out a unit to watch those that had been camped to the west of the lake, and two to stand guard by the cave with Zen and Ani; one of whom was Tru, who had personally asked to be given the duty. He would also change the perimeter guards each morning and night. There was nothing he couldn't do on three legs except fight one on one.

"I will take these three units into the forest and into the East where the tracks lead," Fisher told Zen and Ani. "We will find the cubs," he added reassuringly. "We won't come home without them." Fisher turned with a flourish of his tail and trotted towards the eastern horizon with his wolves.

Pieces was left standing alone with his charges. "OK. We've got work to do. If I'm to be gone on the search party with Washer, those vegetables from my winter cellar will rot. This zoo needs to be fed." He was angry with himself. He had felt danger when he had seen those wolves on the rise that morning. He had let sentimentality replace his instincts. He had seen those eyes before and now he remembered where. Venger. He felt old. Would he ever be able to trust his inner feelings again? Just when Khoa had proclaimed him so good at seeing things, he lost it.

The little line of owls followed behind him dutifully as he led the way to his stash. Animals stopped and stared at the little parade as it crossed the town square and then down the little path to his root cellar. Here he stopped and issued orders to his tiny charges. "I will go down and throw the stuff out. Then we will deliver them. These first ones need to go to Ani, Zen, and the cubs."

After throwing about two dozen vegetables out, he retreated from the hole. To his astonishment there were only a few vegetables lying on the ground and no owls. Before he had time to panic, Pieces saw them fly back in, each pick up a piece of food and fly away towards Khoas' cave. These owls were industrious. No slackers here, he thought. Maybe he was being too ungenerous towards them because of his feelings towards their mother. She had trained them well. Maybe he was being too hard on her as well. After all, it was she and Swoop, who had flown off to tell Khoa what had happened to the cubs. She had changed after the great storm. She was no longer just a snoop, but was a helper.

So the days continued in the Wilds. Babies were kept in or close to home, and though it was the end of summer, school was delayed in starting. Serious made the rounds to houses under armed guard to keep the younger ones caught up and the older ones learning new ideas.

It was almost evening and Ani stirred with the last twilight calling of birds. The wolf rose slowly. Her cubs were still asleep; tangled about each other. They shifted with her movement, but did not wake.

Once outside the cave, she looked to the north. She could see the faint outlines of hills in the distance. Trees stood like dark silhouettes against the sky. Towards the west, the last glimmer of gold slipped below the mountain ridge. Her ears picked up movement directly ahead of her, and she stiffened her stance. Instinctively, Ani lifted her nose to get a deeper taste. When she caught the scent she relaxed. It was Pieces, Washer, and the little owls.

Ani saw the twigs and grasses each one of the chicks held dangling in their mouths.

"Still working?" she said to them.

"No. Mama told us to never come empty handed to the cave," Swoop J said.

All the others nodded.

"Aren't they just the cutest?" Pieces beamed.

"You've certainly brightened, Pieces," Ani said, hinting at his change of attitude about the owls.

Zen came out with the all cubs romping behind her.

"The owls told me the story of how Who-Who changed," he said, a little ashamed.

"Can they tell us?" Savor asked.

"Yes, can their story be our story tonight?" Tor Jr. clamored.

"Ask them," Zen said.

"We would be honored to entertain the king's family," Toots said before he was asked.

After the seven cubs settled into their place, Toots began the story.

"It was the storm that changed her."

"The big one this summer that took all the trees down?" TJ broke in.

"Shh! It's not polite to interrupt," Zen said.

Toots nodded and said, "Yes, in our part of Fienix Forest, the brunt of the storm clipped the topper most part of trees clean off as if they had been cleaved with an axe. Most of the limbs which were trimmed away were never found. Every sort of flying bird, big or small, and any creature that had nested in the trees was carried away."

The cubs leaned in closer to the owls with gasps, oohs, and aahs.

"Were you scared?" asked Ginny.

The little owls all nodded and Olive said, "Mama's cousin was lost along with all of his family. Our aunts and uncles disappeared, too."

"Our neighbors, the squirrels, never came back either," one of the other owls added.

"Mama was devastated by the loss of her family members. Papa said she has never recovered totally from the shock left by the aftermath of the storm. Not one twig or feather from a nest could be scavenged from anywhere nearby. She just couldn't get over how everything and everyone in that section of the forest had just vanished," Toots said.

"Mama never slept through the night after that. She sat up and called for her family night after night, but they never came back," Olive said.

"That's when she began to tell everyone she met the story of how Khoa had saved our lives."

"He did?" Tristian asked, looking at Ani.

"How?" the little cubs began questioning.

"Your father, the king, ran all the way through hail and thunder and lightning to get to us in the forest. He was battered and bruised when he reached us. We could hardly tell he was the king."

"I don't remember that," Savor commented, looking up at his mother beside him.

"You were just tiny babies then," Ani said, caressing him with her paws. "You hadn't even been out of the nesting yet. Hadn't taken your first steps."

At this point, Hoot-Hoot came forward, "Mama always says," and he began to imitate Who-Who, 'It was his matted and bleeding body that shook me into my senses, that scared me into changing my mind enough to turn and leave with him. I saw how much he gave. And then Papa always says, 'You didn't expect that from the King, did you?"'

Toots came up by his brother and said, "And then Mama always answers him," 'So be it.' "

"It was only us and a few other families that listened to Khoa's warning. Now our mother tells everyone she meets about what Khoa did that night, and about how he helped us rebuild a new nest lower in the branches right here in the Wilds," Hoot-Hoot said.

"Yes," Swoop J said, "But her favorite story to tell is about how Khoa, the King, told us children to help ourselves to whatever we wanted from the pile of treasures outside of this cave. One time we had taken so much from the pile home with us that Mama took some back, but Khoa had told her,

"Whatever is mine is yours. You can have it freely. Not just for this time, but in the future."

"Mom watched very closely to all the king did. Not only had Khoa helped us, he had helped every beast that had survived the storm. She had watched as your mountain of treasures became emptier and emptier. But then a strange thing began to happen. Animals from everywhere brought new things and restored the pile higher than it had been before. We flew by the cave every week. We weren't here to take anything from the treasure pile, but to make sure that Khoa was still around," Swoop J said.

Hoot-Hoot continued, "Mama wanted to make sure she could find him. It particularly gave her a feeling of security to see the wolf family, as she called you, about the outside of the cave."

"Mom brought something to the cave every week after that. She said, 'who knew what animal might need a twig or two?" Swoop J added.

"It gave order to her world, she said," reported Olive.

Just then Washer looked up and commented, "Well, talk about the owl, and there she is," he said, pointing to the sky and northward.

Everyone stood up and waited for the birds to land. "They've returned sooner than I expected," Ani said.

"Yeppers, but is it good or bad?" Pieces said, almost under his breath.

Even before the two owls landed, they could hear Oh-Oh say, "Khoa's a few hours behind. We did not tell him the news of the missing cubs, only that he was needed home at once. We did not want him to travel with bad news on his mind."

"And Tor? Was Tor with him?" Zen asked eagerly as the pair landed.

They both shook their head.

Ani looked at Zen. "Khoa will have news."

"They were pulling a hurt wolf on some branches," Swoop said.

"Funny thing though," he added. "They were already on their way home."

"They must have found the others and were heading back," Zen said. A new sense of relief and hope entered her.

News traveled fast and the Wilds stirred to life as animals came out to wait for the king. It would be safer now.

The animals had set a watch to announce the king's return, but almost everyone in the Wilds was looking northward. At last the army was seen on the ridge that lead down in to the Wilds.

The closer the army drew it was easy to observe the cadence of their march. It was slow and their posture tired and worn. The exuberance of the animals faded as the wolves marched into the square. Whispers ran through the crowd.

"Only Khoa is leading them."

"Only one army."

"Something's wrong."

Food had been readied for Khoa and his warriors, but not one of them ate. They watched in silence as a healer wolf took Winter off. He was the only one from Tor's army who had returned with them. All sat listening to Khoa. Even the cubs sensed the heaviness of the moment and were quiet. He told them all of what Winter had related to him.

"We are going to gather and train our army into a force that can go against over a thousand. We will remount the attack before they come against the Wilds. This is not their home. It is ours."

He waited for the response from the crowd, but none came. He knew looking at their faces that it was not just his news that had silenced them. Ani called him over to her side. "I have something else to tell you."

As Khoa walked over to her, he noticed the quietness of the cubs. They had not moved.

"What's going on? No one happy to see me?" but not one of them stirred. He looked over their faces, his nose seeming to count each one. Hmm. Not all of the cubs were there. He counted again, his nose moving slower this time. "I only count seven. Where are all the cubs?"

It was at that point that Ani broke down and let the tears stream down. The animals watched for a moment and then, urged by Pieces and Washer, began to slowly walk away.

The next morning Khoa was up before the sun and on his rounds. It was good to be home, but he couldn't get the heaviness out of his heart. He moved, but he felt no life in his heart. The trees, the lake, even the meadow that was awash in the radiant colors of the flowers he loved were grayed like they wore a veil which muted and dulled their brilliance. His grandfather's namesake was gone. Tristian, he called in his heart. He let the names roll off his tongue. Tor, Challenger, Scout, Stasher. He had felt this empty aching for his grandfather, and a week ago for Tor, but their deaths had come one at a time. Now there were many, and all at once. Tristian had been a magnificent wolf. Somehow seeing the old wolf in his mind, made him hear his voice. 'I am still in your heart, Khoa. Carry the others there.' Yes, that was his grandfathers' voice alright. That is what he would say if he were here.

A voice interrupted his thoughts and startled him. "Khoa! Up on the ridge." It was Tru. He needed to be more alert. He hadn't seen the wolf come upon him. He hadn't even heard anything. Until this moment he hadn't realized where he was standing. He was no protector, no warrior in the state he was in. He needed to find his strength, his balance. Again Tristian's words came to him, 'Now you will find that it takes strength to live, to fulfill life's destiny.' Yes, he was learning that, and it was a bitter lesson.

He struggled to make sense out of what Tru was saying. The wolf was pointing upwards. As he loped up the incline, he saw that Tru had dispatched the morning patrol to relieve the night sentries. Overhead he saw Swoop fly in and land. In the sky was a host of various kinds of birds. There were over two hundred eagles, osprey, owls, blackbirds, and robins.

"You said last night you needed recruits," Swoop announced, and flew away from the rest of the birds. He lowered his head and bowed his wings forward towards Khoa. All of the birds followed suit, and it touched the wolf's heart.

Turning to Swoop, Khoa said, "We sure could use your speed of flight to send a message to Fisher and to peek into the Blackstone fortress for Tor and his army. Things are changing quickly."

"Done."

"Come with me first," Khoa said, walking away. "I'll brief you on what we've already planned. We've got a temporary headquarters set up in the school."

He stopped and turned to Swoop, "Can we have some of your trained couriers now?"

"We will do anything you wish."

To Tru he said, "I want you to send out the trained birds to all the towns and get recruits. Tell them to report to the Wilds."

"And their families? We can't ask wolves to leave them alone."

"Tell them to bring them with. They will be protected here."

By early afternoon, Khoa watched the animals he had asked to build a wall around the outer edges of the town. Now there was only a small structure around the field where they trained, but it was not tall or fortified enough to stand against the thousands that would be coming. The new walls would protect them on three sides from attack and the lake was behind them, he thought. They would use the lake both as a line of defense and a means of escape if necessary. He needed to have rafts built and a fall back fort across the lake they could retreat to. The beavers had cut down trees from the outer edges of the forest, thinning out the diseased and decaying ones. Khoa was surprised at how much work had been done. Walls were going up. They would hide the lake and provide a false front from attackers.

Standing on the ridge he thought of the words in the Book. *First nature, then spirit.* It seemed like a double attack to him at the moment. What it meant was there were two things that hit you, not just one. As far as he could discern, the first signal came out of a blue sky like a sudden storm comes in the mountains. Then the second sign hangs over your head like a great stone until it drops. That's where he was now, he thought. What good was this warning system? He must not be reading it right. It was bad news the way he was thinking about it, and yet the Book said it offered wisdom. Right now it was a big stone of doom that weighted him down. There was nothing he could do to stop what was going to happen. It was like trying to stop the moon pulling on tides. Whatever it was, it was as natural as nature itself. It was a law. Like the sun coming up and going down. Like breathing in and out. Nothing could stop it. Just like nothing could stop the snow that came in winter, or the rain from falling. Just like the dream. Just like Tor. They were simple everyday things, but they held a greater mystery than that; the mystery of the force that controlled them. It seemed like he almost had understanding, but it kept slipping away in front of him. It kept one step ahead. An inner voice said, 'You're almost there.'

As he stood on the ridge he looked up into the sky. The sun was now low in its arc and slipping lower. In his field of vision he could see Ani loping up towards him.

"You have that look on your brows. They're knitted together. What's troubling you?"

"I wasn't a very good parent. I didn't give Tristian enough love, knowledge, anything. I didn't equip him to live in a world beyond here."

"You gave him enough. You gave him what time allowed you to."

"I should have taught him more from the Book, more about the Alpha."

"You gave him more than you know, Khoa. You gave him a seed just as Grandfather Tristian gave you a seed. Now let it grow. There's nothing else to do."

Khoa knew that what his mate was telling him was the wisest advice he could hope for. He needed to trust in the

Great Wolf. He needed to let it rest in his hands, and that was the hardest thing he had ever needed to do.

"I won't try and make it sound easy, Khoa. The cubs will have quite a different experience with the black wolves. It'll be quite a change of life for them outside the Wilds," Ani said.

"You don't need to tell me that. I lived with the black wolves. I know the manner of life they will be exposed to if they are even alive."

"You survived, Khoa. I survived."

"That was different. We were older. We knew something of what the black wolves were like."

"Who helped us survive?"

Khoa didn't answer. He knew what his mate was telling him. She was staring at him, waiting for an answer and finally he said, "I know what you're saying is the truth. I need to trust in the Great Wolf. I need to let it rest in his hands, but I don't know if I can."

"You don't really have a choice, Khoa. Neither do I. Neither do Zen or the cubs. Life is what it is right now. You can't change it."

They stood alone on the rise for a long while before Ani came and rested her head on his back. "Maybe it's time I started listening to myself instead of everyone else."

"Like it or not you have been called to be the one to do it," she said, taking her head off his back to look him in the eyes.

"What if I can't? What if I fail?"

"You're not Tor. Don't try to be. Lead them the way of Khoa."

"My heart is gone. How can I lead anybody?"

"Give your heart to the Great Wolf. Call out to Him. Let the whole Wilds hear you call. Call loudly. Break the darkness with it," Ani urged him, nipping at his shoulder, but he only stood there.

"I can't. Not right now."

"You are just a wolf, Khoa. Don't think you are anything more."

"I know I am just a wolf. That's what I keep telling everyone. Maybe I know my limitations better than anyone. Since finding the Book and going in the Way, I have been pushed into everything I never wanted to do."

"And me and the cubs?"

"I may not be who you think I am," Khoa said and ran off the hill.

Ani looked after him and thought of the night she had seen him in the snow on the top of the ridge. This was a different Khoa. One she didn't know. One that frightened her.

So the days passed in a haze that made them all run together and Khoa dreamed many dreams. It became so he could not tell his waking life from his sleeping life.

This night he dreamed he was in the tall grass by a brook. He thought he should know where he was, but he wasn't sure. Some things were familiar and yet others weren't. It was summer and he heard the water coursing over the smooth boulders. Its current was brisk for the spring snows had just melted in the high mountains. He drank from the waters and it was icy and refreshing. Instead of his own reflection in the water he saw the face of the Watcher looking back at him. Suddenly she emerged right out of the water into a full wolf before him. As she walked, each step speeded up time into the blinking of an eye. With her first step it was autumn. Her second step brought winter, and then night came with her third step. As she continued to walk closer, it seemed to Khoa that the seasons still passed, but he could no longer see them in the darkness; only feel and smell them.

"Why is it the night not passing?" he asked in the dream.

"It is the season," the Watcher answered.

But there is no such thing as a season of night his mind told him. Khoa thought he had said it out loud to her, but when she didn't acknowledge it with a reply he decided he had only thought it. There was no time to dwell on it for he saw his pups and Tor's running before him in the meadow. All nine of them were there, and next Challenger and Tristian were tumbling down a hill side by side in the darkness. He could see the two looking at a sky filled with stars. Then the sky changed from just a jumble of stars into the shape of the warrior squirrel riding through the heavens, its sword drawn high. Instantly a streak passed by them; a falling star which cast rider and horse to earth.

Khoa turned to the Watcher. "What does this mean?"

"All stories are in the sky. Isn't that what you taught them?"

"Yes, but what does it mean?" he asked her again.

"You have seen what is not, but as it will be. It is the answer. Remember it is the Great Wolf who raises up kings and sets them in the sky."

CHAPTER 6
PAX

Khoa headed for the lake earlier than usual the next morning. He did not go directly to the spot where the animals met to form the patrols for the day. Today he wanted to just walk along the shore. He needed to think. Each day about twenty animals walked the perimeter of the wilds and sometimes beyond to keep the citizens posted as to what animals were in the area and what their business was. Now, there was a need to have the patrols go further from the wilds, but it was the dream that was foremost in his mind. Where was the Watcher when you needed her? She had come to him in the dream, but given him no answers. Her voice came to him again. 'The Great Wolf sets up kings. He knows all things.'

I know the Great Wolf does all things, he said to himself. Why did the warrior squirrel fall to earth? Did that mean he was going to fall in battle? Was the Wilds going to be lost now that Tor was gone? There was no answer in the dream, only more questions that seemed to lead him in a circle. It was just a dream, he finally told himself. Why was he even trying to get something out of it? A voice came to him. 'You have the answers, Khoa. Just not the ones you want. Your ears do not hear because your heart tells it not to.' Here was that thing of hearing with your heart again. Tristian had said that the heart hears. The voice spoke louder over his thoughts. 'Listen, Khoa. You seek the Watcher, yet drive her away. She cannot come when the heart does not hear.' The time for listening was over, he told himself.

Khoa had walked some distance, and as he was just rounding the point, he could see Washer was out there. He was fishing from the furthest most rock that jutted out into the water. Reeds grew all along the rocky outcropping, and the fish liked to hide in it, the raccoon had told him. The raccoon was an early riser. He liked to fish alone and he liked the way the mist hid everything around him. It seemed to bring a stillness upon everything, he had once told Khoa.

The wolf had been staring after the raccoon, and the animal must have sensed it because he turned around to look towards the shore. Khoa waved and the raccoon immediately greeted him back. Washer bent forward to pick up the end of his fishing stringer. He pulled it along behind him.

"Breakfast?" he asked approaching Khoa.

"I could use a few."

"Trout's your favorite, isn't it?" he didn't wait for Khoa to answer. "Course it's only the lake variety. I haven't been fishing the streams lately."

As Washer unhooked a few of the fish and tossed them over to the wolf he said, "They're on the house. That is as long as you can give me some needed advice."

Khoa was aware of how focused and intent the raccoon's eyes were as he was talking.

"Well, I don't know what you're looking for. Maybe I better not eat the fish until I know if I can help you," the wolf winked.

Washer looked away, knowing he had given Khoa the wrong impression. "Eat away. Everyone thinks better on a full tank."

"Once they're gone, they're gone," the wolf warned.

"I'm thinking of switching my patrolling day permanently. Do you think that's a good idea?"

"You mean so you won't have to be around Serious?"

"Exactly."

"It's been six months since your little tiff. Don't you think it's time for you two to mend fences?"

Washer walked away from where he was standing and down to the shore. He had a big fish in his hands, and he began washing it in the waves as they hit. "He's a hard hearted rabbit."

Khoa watched as the raccoon took a bite of the fish, chew while he waited for the next wave to roll in, then dip the fish again, chew, wait for the next wave, dip, bite, chew. Wait, dip, bite, chew. Wait, dip, bite, chew. When it came to his eating habits, Washer was very fastidious and proper.

"If that's how you feel, Washer, then you've got your answer."

Washer threw what was left of the fish into the next wave. "Truth is I miss him," he said, turning around to face Khoa.

"Then form a pax with him."

"Pax?"

"It means peace in the ancient language."

"But how? What do I say?"

"Tell him what you told me, that you miss him."

"Should I write him a note or tell him out loud, nose to nose?"

"It might be wiser to write him a letter."

The raccoon scratched his chin. "You mean, safer." He didn't look at Khoa, but stared out over the lake, thinking. "Yes, you might be right. He might take a nip at me in a nose to nose encounter."

Washer turned to face Khoa and walked over to him on all fours before standing on his hind legs so he could see into the wolfs eyes. "But then again, he might not read a note. He might just throw it away. He's a hard hearted rabbit, you know. Which should I do?"

"What's a nip between friends? Life's short. You never know."

The raccoon looked away from the wolf's direct stare. He knew what his friend was saying. You never know when the one you love is gone in a flash, when life turns suddenly, like it had for him and Ani in losing young Tristian and for Zen in losing Tor and Challenger.

"Yes, I see what you are saying. Better to make a pax while you can. Better on the conscience, too."

"You need to decide, Washer. I can't do that for you."

From behind him, the raccoon could hear the padding of feet drawing nearer. "Oh, oh. Here comes the patrol. My cue to leave," he said getting down on all fours again. He made tracks in the opposite direction.

"Why don't you face Serious now and get it over with?"

Washer turned briefly back towards Khoa, "I need time to prepare." He stood up and looked towards the approaching group. "Boy, they sure are noisy this morning."

The raccoon was right, thought Khoa, and he knew why. War was on the horizon. As he watched his friend leave, he felt a sudden let down. There was great energy in the air around the patrollers. They walked in quicker steps, talked in louder voices. It was as if they pulsed with expectancy. They were tight, alert, and coiled. Khoa sensed that if a fight were to happen this minute, they could respond in seconds, and emerge untouched and victorious.

They stood looking at him with eager anticipation. He felt a sudden let down. He had come out early to walk, to be alone and to think of a plan to give to the patrol when they arrived, and solve his own problems. He wished the raccoon would have made the pax with Serious. At least then he would have accomplished something this morning. Pax? 'Yes, that was the answer,' the voice whispered. 'Peace. Peace at all costs.' That was not what was in his heart. He wanted to hit the dark wolves with all he had. He wanted his heart to even the score.

"We patrol as normal this morning. I don't want any lone out breaks of skirmishes. I don't want them to be aware that we are onto the dark wolves."

"What if they attack us?" Corker asked.

"Then you have no choice," Khoa said as he made his way to the front. The white wolf was thinking that there were a lot of young animals on patrol. There were also the new wolves to train. They needed to know where the outposts were and learn the signals. He called Scout and Winter over to him. "I'm going to change the roster this morning. Mix it up a bit." Amid the groans from the ranks, Khoa continued giving his orders. "If there's trouble, I want all of you to be ready to stand beside anyone you find yourself with. I need to put the new wolves in with your units and some of the elite garrison in with you as well." The white wolf quickly looked over the group to see what would be good matches of age and youth. "Scout, I'm putting the smaller animals close to the Wilds."

"OK. Listen up. Patrol one: Serious, Cody, Linus, and Winter."

Khoa continued reading the new rosters until all seven units had been rearranged. As the animals were busy assembling themselves into their new patrol units, and preparing to move out, Khoa said, "Remember don't take them on alone. Report back immediately. Keep invisible."

Someone was clearing their throat and patting his front leg insistently. He looked down. It was Washer again.

"Put me in with my hard hearted chum, will you?"

When Khoa didn't answer, he continued, holding a small envelope up to him. "Please. I even have a pax offering for him. A packet of carrot seeds that Pieces gave me from his secret stash."

The white wolf nodded, but before he could speak, the raccoon was tugging at him.

"Maybe you could call him over here. Act as a referee."

"Anything else?"

"No, that would be sufficient."

Soon Serious was standing face to face with Washer and Khoa. His back rear leg was thumping lightly on the ground. Washer couldn't look him in the eyes and just thrust the seed packet out in his general direction.

"Poison?" the rabbit asked sarcastically.

"Life's short and I…" Washer began, but the rabbit cut him off,

"And you wanted to make it shorter."

Khoa stepped in by pushing Serious aside with his nose. He explained that Washer wanted to make peace, a pax with him, and that he had brought Pieces' prized carrot seeds. At this point, Serious peered around the wolf's body at Washer. The raccoon was still dangling the packet out in front of him. Hmm. Those were his favorite kind of carrots, and he had always asked Pieces for some of those seeds. He had dreamed about those carrots. There must be a catch, he thought. "What do you want in return?" he called out to Washer.

"To be your friend, again."

Serious looked at Washer and then at the seeds, but didn't say anything.

"Khoa made me realize that life can change in an instant. I wanted to make each day count…," here the raccoon paused, "with everyone."

"You want to ease your conscience, you mean."

"No, my heart," Washer said, dropping the packet on the ground.

He got down on all fours, turned, and ambled away.

The sight of his friend's back, and his slow, waddling retreat struck Serious with sadness. He had wanted to end this stale mate of war between them many times, but pride had gotten in the way, and the simple fact that he didn't know how to end it. Now, he had been given the chance to end the distance between them, and he was throwing it away. Tears began streaming down his face. "Washer! Washer!" Serious called, hopping after him in a halting fashion. When the raccoon didn't stop, he called out a single word, "Friend."

As soon as he noticed that Washer had stopped walking, Serious went into dash mode. He sped by the seeds on the ground and was in front of the raccoon in a second. They stood looking at each other. "Pax?" Serious asked, offering his paw. The raccoon hesitated, but then noticing the tears in the rabbits eyes, stood up and took his friends paw. "Pax," he said back.

CHAPTER 7
CAPTIVES

Tristian woke in darkness and to terrible pain in his head and stomach. At first he thought he must be going blind. Hazy light was visible, but black dots or spots obscured his sight. What was wrong with his eyes? He reached a paw up to rub them, but found that something was confining his movement. He could see his paw clearly in front of him. Tristian looked again beyond his paw and saw the patch like vision again. It was like a rough weaving of sorts. The pup could vaguely make out light through the tiny holes. It smelled musty and of earth. Dirt clung to his tongue as he licked against its sides to get a better sense of his surroundings. The aroma was not unlike the vegetable smells that came out of the rabbits' garden. All of a sudden, his thoughts led him to a picture of Pieces' storage room and the bags heaped up in that area. He was in a potato sack.

A voice boomed out, "Let's get moving," Suddenly the ground began to tremble beneath him. He was jolted forwards and back. The earth was not smooth under his belly. He could feel only hardness underneath him. No grass cushioned him as he was jounced to and fro. In the partial darkness he traced the outline of the hard lines with his right paw. The lines seemed to form little squares all around him. He was in a cage of some sort. Then he suddenly remembered seeing the two wolves' reflection behind him in the stream. Could he have possibly been sleeping all this time? He had never slept so hard. Did they know he was there? Why was the earth moving under him? His heart trembled and shook. He was afraid to move. He lay perfectly still, listening to his heart, feeling it jolt with each new bump beneath him. Tristian felt frozen. You're a coward, he told himself. You're afraid because you're alone.

He thought of the cave, of his brothers and sisters, and mother and father. He had only known safety and laughter. Now the first time he had to face danger, he fell back. What had his father told him when he asked him if he had been afraid in battle? He had answered 'yes', and then said, 'You can either fight or die. The choice is yours.' It was really that simple, the cub decided now. Fight or die. He inhaled a great breath and he let it go, which gave him a great sense of relief. He had met his fear and pushed past it.

"Hello? Who's out there? I'm in here." Somehow he found comfort in the sound of his own voice.

"Yes, we know you are in there," the same voice said amid laughter.

"Let me out. I need air and water."

"Get over it," the voice came back.

"The little king is giving orders." It was a different voice this time. More laughter erupted.

They were aware of who he was, but who were they?

"I need water."

A voice next to him cut him off, "Save your breath. You'll get water when we get water."

Tristian recognized the voice. "Ras?"

"Maybe. Maybe not," the mixed wolf taunted.

"Why's the earth moving?"

"You afraid or something?" the cub laughed, and then added, "It's a cart, stupid."

"I can't see so well. I'm in a bag, you know."

Tristian had never ridden in a cart before, and if this experience was an indication of what it was like, he didn't want it again. He tried to remember the pictures he had seen in school books of carts. In the stories he had read, animals put goods in them to haul to market. He tried to glance around him to see if there were more bags. There were.

"Boy, king's son or no, you sure are stupid."

"What are you going to do with me, Ras?"

The wolf snickered. "Name's not Ras."

"Okay," Tristian answered.

"You know why they put kittens in bags don't you?"

"No, I've never heard that."

"They put them in bags to drop them in the river."

Ras' voice set him on edge. He could feel his hairs bristle against the closeness of the sack and heat course through his body making him sweat. Suddenly he found himself struggling for breath. The white wolf pup began thrashing around inside the bag. He had to get out of there. Now. He had almost drowned once, and he didn't want to go through it again. It was more than fear that had made him try to escape. Tristian wanted to strike out at the dark wolf. He wanted to hurt him in the same way he was being hurt.

Through the weave of the bag the wolf pup could barely make out a wolf coming closer to him. He saw a paw coming down towards him and tightened his muscles in anticipation, but instead of striking him, the paw patted him a few times over his back.

"Stop jumping around in there. You'll use your air up." The voice was kinder than those who had spoken before, and it whispered. He had to stop moving in order to hear him.

"I'm not going to sit in this bag and be drowned in the river." He knew his voice belied his fear and stopped talking. His voice wavered like the quivering in his stomach. He repeated the words, 'fight or die' in his mind until he felt strength replace the fear and shouted, "Kill me now." The forcefulness in his voice surprised even him.

"No one's going to drown you. Just lie quiet. Strider was just having fun with you."

"So that's his name, Strider. Not Ras. Who's there? Who are you?" Tristian whispered back.

"Stoner. Now, just lie quiet. I'll get you water to drink when we stop."

Something about Stoner's voice calmed him, and told him that perhaps this new wolf could be a friend, an ally. He needed a help mate right now. He would have to find that out.

"Who are you? Who do you belong to?"

"I'm Strider's brother, if that's what you're asking."

Strider's brother or not, Tristian knew that the wolf was right. His anger wasn't going to get him many results in the present situation. It was only making him hotter and more thirsty. He put his head on his paws, but the musty odor of the sack bothered him. He needed to think about what was going on. What had the trainers back in the Wilds told him during the mock battles he and all the others had competed in? Fighting wasn't just fighting. It was thinking. A warrior was able to think on his feet. It made the difference between life and death. Yes, there were things he needed to figure out. There wasn't much else he could do in the present situation.

He thought back over the short history of his life. He had been with his family and they had shown him that very day in nature held something new. Even the sky wore a different hue each day; its color changing with the rising and setting of the sun. He had seen the sky in every color it could paint, especially blue. He thought back to the day he had been taken when he had first seen that deepness in the sky. That perfect blue. The Great Wolf's blue. Something else nagged at him from that day. *You heard it,* the thought came to him, *just like you are hearing it now. That day you brushed it away as only a thought among many, but now you know it was a voice.* It distinctly said, 'remember it. You will need it.' Remember what, the color of the sky? The voice? In his mind's eye, he drifted back to that scene on the rise. He could see that blue spread out over the sky like a precious jewel that he couldn't take his eyes away from. He had been mesmerized by the simple beauty of it. Even now, just remembering it, was soothing and hypnotizing. He let himself drift into it and was soon asleep.

Tristian woke to the sounds of harsh voices. Where was he? Where was he going? More importantly, what we're they going to do with him? Something hit against him. It was not forceful, but there was movement. Tristian could hear thrashing and tumbling near to him.

"Get me out of here. Get me out, now!" a voice demanded. He knew that voice. It was Challenger. His heart raised up. He had needed an ally and now he had one. The next time the body came crashing into him, he tried to grab at it and hold it, but the gunny sack prevented him from using his paws through its thickness.

"Challenger," he said as the bag rolled away from him, "It's Tristian. Hold still."

"Tristian?"

"Try and look through the gunny sack. I'm right next to you."

When his cousin didn't come forward to release him, Challenger shouted, "Let me out of here. This isn't funny."

"I wish I could. I'm in the same fix as you are."

Challenger looked through his sack and could make out the image of a lump next to him.

"What's going on? Boy, my head sure hurts."

"We've been captured by the black wolves."

In a flash it all came back to him. He had been jumped on from behind in the forest by wolves he had not seen, something had struck him on the top of his head.

There were sounds of footsteps coming nearer and voices.

"Shhh!" Tristian warned as the cart suddenly stopped.

"I think the natives are growing restless in their bags."

"Well, it's almost dark. We can let them out for a drink. They won't see much, now."

Tristian heard the latch on back of the wagon being released. He tried to ready his muscles and get to his feet, but the sack was too small for him to stand up in. He wondered if could get up at all because his muscles felt weak and heavy. Next, he felt a nose prodding him from behind while something jerked at the bag from the front. Some wolf had taken the bag in his teeth. He could smell its breath as he was being pulled across the wagon floor. The wolf released the bag for an instant before taking hold of it again. This time the bag came forward with force and he felt himself falling. He hit the ground with a thud.

"Okay, untie the bag." It was the same voice Tristian had heard earlier in the day.

Again the teeth of a wolf worked on the knots of the bag. Get ready to spring the pup told himself, but his muscles didn't respond. They felt weighted in place. How long had he been trussed up in this bag?

Tristian felt the bag being pushed down around his head. A rush of wind touched his sweated fur, and he breathed in deeply, filling his lungs with the cool night air. Before he knew what was happening, the cords on the bag were cinched tightly around his neck. Only his head remained out of the bag. The pup could see that no other wolf had been taken out of the cart. He stood alone. The night sky was gray and troubled. Clouds covered the moon; its light faint and hazed.

The sky was as heavy as he felt. He thought of the night skies he had seen at home outside the cave. They had been black like the patches of fur on his fathers' back and tail, and the stars had beckoned warmly into a future that promised glory. All's safe. All's as it should be, they seemed to tell him. The stars had talked to him, promised him that they would always be there guiding the way. Tonight they were silent and as invisible as if they had been erased from the heavens like words or numbers on some giant blackboard. Maybe the stars had died and simply dropped to earth. Whatever had caused it; their shining was gone, and it took the light out of his heart.

A paw pushed his head down towards the ground. There was a bowl in front of him. Tristian could smell the water, but he was no longer thirsty. So they had offered him drink and did not intend to drown him. He almost wished in that moment that they would drown him. Suddenly his head was pushed into the bowl of water. It felt cold and refreshing to his parched lips, and once he had tasted it he couldn't help lapping up the rest. The sudden plunge head long into the water had sent a fear into him. It seemed to energize his mind and body. The thought struck him, 'when presented with life or death, choose life.'

Immediately after he had finished drinking, the noose of the bag was loosened just enough to push his head back into it. Tristian lay on the ground listening as each wolf and bag was dropped. He had recognized the voices now of Conner and Trin, Ras, well Striker, and his brother, but didn't know who the others were. Whoever they were, they knew what they were doing to prevent escape.

The days continued in confinement, and each night they were given water. He had just had his nightly drink and was cinched into his bag on the ground for the night. As usual he became very drowsy and needed to sleep. That was odd, he thought, for just minutes ago he had been wide awake and his mind was going a mile a minute. There must be something in the water. Yes, that was it. He always felt like he couldn't move a muscle shortly after drinking. All he wanted was sleep. Tomorrow he would not drink. Seeing the sky each night awakened a home sickness in him and he thought about the cave, his brothers and sisters, his mother and father and pictured each one in his mind. His mind drifted back to a night Pieces and Washer had come to cub sit with them.

"It's time for bed, little cubs," Pieces said, closing the book.

"Grandfather Pieces, don't stop now," he had said. "I'll be listening for things all night in the quiet."

"You take these stories to heart, don't you young Tristian?" the rabbit had asked.

"They're just stories. Nothing's true about them," Savor interrupted.

"You might be surprised, little wolf," Pieces said.

"Savor was real. He was your grandfather," came Washer's voice from the doorway.

"We know that. There's his namesake," his brothers said, kicking at him.

"The things he did were real. They were just as real as he was," the raccoon continued as he came closer and pulled the blankets up around the three male wolves, but they sprung back up almost at once, tossing the coverlets into a heap again.

"Then why isn't our cave burned inside?"

"Yeah, and why is the Wilds still here?" asked Savor.

"It was a different cave and a different part of the Wilds," the old rabbit shot back at them. "Now, lie back down."

"Just bedtime tales," his sister Jen had laughed. "Whoever reads the story just puts grandfather's name in it to make it seem real."

No," said Pieces pushing Jen back down, and covering her. "It's all real. Why, he was just as real as all of you."

At this all the cubs began to snicker.

"How do you know Grandfather Pieces?" asked little Anna.

"I was a part of it. It was Savor who saved my life."

"You were the rabbit saved from the fire! The stories are true," Tristian shouted, but Jen ignored him and asked, "Where's your brother and sister now, Pieces?"

The old rabbit looked down and stared into the distance. It took a long time before he answered.

"Gone. Dead. I don't know."

"Pieces?" Tristian asked softly. He waited until the rabbit looked at him before continuing.

"I'm sorry."

"We're all sorry. You look so sad," came the words from Jen.

"No. No, not sad. I was just thinking how much your brother here looks like your great grandfather Tristian," he said coming closer and patting the cubs head.

"I do?"

"Yes, you have the thickness of stature he had, his size, and the markings on his chest. He had a white chest with two sets of black rings on it just the way you do."

"I thought he died before Khoa came to find all of you by the river."

The old rabbit nodded. "You know that part of the story well, but I saw Tristian move the great chasm when we fled the Wilds the first time."

A great clamoring started among the young pups.

"Tell us about that."

"Why haven't we heard that story?"

"There are a life time of stories. By the time you hear them all, you will be older than the sky itself."

Washer was standing next to Pieces. "No more questions. You'll have us up all night."

"One more question?" It was Savor. "Do I look like Khoas' Savor? His father?"

"Yes, cub, you do. I remember Savor, but not just because he saved my life. He was a beautiful wolf. Striking he was. His colors were deep," the rabbit continued.

"What do you mean, his colors were deep, Pieces?" the raccoon said tauntingly.

"Stop interrupting!"

Washer waited awhile before saying, "Well."

Pieces threw him a side long glance, but continued, "I mean where he was white it was brilliant white, and where he was black it was so solid you couldn't see through it. Deep."

His father, Khoa, was those colors, Tristian thought now. He was brilliant white and the patches of black on him were deep, like the night sky. He struggled to rearrange himself in the bag by stretching. He held onto the picture of his father in his mind's eye until sleep erased it.

When Tristian woke, it was to the sounds and movement of the cart over the uneven ground. Other than that there was silence. They had been prevented from talking when they were awake by being hit with a stick by whoever sat next to them. Not even their captors spoke. He had not heard Strider's or Stoner's voice since that first day of his capture. Tristian thought back to the first time he had ever laid eyes on the mixed wolves. He was angry with himself now. Something had told him they held a force he should not tangle with. He had ignored his inner self, and trusted to his own sense of fairness. Now he found that all wolves did not live by the same code. Even if you treated some wolves honorably, they would not reciprocate in a like manner, could not. How could he have expected a stranger to know the moral codes he and his pack lived by? It never occurred to him that some wolves had never been taught to obey a set of rules. A voice whispered, 'teach them.' He chose to let the thought fade from his consciousness. He wanted nothing to do with his captors except to give them a taste of their own treatment.

Each day became like the last and it was always towards afternoon that he woke. As hard as he tried not to drink the water he was offered each night, he found that his thirst overpowered the resolve in his mind. He would die without water. Tristian waited until he heard movement from the bag next to him.

"Challenger, that you moving around?" Both wolves waited to see if the guard was around to whack them with his stick before they carried on with their conversation.

"Yes, but I've never slept so much in my life. It's like I can't wake up."

"It's the water."

Just then a yell came from outside. "Whoa up there."

The cart stopped suddenly. They listened as the wheels of the other carts behind them became silent.

A voice from somewhere in back called, "What's the matter? Why're we stopping?"

"Bridge is out. It's rained a bunch lately." It was Strider who answered.

Tristian could hear the footfalls of a few wolves passing the cart and then stop.

"The water's not that fast," a voice jeered. "I'm not going to let that river stop us. Get going."

"Drake, the river's too deep and too fast for these carts," Strider warned.

"Yeah, they're put together with toothpicks. They're just toys," Stoner said.

"Get out of the way. I'll show you cowards how this is done. Anyone else care to go with me, or are you all cowards?" Drake dared them as he headed back to his cart.

"No gamblers?"

Another wolf stepped forward. "I'll go, Drake."

Drake picked up the rope by the loop he had been pulling the cart with and then slipped it over his head and onto his shoulders again. He pulled the cart up to the river's edge. The other wolf did the same. The cart Tristian was in began to move.

"Challenger, it's our cart."

The cart stopped again. The two dark wolves stood inches from the water adjusting the ropes and making sure they were secure.

"Simple. See?" Drake said, turning back to the others behind him before looking at the wolf beside him. "Ready?"

The wolf nodded, and Drake stepped into the current. The wolf was able to wade at first and then began to swim. Seeing that it looked to be safe, the second wolf headed into the water.

As he felt the cart move again, Tristian's heart stopped. "Challenger, we're going into the water."

"I can feel the water pushing at the cart," his cousin answered.

At that point, the first cart began swirling downstream. Drake swam as hard as he could, but was powerless against the current. The cart was tipped onto its left side and swept under. Seconds later the cart bounced back up end first to the top of the water. It was empty of cargo. The cages, being heavy, had sunk out of sight.

The second cart ran into a snag of logs that was being pushed down stream, which helped keep it afloat. The gray wolf struggled desperately to climb onto the raft like structure of logs, but the heavy load of the cart kept dragging him backwards into the water, and the rope that was tied to him was too short for him to climb onto the logs. The cart was afloat and bobbed behind him in the water. Suddenly the log jam slammed into the bank on the other side of the river, flipping the cart almost on top of it and knocking the cage door open.

From the side of the logs to which he clung, the dark wolf watched as a small raccoon jumped onto the logs from inside the wagon. Somehow the animal had managed to undo the bag with his hands and free himself. The little animal jumped back onto the cart and grabbed a bag and began pushing it until it rolled down the pile. He worked quickly, pushing bag after bag down from the heap and onto the logs. Tristian felt himself being tugged at clumsily before he began rolling downward. *In seconds he would be in the water,* he thought. He waited for the splash and the feel of cold water to rush over him. *He would never see the Great Wolfs blue again.* Just as he pictured the sky in his mind he felt himself hit a hard surface and roll into something soft. Next, another soft object hit him from behind.

The little raccoon worked faster, but he was having a harder time with this bag as he was clearly tired and spent. "Who's ever in the bag, roll to your right. Help me. I'm a raccoon. I'm trying to save you from the water."

He felt the animal in the bag move and felt it pull away from his grip. He paused for a minute to get his breath, but as he did, the raft was swirled away from the banks for an instant and then back into it again. The impact jolted the cart free from where it had been wedged into the raft of logs. The raccoon watched from the safety of the logs as the wagon floated on the water for a moment and then went under, taking the gray wolf with it.

Strider, Stoner, and the others looked helplessly from shore. They could make out the shape of the raccoon sitting on the raft. He was busy untying the bags. Soon two other animals emerged free on the log jam. They started helping untie the pile of bags that were on the raft like structure. Everything had happened in a matter of minutes.

"We've lost more than a third of all the animals we captured," Stoner said.

"That's not the worst. Drake had all our medical supplies and food."

"Father will have us in the quarry's for this," Strider said spitting.

The chattering and shouts of freedom from the raft made the two wolves redirect their attention to the survivors across the river.

"There they go," Stoner said watching as the raccoon, the badgers, beavers, and the white wolves jumped from the raft onto the opposite shore.

"What are we going to do?" Stoner asked.

"Wait for the river to go down, so we can cross. We'll get them then if a patrol from the fortress doesn't pick them up before."

"That may take a week or more. Hey, we could built a raft," Stoner suggested.

"I'm not riding on it. Not after what I just seen. You go. You drown," Tacker said spitting at Stoner.

Strider was at Tackers' throat and had a grip on it. He held on, his teeth digging deeper into his fur. "Okay. Okay. You win," Tacker whispered as loud as he could with Strider at his throat. After Strider let go, the wolf backed away and said in a hoarse voice, "I was just funning with you."

"Where's Conner?" Strider asked looking around.

"Where do you think? Drunk in the wagon," answered Stoner.

"Drag him in the water and sober him up."

Strider turned from his brother and spoke to the others. "Get those beavers out and to work."

It was the noise and commotion below which alerted Traveler, Scout, and the warriors as they stood on the top of the hill. They had been heading for the river to drink when they had witnessed the sinking of the carts. They had watched as the raccoon had saved and untied the bags to free the animals.

"So that's how they've been stealing our families," one wolf observed.

"Scout," Traveler said, "Let's go up river and have a look. I could have sworn I saw some white wolf cubs head north into the trees on the other side of the river."

Even above the river where the white wolf army had camped, the sound of the waters roar was loud. It would cover what little noise Scout and they others made. After searching over an hour for signs of the animals across the river, they gave up.

"We couldn't get them across this stream again, anyway. We'll have to wait." Scout said.

The other wolf nodded. "Time to attack."

"Yes, coming from the direction they did, those cubs could only come from a few towns. The Wilds among them, I'd wager."

Back at the camp, they made plans to raid the camp just before dusk. There were only about five adult wolves and four younger ones, so Traveler took twenty warriors and had fifty of the new wolves back them up so they could learn the maneuvers. The warriors formed a half circle that hemmed in the carts and the dark wolves with their backs to the rushing stream. The enemy would have nowhere to flee except into the water. On Travelers signal, they rushed. Conner came forward a few steps, teeth barred and sounding a low growl. He looked straight at Traveler.

Hearing the second charge come forward, Conner lifted his head to see fifty more wolves make a fence behind the first line of warriors. He stopped his forward advance and lowered his ears to his head to show he was no longer a threat. "No use getting hurt," he said backing away.

Traveler went over to the carts and looked at the wriggling bags. "What are you hauling in the cages?" he turned around to ask Conner.

"Thieves and murderers, mostly."

"Pretty small bags," Scout continued.

When the mixed wolf didn't answer he said, "Untie them. Let's see these bandits."

The dark wolves stared at each other, but didn't move. Traveler took a bag off the cart and untied it. Two white wolf cubs wriggled their way out. One of the cubs shouted, "Traveler! Scout! Where did you come from?" They both jumped on Scout playfully.

Evidently they recognized him, but he didn't know them. "Whose cubs are you?"

"Taylors. Is he with you? I'm Cody and this is Patches."

"No," Scout said. "Didn't he make it to back to the Wilds?"

The two cubs eyed him in a confused way with their heads tilted. "Should he have?" asked Cody. "He was with you when he left."

"We were hoping he did. He was not captured with us, but was out scouting that morning."

"I'm sure he is there now," Patches said.

"Khoa left to find you before we were taken."

"He did? Get something to eat and drink. We will talk later."

"Yes, we haven't had much food since we left the Wilds."

"Boys, how long have you been gone?"

"Forever." Patches said.

"Two, three weeks. Maybe less. Maybe more. I lost track," his brother said.

Scout turned from the cubs to the wolf on his left. "Send a runner to the Wilds. Tell them we are coming from the East with presents. Give them our location. We should arrive in about a week or more," Scout said to the sergeant, "and then help get the rest of these bags untied."

The sun light vanished earlier within the confines of the forest and it was nearly dark when the young sat eating and drinking with their rescuers. A few faint streaks of pink and purple were visible in the open sky above the river. The orange circle of the sun was hidden behind the tall trees.

There were twenty some little animals around the campfire, and as Traveler and Scout tried to take stock of who was who, Cody told them that Khoa and Tors' cubs had been among the animals in the carts that had gone down in the river.

"Tristian and Challenger! But how?" Scout asked.

The two little wolves told how Khoa had left and about everything that had happened to them along the way.

"Yes, Khoas' cubs would have been born," he answered, reflecting on the length of their absence. Just when he thought he couldn't feel any worse, the stretcher which bore Tor's body, was being carried past. It was set down just outside the light of the fire and Scout continued to look at Cody. "Was Challenger the only one of Tors' cubs with you?"

"Uh, huh."

"Can you tell me who else was in the wagons?"

Cody gave him a short list of names of the animals and to whom they belonged. "But there were dozens of other animals from other towns I didn't know. They rode in other carts. We met up with more wagons in the forest."

"That's good for now," Scouted said and patted the cubs head.

Patches had just gone to the stream for a drink and was coming back to the campfire. He noticed the stretcher with the large wolf beyond the light of the fire. Being curious, he ventured over to look at it. It must be one of the wounded, he thought.

Scout was watching the young wolf as he eyed the stretcher and moved towards it. "Don't look, cub."

"I have to. I want to be brave."

Scout nodded that he understood, and let the cub go up to look. Patches took small tentative steps forward until he was standing above the stretcher. He couldn't believe who he saw.

"Tor. Mighty Tor," he said just above a whisper and ran back to Scout, his tail tucked tightly between his legs.

"First, Khoas' Tristian and Tors' Challenger. Now Tor, himself. He isn't really dead, is he Scout?"

"It'll be alright, son," Scout said licking his head.

"No, it won't. Nothing will ever be alright again. If Tor can die, then the world doesn't make sense. Kings don't die," the cub said sobbing into Scouts fur.

Hearing that it was Tor, Cody and a few others went up to see if it was true.

"He doesn't look dead," Cody said.

"Maybe kings don't look dead they way other animals do," the beaver answered.

"What's dead look like?" the squirrel asked, looking up at the beaver.

"Not breathing. Not moving. Cold," Conner said lunging towards the group, which made them jump back.

"Like him. I been throwing rocks at him. He don't move. He's dead."

Traveler, having seen the prisoner lunge at the children, came and knocked the rocks from his paws and moved him further away.

"I won't let you dishonor our dead."

"So your king is dead," Conner laughed. "Don't take it out on me."

The squirrel was shaking his head. "The king's not dead. I'm right next to him on the ground. I can feel his breath. It's warm."

Hearing this, Scout ran over to the crowd around Tors' body. "Okay, let's move away," he said, prodding the animals with his nose. "Who let the tarp fall off Tor's body?" he asked, pulling it back up to cover Tors face.

"No," protested the squirrel, "don't cover him up. He's alive. The king's warm. Feel him."

The squirrel was so sincere that Scout put his front paw next to Tor's mouth, and then moved his paw to Tor's side. Next, he laid his head down on his chest, listening. He could feel slight movement, a faint heartbeat. He looked back at the squirrel, who had moved up closer again. "He's barely breathing, but he's breathing," he told the little animal.

Scout stood up and yelled, "Get me some water, quick! Bring some light over here."

Stasher and the wolves were deep enough into the forest that they were sure they could not be seen from the shore. They had gone in a northwesterly direction, which was opposite to the direction they had been traveling in the wagons. All but two of the wolves had left Stasher once he had fallen behind. Since he was a small raccoon, he could not keep pace with the wolves. The others were way ahead of them now, and closer to safety, he thought. He was tuckered out and winded as he stopped by the side of a tree. He looked at the other two wolves.

"So much for hometown loyalty," he said, watching the cubs and others from Fen Forest disappear. "Go ahead if you want."

"No, you stayed back on the cart to save us. You untied the ropes to our bags at the risk of your own life." It was Challenger, the bigger of the white wolves, who spoke.

Tristian nodded his agreement. "We go on from here together."

CHAPTER 8
BACK FROM THE DEAD

It was the sound of birds that woke Scout the next morning. He had stayed by Tor all night to see if he would awaken, or be given into the Great Wolf's hands, but had fallen asleep at some point. Now Scout lay with his eyes still closed and tried to pinpoint where the birds were. Their voices seemed to be directly overhead.

"White wolf cubs," he heard one of them say. The next words he caught were, "Army of hundreds." They were being spied on, he judged. Slowly he opened only his eye that was towards the ground, and searched for his weapon. His slingshot was two feet away. It was too far for him to grab it without sending the birds flying before he got his shot off. He spotted a stone that lie inches from him. It was big enough and would bring one of them down, he thought. As he waited for the right moment to snatch the rock, he caught the phrase, "Tell Fisher, runner, and Wilds." They were friendly spies.

He leaped immediately to his feet shouting to the birds, "I am Scout, warrior wolf of the Wilds." His voice was so loud that one of the birds lost his footing on the branch and had to flap his wings to regain his balance.

"What are you doing with all these young animals?" the other bird asked.

"We rescued them last night."

"Yes. They saved us," Cody affirmed with a smile.

"Beyond lies Tor, one of our twin kings," Scout said, and watched as one of the osprey flew over to investigate.

"And who is your other king?" the bird asked him while hovering in front of his face.

"His brother, Khoa, of the Wilds."

"Anyone can say a name," the osprey said, flying back to his perch in the tree. He was studying Scout from his head to his tail. "You are a mixed wolf."

"There are white wolves among us," Scout said, pointing to the other warriors.

"True."

"Well, I heard you say Fisher. He is a warrior wolf of the Wilds. He knows me."

Splash said, "Come with us."

Within seconds the whole camp came to life and the bird said, "We will take only this mixed wolf with us."

Scout turned towards the waking warriors. "Wait. I will be back with Fisher."

"Or he with you, dead," the osprey warned.

"Keep the watch on Tor."

As Scout followed the two birds, he thought of the Wilds and of those he knew. It had been almost six months since he had seen home. His thoughts were jumbled and his nerves worn. How was he going to tell all the animals their children were gone, their fathers and husbands, dead? And what about Tor? Would he live out the day? He had checked on him the day of his death, and in the weeks that had followed. He had been cold as stone. It had even snowed in the higher elevations. They had placed branches over Tor and he had not moved. How could this be?

Suddenly his mind went back to yesterday and the wolves that had escaped. Whose cubs were they? Being cubs, would they manage to survive for long? He looked back towards the east and the river. He didn't hold out much hope for the young cubs, but he petitioned the Great Wolf for all these things. 'They are beyond me,' he pleaded.

One of Scouts questions was just being answered on the other side of the river. A band of dark wolves had come upon some wolf cubs in the forest. The young white wolves were running and nipping at each other completely unaware of the danger closing in on them. The dark wolves tightened their circle and moved in for the kill. The white wolves lay dead.

The leader, and the blackest wolf among the pack said, "They didn't even know we were here. We struck with such quickness," Batter announced with great pride.

"There are other animals about somewhere," another dark wolf said. "I saw others running behind these when we first spotted them from the high ground yesterday."

"Let them go," the leader, Batter, said. "We've practiced enough for today. What are other animals, when we have killed the white wolves?"

It was the second night Scout and his warriors had made camp by the stream, but tonight they had Fisher and his patrol with them and a healer wolf to tend to Tor. It was immediate upon their return that Tor had survived. There was excitement around the camp and the warriors moved with a new resolve; Tor had opened his eyes and spoken.

Tonight Fisher told them not to light a fire and set wolves up and down the banks to watch across the river for the enemy and the survivors. He had also moved the company of wolves farther into the woods and away from the beaches. Everything seemed to be in order and Fisher went to report to his king.

Tor was startled and stared at him a long time. "It's good to see you, old friend. A true warrior wolf."

"You have made it, too. Back from the dead, I understand," Fisher answered, patting the wolf.

"Not yet. I'm not back on my feet, but I am back to the pain in my body," Tor said, and tried to brush the healer away, but the wolf would not move from his side.

Scout and Traveler came up to join them. "I was thinking earlier today," Scout said, "just how it could be that you are

146

alive after all these weeks. It snowed up in the mountains and was cold most of the time we traveled. You did not move. You did not breathe. I checked."

The healer broke in on their conversation. "It is the cold that kept him alive and kept his wounds from bleeding."

"We almost took the shorter route over the meadows," Traveler recounted.

"Be glad you didn't. Be glad it snowed in the mountains."

"You make it sound like a miracle, healer," Tor said.

"Your words not mine. I only know that if they had taken you through the meadows in the heat, you would not be arguing the point with me now. You would have bled to death. The miracle was not in the science of heat and cold, but in the path that was chosen."

"I trust what you say is true, and now it's time I heard what has been going on," Tor said to the group.

Fisher stepped forward to speak. The king listened lying down, and with his eyes closed until almost everyone had reported. It was when Scout spoke about Challenger and Tristian that he opened them, and tried to get up.

"No, you don't, Tor. You'll rip those stitches out," the healer said, pushing him back down and standing above him.

"They may still be alive," Scout said. "We saw dozens of animals escape and there were white wolves among them."

"Is this truth, or words meant to soothe an ailing father?"

Traveler spoke up. "Only truth comes from Scout. White wolves were seen heading into the forest. They traveled just inside the forest like warrior training teaches."

"Then there is hope," Tor said quietly.

"There was a gallant raccoon who heaved bags from the cart when it was tossed onto the log jam," Traveler recounted.

"You should have seen him rolling those bags down with the animals in. He stayed with it until the cart and the logs jounced into the bank a second time and got knocked into the water. He saved over twenty animals. Those white wolves among them."

"I sure would like to have that little guy among my warriors," Fisher said.

"This calls for a toast. Bring some water, healer," said Tor.

The water was poured out and Tor said, "A hero's welcome and reward for the brave raccoon!" The warriors all shouted as they raised their glasses and repeated Tor's next toast. "To the Great Wolf who holds up one and lets the other go. Who can know?"

At that moment and across the river, just within the forest of Vale, those animals being toasted stopped dead in their tracks. Blood. The smell of it was strong in the wolves' nostrils.

The raccoon stopped beside them. "What's wrong?"

"Something's happened. I smell blood. At least I think that's what it is," the larger white wolf said.

The raccoon stood on his hind legs and sniffed deeper into the air. "Awful," he said scrunching up his nose.

"Listen. Do you hear anything?" Challenger asked.

Both animals shook their heads.

"I'll go first. Wait for me."

"And if you don't come back?" the little raccoon asked.

"Run," he said, crouching low to the ground and stalking forward.

He was on the right trail, he told himself. The smell was growing stronger. He paused for a moment and lifted his head to listen for any sounds. When he heard no noises and saw no movement, he continued forward until he spotted the humps on the ground. As he moved closer, he could tell they were bodies of wolf cubs. He shook himself and loped back to his friends.

"Our speedy pals from the carts. They met something bigger than them."

"Are all of them dead?" asked the raccoon.

"Say, you sure are a chatty kind," Challenger said, and looked at the little animal closer. "We don't even know your name."

"I'm Stasher."

"Stasher?" Tristian said, laughing and leaping about in small circles.

"It can't be!" Challenger said and nipped at his cousin, joining in his romp.

"What's the secret? You act like you've heard of me or something."

"We have," the wolves laughed.

"Then I take deep offense at your making me out to be the cat's catch."

"The what?" Tristian stopped chasing Challenger. "We're making you out to be what?"

"The cat's catch. The mouse's cheese."

When Stasher saw that he still didn't get it, he said, "The fool."

Looking at Challenger first, Tristian approached the raccoon. "No. No, we weren't laughing at you like that. We were laughing because we were glad to see you."

"You were?" Stasher said relieved, but then a frown came over his face again. "Why?"

"We were waiting for you."

"That's not even a remote possibility," he said, and turned his back to the wolves. "Why would two wolves be waiting for a raccoon?"

"You were coming to the Wilds, right?"

The little raccoon turned back around at this point and said slowly, and with a bit of surprise in his voice, "Yes."

"You're from Fienix Forest."

"Yes," the raccoon affirmed.

"And you have an uncle named Washer."

"Yes," Stasher said softly and thoroughly amazed.

"Don't you see?" Tristian fairly screamed at him.

"Uh, uh."

"Your uncle is our uncle, too," the cub beamed.

The two wolves watched as the raccoon rolled over on his back in the grass and bellowed in laughter. "That comes close to the dumbest thing I've ever heard."

Tristian came up and poked at Stasher. "So you think we're lying to you?"

The raccoon continued to roll and kick, and nod his head wildly. "Yes. That's like asking a smiling cat if he swallowed anything when the bird is gone."

"Come on, Tristian. Let's go. He's not listening."

"Tristian?" Stasher said standing up. "Khoas' Tristian?"

"Yes, Laugher. And this is my cousin, Challenger, son to the twin king, Tor."

"Hee, hee, haw. I've been laughing at princes," he said bowing.

"What a day," the raccoon said, running to catch up to them. "You are Washer's nephews."

"Get back down. I liked you better rolling on the ground," Tristian said.

As they walked along the forest, Stasher asked, "Do you know any of the stories Washer told?"

"Of course. Which ones?"

"The ones where Khoa would give Uncle Washer and Pieces a ride."

The two wolves looked at each other.

"We'll make better time," the raccoon added. "You owe me anyway."

"For what?" the wolves said together.

"Hmm. How quickly you forget the mere trifle of saving your flea ridden furs."

"Alright, Laugher, get on," Challenger said.

"Oooh. Oowe," the raccoon groaned.

"What's the matter?"

"My side hurts."

"Good," the littler wolf cub said.

Khoa had decided to follow after Winter's path, and was trying to enlist warriors for the fight against the Blackstone Fortress. He had picked up very few wolves willing to fight. He was now in Fienix forest and had met up with Washer and Pieces. The town's animals didn't want to fight. They didn't, or couldn't see the dark wolves as their enemies. It was as if they had one mind and could think only one way.

"They have our children. The dark wolves said if we didn't fight them, our cubs would be safe."

"Are your children here?"

The animals hung their heads.

"They are dead to you, anyway. They are not here to touch you, talk to you, are they?" Khoa continued.

"No, but they are alive."

"Are you sure of that? Are you sure that wolves who would come and put you under siege and hunger like this would keep their word? The only ones you have saved, is them."

"What do you mean, saved them?"

"You have saved them from fighting you to conquer you. How many lives have they lost in taking your towns?"

No one answered and Khoa said, "It was free for them, but it cost you your children, your town, and your freedom."

"That's alright for Khoa to say. He's the king," one mother wolf got up to say.

"That's right," another wolf said. "He has nothing to lose."

"Besides that, the dark wolves say it was the white wolves who stole their kingdom. How do we know you won't decide to take our home as well?"

The animals were in a crazed state and Khoa thought it better to end the meeting.

Khoa called out loudly, "I have your answer."

The animals looked at him and their voices quieted down. One by one they began to leave, talking lowly among themselves.

Washer came up to Khoa. "Why didn't you tell them about Tristian? About Challenger?"

"It wouldn't have made any difference."

"How do you know? Why let these cowards think you have no reason to fight? I'm going to tell them, if you won't."

Khoa grabbed Washer. "No." The two stared directly into one others' eyes. Washer had never seen that look from Khoa before. "Okay. I won't say anything, but I don't understand why you don't tell them."

"Their hearts are frozen in fear. They have no heart to fight."

"But you and I know that their children will be killed anyway."

"They choose to deny it."

"You're wrong, Khoa. You're letting them keep their delusions. You're letting them think the white wolves stole the Wilds."

"No, Washer. The dark wolves lie has become a comfort to them now. It's what keeps them going."

The raccoon could only look at him so Khoa asked, "Tell me, old friend, how do I break that spell of delusion? We are among them and they can't see the difference between us who walk in the Way, and that of the black wolf who destroys them."

Pieces had come up behind them. "Yes, it is like a spell isn't it? Everyone seems to act in unison. How is that?"

"They would be given to have one mind," the raccoon muttered under his breath.

"What?" Pieces asked.

"Nothing."

From behind them Climber called, "Washer, we're heading back home. Coming?"

As they walked along Climber said, "I have great respect for your king. He didn't press the animals. He let them choose."

"Do you still think you can just go and find Stasher and take him without having to fight?" Washer asked his brother.

"No, but I don't know whether I can travel with you now. I would be going against the town."

Washer stopped and looked at his brother. "Do you travel with us or not?"

"I have to think on it."

Inside the stump, Louella had prepared a meal. She went about her duties, humming lowly under her breath to lighten the pall of silence that was on all of them. It was another way of not talking. The smell of cooking was comforting, and all the animals kept the thoughts of what was on their minds to themselves. They knew better than to share those just now.

Outside, shouts and sounds of running reached their ears and then loud knocking was heard on the stump door.

Someone yelled, "The army's back! They have cubs, little animals of all sorts with them!"

Everyone but Louella raced to the door which Climber held open. CJ stood behind him as the others raced through.

"Coming mother?"

The raccoon shook her head and looked up. "I need to clean out the larder of fish and vegetables. There's mouth's to be fed. CJ, you stay back to help me."

"But mama," the cub pleaded, "Stasher might be there. I want to see him. Please!"

"Ah, yeah, go on with you, then," Louella said, wiping her paws on her apron.

"Don't you want to come?" Climber asked.

"I couldn't take it if he isn't with them," she answered without looking up. "I want my tears to be private."

Shouts of joy were dying away as Climber and the group reached the gathering. They watched as the only two animals from Fienix to be returned to their parents were taken home.

The crowd was quiet as Scout and Traveler told of their months of captivity and the near execution of Tor. It was a short recap as the shouts from the parents, who wondered about their own children, became louder. "Where are the others?" a wolf family cried out. "We lost two sons, two white wolf cubs."

Scout stepped forward to quiet them and told them the story of the carts in the river and the heroic act of the little raccoon who had freed some of the wolves and other animals before they were swept away.

"There are other young who may still be alive. We will set out to find them."

"Stasher," CJ said to his father.

"Maybe," Climber answered.

"How many raccoons were among you?" CJ called to the animals who had told the stories.

"I know of none except the one that was told of, but there could have been more," the beaver answered. "We were kept in bags and could not see all those around us."

"We weren't given much food or water either," the squirrel added.

"And if we asked for water, we were beat with sticks," another animal testified.

"Yes, and at one point we were told that we would be drowned like cats in bags by those dark wolves over there," cried the beaver as he pointed to his one-time captors in the cages beside him.

The crowd of parents let out angry cries and rushed forward to the cages.

"Let's drown them now," one of wolverines bellowed.

Khoa rushed forward and began pushing the crowd back. On his command, his warriors formed a wall in front of him, and the animals fell back.

"I know you're disappointed, angry, and full of fear, but there won't be any killing here today."

"You don't have any say in this, Khoa," Tangler, the wolverine, said.

"That's right. Your cubs are all safe back home. Move," said a wolf, coming forward with his head down.

The young beaver jumped out in front of the snarling wolf. "Wait! Wait!" he said waving his arms to stop the animal.

The other animals, who had once been captives with him, ran to stand by him. "Khoas' Tristian is among the lost," the beaver said, "and so is Tors' Challenger."

"Is that true? Your son has been taken? And Tor's son, too?" the wolf asked while looking at where Tor lay on the tarp.

Khoa nodded. "Go home. They will have a trial. They will have justice and a chance to speak."

Seeing the beaver in action, Washer poked Pieces and began jumping up and down. "I like his style. Stopped'em in their tracks."

The raccoon rushed over to the beaver and exclaimed his praise, but the animal was not having any part of Washer and walked away without a word.

"What's the matter?" the raccoon asked.

"I don't need you to validate what I have done."

Washed walked back to where Serious and Pieces were standing, his fur visibly ruffled. "Didn't look like that beaver thought too much of what you were saying," Serious said.

"Short friendship," he said and changed the subject. "Let's go see how Tor's doing. That'll give Climber and Louella a chance to talk alone."

"Looks like there's a crowd over by the schoolhouse," Serious said, pointing off to the left.

When they reached Khoa and Tor, the two wolves were staring in the opposite direction.

"You think there's going to be trouble?" Washer asked Khoa as he looked at the approaching crowd.

"If there is, it's already heading this way."

The raccoon and his friends watched as the animals headed straight for them.

"I'm ready this time," Washer said, standing on two legs and punching his front paws into the air.

"Think fast," Pieces called and landed a good one in Washer's stomach with his back kickers.

By the time the raccoon was back on his feet, his two friends were gone, and the wolf who had started trouble before was talking. Washer scrambled on all fours over to the crowd.

"We're not here for trouble," the wolf named Scrapper announced to Khoa. "We have decided to join your search."

"There will be fighting," Khoa said, looking around into the faces of those who stood in front of him. "Lots of it. Some of you will die."

"Our children are dying now. Let it be us instead of them."

"You were right, Khoa. The dark wolves held us in fear on one side and our children on the other. We were in the middle with nothing to bargain."

"Let them fear us," Scrapper said, and all the animals took up the cry.

"The black wolves do not give way easily and they have entrenched themselves in dozens of small towns like yours," Khoa said. "We will have to take back all towns taken by the black wolves. I'm not going to hold anything back from you. It's going to be a long campaign."

"Why don't we hit them from all sides at once?" Tangler asked.

"It would do nothing but divide our forces. There are too many towns. We don't have a large enough force. We need to secure our children. That must be done first."

Khoa looked at the crowd. "And what do you say about the white wolves taking the Wilds?"

"After hearing Scout, and the white wolves who were taken captive in the Black Mountain Fortress, we have come to our senses. The white wolves have always lived there. There is no history of black wolves in the Wilds except in war."

The friends had listened to the wolves make their plans for hours and Washer was getting hungry. He just remembered that lunch had been interrupted. Pieces had fallen asleep under the tree where Tor lay in the shade, and Serious was nibbling grass, which made him hungrier. The sun had disappeared under a spread of dark clouds and a mist like rain began to fall. It was time to head back to Climbers, he thought, and went to gather his friends.

The next morning was a cold, gray day that misted rain. Wind blew the leaves from their branches and the wetness packed them onto the earth. Nothing spoke of green now, or sun, or light. The sky was dreary, the trees black and bare; their elegant dress of leaves fallen away; exposing their limbs like thin skeletons reaching into a darkened sky.

Washer and the two rabbits were sitting outside Climber and Luella's stump. They could hear Luella crying, and Climber trying to soothe her. "We'll find Stasher. You heard what Washer said, "Even Khoa, the King, is going out looking for him."

"Only because his son is missing, too," his wife said knowingly. She lifted her head to look at him and wiped away her tears with the corner of her apron. "Yes, we aren't the only ones to be suffering," she added, trying to be practical.

Climber was quiet while he watched Luella dry her eyes on her apron. He approached her and put his paws around her. "Washer can be a rascal, but he is a raccoon that is good to his word. If he says he will help us look to the ends of the earth, then he will."

Just then the door opened and Luella, still wiping tears from her eyes said, "Please come back in. There's carrot and rutabaga soup." The raccoon noticed Pieces shivering, and heard his teeth rattling. "CJ, bring my shawl."

In a moment, Luella was wrapping it around the old rabbit. "It's a raw wind out there today," she said. Pieces liked the raccoon more all the time. He really liked her. She had never even winced or seem to notice his missing patches of fur or his ear, and that counted for a lot with the old rabbit. Of course, he looked better now that Ani and Zen kept up his grooming and had provided him with a tail to swish. Still, it had been awhile since they had trimmed him what with all the excitement, so he was beginning to look pretty tattered in spots. Serious and the raccoon had told him that. Good friends that they were.

CHAPTER 9
MIRACLE IN THE RAIN

It was mid-autumn and most mornings came wet and cold. Grayness wrapped itself around the forest as thin shades of mist drifted upward toward an unseen sky. Tor and the wolves had been given shelter in the school house and the pavilion when the weather had changed. It was now their headquarters. Winter and other wolves had joined them from the Wilds. Tor could train wolves even if he wasn't ready to fight.

As Khoa stood outside the school, he felt hemmed in by the surrounding landscape. He couldn't see very far into the forest for it was thick with foliage. The enemy could hide well in its denseness. It was not like standing on the rise in the Wilds where he could see for miles in all directions. Here, he felt trapped and claustrophobic with trees hampering his view in every direction. The animals had cleared very few trees and had built their town and homes among them in an effort to preserve the forest's natural beauty. They had done well, and the trees grew thickly; obscuring the view at every turn.

Khoa heard Washer and the others before he saw them. "Winter, assemble your groups. Give them their orders," he called back into the school.

Winter came out at once to stand by him.

"You might have some trouble with a few of them when they find out I've gone without them."

Winter laughed. "No need to mention any names."

"Give them their assignment. Make it sound important. That should let you off the hook somewhat."

Khoa padded quickly over to the line of wolves and said in a quiet tone, "Warriors right," and he went to the head of the column. His men in formation behind him, he led them into the cover of the trees.

Just as the tail end of his army disappeared into the forest, Khoa heard Washer ask, "Where's Khoa off to so early?"

"Maneuvers," he heard Winter reply.

It had been arranged that Winter and Tor would stay to train the new recruits in Fienix until Tor was well enough to travel back to the Wilds with part of the army and the women and children of Fen. He would also take the cadre of beavers that had helped them at the river to build up a strong hold in the Wilds. Scout would stay here in Fienix, making it an outpost between the Wilds and the surrounding towns. Climber and his party would take the children back to their respective homes and enlist as many wolves and builders as was possible. Khoa would help Fisher look for the cubs.

When Winter and Scout had finished explaining the details of the plan to the animals, they began directing them into their respective groups. Winter spotted Washer and his two rabbit friends heading straight for him. Instead of retreating from them, he decided to meet them straight on.

"Washer and company! Just who I wanted to see. I have some things to go over with you."

Washer was taken back with surprise. "You do?" he said looking at the others.

"Well, we have things to go over with you, too," the raccoon retorted in a stronger voice, having regained his composure. "Khoa left to find the cubs. Left us behind. We have come to protest."

"Come with me," Winter said turning and heading into the schoolhouse.

The group, along with Climber, followed after him in a marching and deliberate style.

Inside they saw Tor struggling to his feet with the aid of the healer wolves and stopped.

Pieces sat up on his hind legs and asked, "Are you feeling better? Good to see you getting up and around."

Tor didn't answer the animal directly, but said, "Doing the part I've been given to play." Once he was standing, he looked directly at all of them and said, "Until I can do more."

He walked over to where the group was standing. "Tell me, do you have a part in this grand undertaking? I'm interested."

After they told him what plans Winter had unfolded to them he nodded. "So you have orders. You are more fortunate than me. I am not being included," he said with a wink to Winter.

A long silence followed. "Well, you can only do what you can do," Washer said.

"Yes," Tor nodded, "but it's hard to accept when you want to do more."

He looked at the animals and then at Winter. "I'm sorry. You must have business to conduct with your soldiers."

"Yes, I was going to give them the secret route they are to take so we will know where to locate them in case something goes wrong."

"Military strategy is important. We wouldn't want to lose these valuable veterans."

Winter walked over to a crude map which had been given to him by the town and the group followed him. He looked at Climber. "Is this an accurate map of the area as far as you can tell?"

Climber studied the map and looked up at the wolf. "Very."

They went over the route several times until the animals had it memorized. "Leave as soon as you are able," Winter directed.

Once the group was gone, Winter said to Tor, "Thanks for helping to quell the riot."

"I heard their comments as they were coming in. I have the ears of a wolf, you know."

Outside the schoolhouse, Scout was putting the new wolves through drills as Washer and his group made their way around the open area of the training ground. Four rows of wolves stood at the ready.

"First line forward," Scout ordered and the group moved forward in a half circle.

Serious turned to Washer and Pieces as they continued across the training ground. "The king said we were valuable veterans. Did you hear?" he asked proudly.

"I know what valuable is, but what's a veteran?" Pieces asked.

"Old hat," answered Washer. "Been there. Done that."

"Veteran usually refers, but not always, to those who have fought in previous wars and lived to tell about it," Serious explained further.

"I like the way Washer explained it better. It was simple. To the point," Pieces stated.

The younger rabbit scowled at him.

"He gave me an example."

"Example? How?" Serious demanded. "He gave a very generalized definition. Why, it could have meant anything."

"That's why I could understand it because what Washer said was so, … so broad, so…."

Washer interjected to help the rabbit out. "So comprehensive."

"Yeppers!" Pieces said. "That's the word."

"Definitions are meant to limit, to fix a meaning, not broaden it," the younger rabbit corrected.

"I don't know about that, but I know it painted a picture to me because I've been there, done that quite a lot in my life."

"Don't start with me old rabbit," Serious said, beginning to thump.

By the time Washer, Climber and company were ready to head out with their little charges a few days later, Khoa and his troops had reached the stream where the animals had been rescued. The white wolf kept his army in the trees and went out to survey the clearing. The lumber which had been cut earlier to rebuild the bridge lay in piles. Khoa set the beavers to fell more trees and clean them of branches. If anyone happened along the river, all they would see was the beavers at work. They would be ready to build when the waters calmed and receded to their regular banks.

In the trees above, the osprey chirped and talked. Khoa looked up at them. "What have you to report?"

"All sky spies are gone, just as you requested. Just over an hour ago. There are dozens who flew over the waters and into the forest in every direction. Now we wait."

"That's the hard part," Khoa said looking around. They were in a small clearing near the banks and the whole area was surrounded by trees. It was a bad spot to camp. Anyone approaching them would not be seen until they were in the clearing. The forest made an excellent cover. To the north he spotted a ridge. It would give them a vantage point.

"I'm going to take my warriors up to the ridge. We'll be able to see an army coming from the north," he said to Sure Claw." The osprey nodded and brought his wings forward in an arc like movement, and the birds with him flocked away in unison.

A few days later, towards late afternoon when the sun's speckled light sprinkled through the leaves of the trees and dotted the forest floor, a runner reported to Khoa that birds were coming in from the east. Khoa went to the edge of the bluff. From there he could see Sure Claw talking with fellow osprey in the trees. All of a sudden four birds took flight and flew over the pathways of the stream looking down on it. One osprey dived down until he skimmed the surface of the water. He seemed suspended in flight over the water for an instant, but then rose a little unsteadily; his great wings straining under the weight of a large fish dangling from its talons. After adjusting his prey, the bird sailed effortlessly. Khoa had no doubt that the osprey could have easily carried a much larger prey. He kept track of the bird as it flew towards him and dropped the fish to the ground. This process was repeated over and over by each of the great birds.

While his warriors ate, Khoa kept his eyes on Sure Claw and the dozens of birds who flocked in around him to report. Suddenly Sure flew from his spot in the trees and towards the rise. Once overhead, he dove straight down and landed. From the bird's mannerisms, Khoa decided the news wasn't good. "Tell me straight," he told Sure.

"Four white wolf cubs found dead in the forest."

He couldn't help turning away from the osprey's eyes. Khoa wanted to ask Sure if there could be any mistake, but after just witnessing those birds sight fish under the water from great heights, he knew they could not mistake bodies as big as the cubs for anything but what they were.

"I hope they were not the ones you seek."

When Khoa didn't answer, the osprey said, "They also reported a mixed group of young animals traveling together to the north."

"Were there wolves with them?" Khoa asked, turning to look at him again.

"No."

"Thank you, Sure."

"I'll have my group drop some more fish your way," the bird said before flying off.

Khoa nodded. "Send your scouts further out tomorrow."

"How far do you suggest?"

"Until they find the camp of the dark and mixed wolves."

"It's almost time to migrate."

The white wolf nodded. "Just tell me when you need to go."

Khoa watched as the dots of light on the forest floor danced to and fro with the movement of the leaves overhead. He wondered if those bodies that the birds had found were Tristian's and Challenger's.

At that moment, the two wolf cubs and Stasher had taken shelter in an abandoned mine shaft when they heard voices in the distance. They waited by the entrance until the animals came into sight. Relieved that it was their fellow prisoners they sprung out.

"If it isn't the speedy ones," Stasher said.

Teaser, the deer, had run thirty feet before he heard the raccoon laugh and stopped.

"You're lucky we're the friendly type," the raccoon continued.

"What do you mean?" the beaver asked cautiously.

"You're a noisy lot."

"Yes, what Stasher says is true. We heard you a long ways off."

"You haven't learned much since you lost your pals," Stasher said, making a slicing motion with his paw across his neck."

"We don't need to be careful. They don't want us. They only kill wolves," Bodger the badger retorted.

"Yes, we heard them say so," Teaser added.

"Who?" the trio said together.

"The dark wolves who killed the white wolves."

"That can't be true," Tristian said. "They stole you, too."

"They're dead aren't they?" Bodger declared. "And we're here."

Stasher turned to his two companions. "Why do they want to kill you white wolves?"

A sudden crack of thunder sounded above the tree tops and a quick flick of lightning struck a nearby tree, splitting a large limb off and sending it to the ground. Everyone headed back for the cave. Inside they sat staring at each other.

"There's safety in numbers," Slivers said just to end the silence. He looked at the two wolves.

"Well, do you have an answer?" Stasher pushed. "Why do they want to kill you?"

"Not an answer, but a story," Tristian said.

"Yes, that will help make it seem more like home," Teaser said.

"We've got nothing better to do," Bodger said.

Both Tristian and Challenger took turns telling stories about the dark and white wolves they had read about from the Book and stories their fathers, Washer, and Pieces had related to them about their journey back to the Wilds.

Bodger and a few of the others were skeptical about the Great Alpha. "They are stories. Bed time ones. That's all.

"Hey," said Teaser going towards the entrance. "The thunder and lightning have stopped."

"Let's go, then," Stasher said.

"Go where?" Bodger asked. "We don't even know where we are."

"Bodger's right. We should make a plan," Tristian said. "Who's got a plan?" he continued, looking at each animal in turn.

"All I know is we were going in the wrong direction because we met the black wolves," Bodger said. "I vote to go back the way we came."

The animals readily agreed with him and said so.

"We can't go back to the river. Stoner and Strider are there," Challenger said to the new comers. "We were heading north to find another bridge and cross back over before we ran into you."

"We're not going to find anything in the middle of the forest except trees," Bodger scoffed.

"We know what's in back of us," Challenger reminded him. "I'm for avoiding that."

"SShhh!" I hear something," Tristian said, pushing them back from the entrance.

All ears went up.

They could hear the padding of many feet even over the rain.

"They're getting closer," said Teaser jumping back and forth like he was ready to bound off.

Bodger went over and nipped at his heels until he stopped prancing in place.

"There's an old mine shaft," a voice said. "We can take shelter there."

The animals looked at each other and ran deeper into the mine.

"That's the voice!" whispered Teaser. "The black wolf who killed the white wolves."

"The rains stopped now," another voice said. "Strange. One minute it's pouring down so you can't see in front of you, and the next, the sky is clear. I've never seen anything like it."

"Let's get back to the fort while it's day light. We'll head for the bridge tomorrow to see if Stoner and Strider are there yet. I've got a date with a new wolf tonight and I don't want to smell like dirt and wet fur."

The little band in the cave listened until they could no longer hear the footsteps of the wolves and then continued their argument about which way to proceed. An hour later the pouring rains began again.

Tristian got up and went to the entrance of the shaft. "We leave now."

"In the rain?" the group shouted.

"What better time? No animal will be out."

"Yes," agreed Challenger. "We can travel in safety now."

In the midst of all the grumbling Tristian said, "You heard them. They are starting to the bridge tomorrow. You do what you want. We are going north. The Alpha provided the rain so we could escape."

"You think your Great Wolf stopped and started the rain?" Bodger laughed.

"Believe it or not," Tristian answered. "You've seen a lot of strange things, starting with the wagon and the river. And there's another staring you in the face," he said, pointing at Stasher, and then went out into the rain.

"Wait," Stasher called after him. "I want to get on."

After he was settled he said, "This is just like in the stories. Just like my Uncle Washer."

The other little animals were eager to leave, whichever way they traveled, and climbed on to the wolves' backs and on to Teaser. Bodger was left standing by himself.

Tristian turned to look at him. "Coming?"

Without a word the badger hopped up on him and next to the raccoon.

After a few hours of traveling, the wolves stopped. The incline was getting steeper. The terrain was becoming rockier and the trees thinned to a scattering of scrub pines.

"Do you think we should head west now and to the edge of the forest?" asked Tristian. "This looks like a pass."

Challenger nodded. "We need to look along the stream for a bridge. We're getting up into the mountains now, and the chance for there to be a bridge is less."

It was late afternoon and hazy mist drifted through the trees rising to a sky that was just as gray. The wind had picked up; making it harder to walk against the rain.

The animals that rode tried to hide in the wolves' fur from the rain, and the black squirrel was crying. Tristian went over by Challenger to talk to him. "I'm sorry. Say, what is your name?" The squirrel shook his head, and the badger answered for him.

"He don't remember. He don't talk much, either. Just cries all the time."

"If I could cry, I would," Tristian said.

"I'm cold and hungry," the squirrel said suddenly, looking at Tristian. He liked the young cubs face.

"Me too, Squirrel."

Stasher spoke up. "Trade places with Bodger here, and sit under me. I'll warm you up."

The little black squirrel scrambled down Challenger's front leg and up Tristian's leg and curled next to Stasher. The raccoon arched his body over the tiny black frame. Bodger didn't move, so Challenger picked him off Tristian's back with his teeth lightly and set him down next to the beaver.

"Better?" asked Stasher and felt the squirrel nodding his head beneath him.

The group started out again, but this time they headed west.

CHAPTER 10
BODGERS BADGERS

Night fell earlier than usual because the sky was already dark with clouds. The small troupe took shelter under the spreading branches of a large pine tree. Dry and reddish needles lay strewn on the ground and the animals raked them together to make a bed. Everyone nestled into it and lay down except for the badger, who stood looking out from under the branches.

"This rain can end anytime now," Bodger said.

"Hope it doesn't. Your life depends on it," Challenger replied.

"This is no miracle," the badger snapped back at the wolf.

"What is it then?"

"Rain. Wet, miserable rain."

"Where did the rain come from?"

"The sky."

"Who made the rain quit today just as the black wolves were about to use the shaft for shelter? Who tipped the cart onto the logs?"

"Nobody I saw. Any of you see someone stop the rain today?" the badger asked, wheeling around to face them, which made the black squirrel jump up and burrow back under Stasher.

No animal answered him. "Just as I thought," he scoffed.

"Get some sleep," Challenger said. "We leave before dawn."

For two more days the band of animals continued on and so did the rain. On the morning of the third day they came to the edge of the forest and saw rolling hills in an open meadow. The sun was shining down on the long grasses which waved gently in the breeze. There was a faint scent of flowers in the air.

"This is my kind of country. Badger country," Bodger said, looking towards the small mounds. He was standing on his hind legs and inhaling deeply.

"How do you know?" Challenger asked.

"See those holes in the hillside? Those are badger homes. Let's go."

"They may not be up for company," the larger wolf said.

"You stay here. I'll check it out."

The wolves stood where they were, watching the badger disappear into the tall grasses which parted as he made a trail through them. They could see him plainly again as he headed across the expanse of short grasses and up the hillside. Bodger stood for a moment outside the holes, and then disappeared inside.

Within a short time he was in full view again, and there were dozens of badgers who stood around him. He waved at them and they started forward, following the path he had already made in the tall grass.

Once they entered the clearing, Tristian sensed that the badgers were distrustful of them. They hadn't taken their eyes off them.

"You are a prettier wolf than the black wolf," the large badger said, approaching the pups. He looked them both in the eyes and then squinted.

"Look everyone! They have eyes I have never seen. They are the color of the sky," Digger announced.

Every badger drew up close to see for themselves.

"Where did you get them?" someone asked.

"We are white wolves," Tristian said.

Digger turned around to the others. "The legend is alive. It has walked into our camp."

"What's a legend?" Challenger asked.

"A great story that has been handed down."

"A story you don't know for sure is true," an older badger said, walking up to Stasher and the squirrel. He walked with a cane and his fur was grizzled and white with age.

"So you're not afraid of these wolves?" he asked the squirrel.

The black squirrel shook his head and leaned into Tristian's neck.

"Not as afraid as I am of you," he managed to squeak.

Everyone laughed.

"I'm just old. Older than this meadow. Come little ones. You must be hungry," Grumps said.

They sat together and ate. There were piles of worms, little field mice, and fruit. Most of the group ate the fruit and Teaser munched on grass around him.

"Say, what do you call these?" Stasher said, holding up a piece of fruit.

"Apples."

"I'm going to take some of these home."

"Don't eat the seeds then," Digger warned.

"Oh?"

"Give them to me. I will save them for you," Grumps said, and put them on a leaf to dry.

"Not a lot of food for some of you," the old badger said looking at the wolves. "There's a stream just over that hill. I hear the fish waiting for you," he teased.

"You must have good ears," Challenger said.

"No, I don't hear hardly at all. It's just a manner of expression."

"Oh, I get it now," the white wolf said and smiled.

"Go. Eat your fish. We'll all go for an after dinner dip. I have questions to ask you," the old badger said, shaking his cane at them.

Bodger stayed behind with Grumps. There was a certain girl badger that had caught his eye during the meal. She had given him heaps of worms.

Now she helped the old badger up and steadied him as he walked. Bodger walked on the other side to steady him as well. Grumps looked back and forth between the two as they made their way up the hill.

"I'm Bodger."

"Greta," the female badger said, looking around her grandfather.

"Thanks for the extra worms."

"You looked hungry."

Their small talk continued until they reached the top of the hill and the old badger said, "Go on now. I can make it down on my own."

"Are you sure, Grandpa?"

"I'll roll down if I have to," he laughed.

After the wolves and raccoon had fished and eaten and the badgers had taken a dip as they called it, the animals sat in the early twilight talking. Grumps had made them tell the whole story of their journey and asked many questions about their fathers and the Book.

"How is it that you wolves know so much about the legend?"

"Their fathers are the kings, Tor and Khoa," Stasher blurted out.

Gasps could be heard all around and the badgers all rose and bowed.

"No. Don't do that," Tristian said. "No one bows to our fathers."

"Can this be true?" Digger said looking around. "Why?"

"Because, well, our fathers say all animals are equal."

"Animals do not live like that out here in the Meadows."

"Why?" asked Challenger.

"The big feed on the little," Digger answered.

"Why?"

"It's the way it has always been."

"Why?"

"Is that the only word you know?" Grumps asked, but Digger shrugged and said, "We don't really know each other."

"No, Digger. We don't trust each other," Grumps corrected. "We eat them before they can eat us. It is that simple."

"We're all friends," Tristian said, waving his paws around to include all the animals gathered.

"Yes, the legend is true. All animals lay down as one," the old badger said.

It was quiet for a long time before the old badger spoke again. "Tell us how this came to be."

When Challenger and Tristian had finished telling what the Great Alpha had said in the Book about getting along with others and the Great War their fathers had fought in, most of the little badgers were asleep.

Grumps stretched and rose to his feet with a groan. "Thank you. You have been most gracious guests. Time to get the little ones to bed."

"It is us who should thank you for dinner," Challenger answered.

"What dinner? You had to catch your own," he laughed and turned as Greta came to help him back up the hill. Bodger was with her.

"Coming?" Grumps asked the band of animals.

"No. This is a good spot for us by the stream," Tristian said.

"Yes, you might find our badger holes a pretty tight fit."

He looked at his granddaughter. "Get me going, then."

"We will hear more tomorrow," Grumps called back without looking, waving his cane in the air as high as he could which wasn't far.

Stray streaks of purple lingered around the edges of the horizon after the sun went down giving a deeper appearance to the sky. "I'm going for a splash," the beaver suddenly said. "No telling when we might have water again."

Tristian looked after him. "I could use some water." The rest of the band followed him to the banks for a drink and then headed back and settled in for the night in the grass. The sound of the beaver's soft splashing reached them from the distance.

"The only thing that's missing is a campfire," Challenger said. "And then it would be just like home."

"Except everyone we know is missing," Tristian said.

That sentence brought a long silence on the group.

"How long before we get home, do you think?" Stasher asked.

"Well, the trip to the stream where we escaped was several days from home, and now we're above that stream somewhere, so I would say several days back or more."

"That's not bad," the squirrel said and sighed. "For the first time I feel like we're really going to make it."

They heard Slivers come on to the shore, shake himself off, and pad up to them.

"Where's Bodger?" he asked.

"He helped Greta take Grumps up the hill," Tristian said. "He's smitten with her, I think."

"I can see him liking her, but who would be taken with him?" the black squirrel asked.

"Another badger," Stasher answered.

"It feels good to be in the wide open spaces again where you can see the sky." Challenger said.

"Look at that moon rising. It's like having a light in the sky it's so bright tonight," Stasher commented.

"We should be traveling by it," Challenger said. "Now let's get some sleep."

"I thought we were waiting up for Bodger," Stasher said.

"No!" came the unanimous consensus from the crowd.

The next morning the two wolves, the beaver, and the raccoon were fishing in the stream. Slivers was floating on his back cracking clams with a rock on his stomach.

"Let me try one of those things," Stasher called.

Slivers dove down in the water and came up with a clam and threw it to the raccoon. "Get your own rock."

The little raccoon dove down for a rock and tried floating on his back with the clam on his stomach, but kept losing the clam as he struggled to stay afloat. "I'll drown doing this," he finally said.

"Break them on the shore," the beaver called back. "Raccoons can't float on their backs, I guess. It's in the tail. Make a paddle for your tail."

The raccoon threw a few clams on to the rocks and waded out of the water. He picked up a rock and began hitting the clam over and over. "They better be good. This is a lot of work."

"The way you do it, yes," Slivers called back.

"Show me how to whack them," Stasher said, and stopped attacking the clams. As he waited for the beaver, Teaser and the black squirrel came down for a drink. Teaser was galloping and stepped on one of Stashers clams.

"Hey," Stasher called out running in front of the deer waving at him with his paws. "You're walking all over my lunch."

The deer looked down at his feet. "I thought I heard a cracking sound," he said lifting his foot off the clam.

Stasher walked over to the clam. "It's open."

"Sorry."

"No, no. That's what I was trying to do with the rock," he said looking at the deer.

"Stomp on the rest of these," he said, throwing a few more clams by Teaser's hooves.

So the days hastened on with the group eating, playing and teaching the badgers about the Way. One morning while the squirrel was up in the walnut tree getting his breakfast he had spotted two foxes coming from the direction of the forest. They were heading for the badger's holes. He charged down the tree and onto Teasers back yelling all the way. In between his chattering, the deer got the message. He sprang over to the stream.

"Foxes at the holes," the squirrel shouted as loud as he could.

Tristian and Challenger galloped up the hill and saw the badgers on their hind legs standing against the foxes. Their teeth were exposed fully as Digger and the others dove forward at the foxes, mounting their attack. The bodies became tangled and soon the badgers were on the top of the foxes, biting them. The foxes yelped in a shrill manner while trying to regain a standing position. The wolves watched as the badgers charged again and again, backing the foxes up. They were relentless in their attack, ripping at the foxes savagely with each surge until the enemy turned tail and ran.

The two wolves met the foxes as they fled up the hill. Seeing the wolves, the foxes sprang straight up like rockets, but once they touched ground again they veered courses and set a new direction. They were on the run, but the wolves chased them for a distance just to make sure they kept going.

"I've never seen a fight like that," Tristian said when they returned. "You little guys showed them."

"Never back down," Digger said, looking at the two pups.

"He's right," Grumps added, coming out of the hole with the younger ones. "Once you snag a piece of them, don't let up. Keep driving them backwards. Show lots of teeth. Once they've been bitten, they have new respect and don't won't to feel it again."

"Draw first blood," Digger said.

Teaser and the others had come down from the hill. "I'm glad that wasn't my introduction to you," the squirrel said.

"I'll take that as a compliment," said Digger and paused. "I'm sorry to admit it, but I don't know your name."

"I haven't been able to remember it," the squirrel said, looking down.

"He can't run around without a name," Grumps shouted.

"We tried to call him Crier because he cries all the time, but he threw things at us," Bodger half laughed as a nut hit him in the head. "See?"

"Who wants a name of shame?" Grumps asked. "I'm sure he has done plenty of good things."

"Well, he sounded the warning about the foxes, so you can thank him for that," Tristian said.

"Yes, when the foxes heard your wolf calls from the hill, that took the last stick out of the dam, so to speak," Digger said and laughed. "Did you see them when they turned to run in your direction and saw you coming down the slope?"

"They jumped so high, I didn't think they'd land," Challenger said.

"I saw them from the tree and told Teaser and we ran and told the wolves."

When he was able to stop laughing, Digger patted the squirrel and said, "Anyway, like Tristian said, thanks for sounding the alarm."

"That's it. That's his name. Sounder," Gramps said, looking at the black squirrel.

"I like it," he said, and then thinking better of it, added, "At least until I remember my old one."

"Not everyone gets the gift of choosing his own name," Grumps told him.

The little band learned much from the badgers in the coming weeks. Not only did they learn about taking a stand against foxes, but where to find the best worms, and to make extra holes to store provisions in. "Always put a little portion aside," Grumps had told them.

Today the travelers lay sunning themselves in the meadow.

"What a beautiful day," Sounder said.

"I could live here forever," the beaver answered

"A lot of good things have happened here," Sounder affirmed.

"Yes, I found lots of new foods. Apples and clams," Stasher joined in, and looked at the pile of opened clam shells and apple cores strewn around him. He stood up and looked around. "There's everything here. Water. Food."

"Add no rain," Teaser broke in. "Since we have been here, there hasn't been a drop from the sky."

Challenger stood up and looked back at the slope.

"What's the matter?" asked the squirrel.

"Nothing, but I think I'll go have a look over the hill."

He started off and Tristian trotted after him. "Their talk reminded me that we have been here for a long time. Maybe too long."

Tristian remained silent.

They reached the top of the hill. From here they could see the badger holes, the expanse of meadow, and the edge of the forest they had come through.

"What are you looking for?" Tristian asked.

"I don't know. It's a feeling. Like the feeling Pieces had when he saw the black clouds," he said, turning to look at his cousin.

"Something's pulling at me, too."

Just then Grumps came out of his hole followed by his large family. He saw the wolves, waved, and started towards them with Bodger and Greta on each side.

When the old badger heard the news that they intended to leave in the morning, he said, "I knew there would come a day when you would feel the need to leave, but so soon? I will never hear all I wanted to about the invisible wolf."

"Speak to him like we did," Tristian said. "He hears all animals." As he thought about the words he had just spoken to the badger, he thought he sounded like his father. He had heard him say that many times.

"What sort of things would I talk about?"

"About bigger holes, about stopping the rain, about the sunshine, or big, fat worms."

The old badger laughed in his kind and knowing way. "He must be very patient to listen to all that."

The next morning the group headed to the badger holes to say farewell and pick up Bodger. There were hugs and tears all around. Tristian looked at Stasher and Sounder. "It's time," he said, and the two animals climbed on to his back and settled in. Slivers took his seat on Challenger.

"Ready?" Challenger asked Bodger.

The badger moved forward with his head down, but soon looked up at the white wolf. "I've decided to stay here. I've found my family."

"What about your real family?" Tristian asked.

"They went down in that cart. My mom and sister, anyway. Dad went off weeks before we were taken and never came back. I wouldn't know him if I saw him."

"You never said."

"I couldn't talk about it, I guess."

"Thank you again for saving my life, Stasher," the badger said, holding on to Greta.

"We will tell our children about how you untied the bags and saved their father," Greta said.

"You have become a legend," said Bodger.

"Yes, you taught us all about tying and untying knots," Grumps laughed.

"Here, I almost forgot," Grumps said, taking a necklace from around his neck. "This is for you, Stasher," he said, holding it out to the raccoon, but Stasher shook his head. "I don't want any medals."

"No medals here. These are apple seeds I saved for you."

"Uh, yum. Thank you," the raccoon said, looking at the little package of bundled leaves. "Nice knots."

"Handy," he said, putting the braided grass rope around his neck. He touched the packet of seeds that now dangled from his neck.

"You've taught us more than we taught you," Grumps replied.

All the animals exclaimed that wasn't so and began to name off the things they had learned.

"You'll come back for a visit?" Grumps asked almost shyly, hoping for the best. "Bring the kings of the white wolves, the ones who walk in favor with the invisible wolf."

Everyone nodded, but Tristian knew that would never happen. The badgers were a part of their life that would never come again. It was neat and complete just like the seeds that were wrapped up in the package, he thought.

CHAPTER 11
ALL THE VALIANT HEARTS

Back at the site where the animals had been rescued and the dark wolves captured, Gambles was yelling out proudly, "There she is. Ready to cross." It had taken weeks to accomplish their task. A crude, massive log lay across the waters now from shore to shore. Khoa thanked the beavers and called for his men.

"Sorry it took so long," Gambles said.

"You stayed with it. That's what counts."

The beavers had first tried to build a bridge like the one that had originally been there, but every day they sunk footings, new rains came and washed them away during the night. Then they had taken another tact by trying to build dams above the bridge site to slow the waters, but Gamble had told them over and over, "Ain't the right place. All the streams in this river empty into here. It would take years to build a dam high enough to stop them. That's the head waters just up a bit." After weeks of watching the dam started and washed away, Khoa had approached the head engineer, "You're right. There must be another way."

Gambles had looked at him, and scratching at the area above his tail and deep in thought, had said, "Not unless you want to throw a tree across the whole river."

"Would it work?"

The beaver was still scratching his tail end. "It would have to be a big, big tree, and I don't see any of those here. They would be in the older part of the forest."

"Let's try it," Khoa said smiling.

It had taken days, but the beavers had located a massive and tall oak that was nearing the end of its usefulness. They had put ropes around the trunk before they felled it so they could use them to pull the large tree to the river. It took some time to trim all the branches down and get it back to the river. Once at the river, they used the ropes along with fifty wolves and hoisted the massive oak upright again. It towered into the sky. A lot of maneuvering was needed to position the tree just right so it fell straight across the river and not sideways.

The tree had to be big enough to stay in place once it spanned both shores and this giant oak filled the order. They had placed it five feet from the rivers bank on this side and tied many ropes around it, which they then tied to the rooted trees to act as an anchor. This would keep the tree from being swept away by the current once it spanned the water.

Gambles checked the knots on the trees and gave the order for the wolves to let the tree fall. It fell quickly and landed on the other shore with a loud crash. "Perfect," the beaver shouted. "There's five feet left on this side out of the water and looks to be more on the other."

Gambles and some of the other beavers picked up some ropes and walked across the oak and anchored it to trees on the other side as well. The beaver waved back to Khoa. Soon the army was on the bridge. As the engineer watched the wolfs crossing by twos, he said to the others, "Biggest job of my career. And for the King."

Cheering came from both sides and the wolves broke into song.

>"We come from the Wilds
>
>And we take those hides."

"Whose hides?" the sergeant called out.

>"Those black wolf hides," came the roar back and

then they resumed the cadence of the song.

>"Wherever we can find them.
>
>Ain't none too big,
>
>Ain't none too small.
>
>We ain't picky,
>
>We take'em all.
>
>We come to fight,
>
>And make things right.
>
>To set all free,

Who wanna be."

"Where're you from?" the sergeant called out.

"We come from the Wilds."

"Who do you want?"

"Those black wolf hides."

Gambles looked over at his work crew when he realized they were whistling the tune of the wolves. "Trees are calling, and you guys are whistling through your teeth. Let's go! Jasper, take your units and head for the Wilds. Get that fort built like we talked about. Me and the boys will be up river here, building dams so this river won't over flow this way again."

Within a day Khoa and his army had followed the osprey to where the bodies of the wolf cubs lay. They were mangled, and parts had been eaten away. Their fur was pulled from their bodies and matted into the dirt and leaves making it hard to tell the outline of their frames. Khoa ordered graves to be dug and helped his wolves with the task. Each wolf, who dug alongside him, watched him reverently. When the hole was deep enough, Khoa leaped out and helped lower the bones in. Were they the bones of his son? Of Tors? *Great Wolf, give me a sign. I am dead in my heart,'* he pleaded silently. He looked around at his warriors. They must not see his weakness of spirit. He wished at this moment to throw off his kingship and howl until his grief was no more. Suddenly a movement of his troops coming forward in a line brought him back to his task.

Somehow he was able to get words out, but he didn't even hear them. "No one will ever know who these pups were, but they will be forever honored. The valiant four."

His whole regiment whispered back, "The valiant four."

Khoa turned to one of his sergeants. "Finish here. Mark the top stones and the tree with the sign of the half fish, then catch up to us."

The sign of the half fish was made to indicate that an animal of the Way had been there. It was an arced line which made up the top half of the fish. If another follower spotted the sign, he would provide the bottom arc to complete the fish. It would not only let them know where to find the grave, but would let them know if others who practiced the Way had been there.

Some days later they came upon the fortress. From a distance it appeared to rise directly out of the water. A large lake lay in front of it and mountains lay to the left. The right side had spires and spikes around the top of the wall.

"You've got to swim or fly to get in there," Sergeant Jace remarked.

Khoa looked at him. "You may have just given me the answer on how to plan an attack."

"How?"

"Old Deuce's in the details. I don't know, but somehow by air and water."

Khoa watched overhead as the osprey changed their direction, circle three times and then fly back south. "It's like having a living map, following those birds."

"This looks more magnificent than the one Tor told us about in the Blackstone's."

"Just how many of these have they built?"

"Let's take a look from the mountain on the left to get a picture of the inside."

"Tell the warriors to wait here. The fewer of us moving about the less scent we scatter for them to catch."

From their mountain like eerie the two wolves got a full look at the fortress. Khoa took his book off his back and drew a picture of the lay out on its back cover pages. He wrote a thousand plus wolves. Just then three units of wolves came on to the parade ground and stood in rows ten deep.

A wolf, who Khoa had never seen, stood facing the army. "This is jugular training. It is the fastest way to kill your enemy," the dark wolf said, showing them with his paw on his own neck. "This is the spot. Bite it and your prey will drop. Don't look to see if he's dead. That takes seconds. Move on to the next jugular. If you've done your job right he will be dead when he drops."

Khoa watched as the commander wolf turned towards the row of houses. His coat was totally black and it gleamed in the sun. "Bring out the prisoners."

Khoa and Jace saw twenty assorted animals being led in single file in front of the army. "Now you lazy buzzards find out what happens to those who won't work, who've out lived their usefulness. Welcome to the races. You don't have to do anything but run."

The wolf spun quickly. "Can you do that?" he screamed at a wolverine. The animal cowered, but nodded.

"Good," the black wolf said turning back to the waiting wolves.

"Tear Tear. Step forward. Ready for lunch?"

"Haven't you got anything bigger? He's just a bite."

The wolverine, sensing what was about to happen, bolted from his spot. For a moment it looked like he had caught the wolf off guard and started to put some distance between himself and his attacker. Tear Tear stood a moment longer and then raced after the fleeing animal. The wolverine was heading straight for the walls of the fortress, and with a great effort and stretching out of his body leaped onto its sides. His legs struggled to gain a foothold so he could pull himself upward. It was working. He was making it up the wall. He turned to look down as he felt the wolf jumping up behind him.

"You missed, Tear," came the voice of the black wolf. Tear Tear leapt higher the second time and caught the wolverine by his hind quarters which brought him tumbling down. Tear Tear, in seemingly one motion, turned, and was at his victim's throat. A high pitched scream reverberated across the mountains and back until it was a low hollow sound.

"It's murder, Khoa," Jace whispered. "I had only heard stories about the black wolves. Now I have seen with my own eyes and I will never forget."

"There stand the valiant," Khoa said in a low voice. He looked at his sergeant. "Time to get back to the warriors."

"There stand the valiant? There die the valiant, you mean. Aren't we going to stop this?"

"How? It's over a thousand feet down."

The sergeant looked at him helplessly.

Khoa said, "Jump if you want to."

Jace took another look over the edge, and then followed Khoa back down the mountain.

The sounds of the slaughter came from behind them.

"How can you stand to hear that and not want to help?" Jace asked, pulling at Khoa to turn him around. The white wolf turned fully and looked at his sergeant eye to eye.

"One second at a time. The same way I buried my son."

Jace felt the coldness of Khoa's words and had no doubt that the score would be evened.

CHAPTER 12
AVEC LES LOUPS

We've come a long ways," Challenger said, turning to Tristian. They had gotten into a routine in the last week and the wolves only stopped when it was time to rest or near dark. Since it was sunset, the riders jumped down without a word.

"It seems quiet and still just being us," Sounder said, looking at his friends.

"There's not many of us left," Stasher answered.

"Do you think any of the others who ran the other way are alive?" the squirrel asked. "There was over twenty of us who ran off the cart that day and now there are just five of us."

Tristian noticed the fear in his friend's voice and said, "I have asked the Great Wolf to protect them and us. We're still here, aren't we?"

"So they are still here," Sounder said, trying to convince himself.

"Well, we done traveling for the day?" Stasher groused. He didn't wait for anyone to answer and said, "Can we eat or not? If yes, throw me one of those apples from the pouch."

"What's the matter with you?" Challenger asked.

"You wolves keep looking behind us. It makes me nervous."

"Instinct," Tristian said.

"Those dark wolves don't know we even exist. If they did, we would be lying in a heap like those others."

"I think Stasher's right. They don't know we're alive or where we are," said Teaser.

"If they haven't caught us by now, they aren't coming," Stasher said firmly.

"We can't stop looking. It wouldn't be safe. For any of you," Tristian warned. "Do you want to be taken? Do you want to be eaten? Do you want to be killed?" the white cub said, looking at each animal in turn.

"Let him watch, Stasher," Slivers said, shaking his head, his eyes looking bigger than any the raccoon had ever seen.

After seeing how scared Slivers was, the raccoon wanted to agree with him, but rather than admitting it, said, "I didn't say stop looking. Just don't let me see you looking. I get edgy," the raccoon said, patting the wolf's back, and transfixed by the fear in the beaver's eyes.

The animals ate in silence trying to avoid one another's eyes. Each one was looking around at the new land they found themselves in.

"I wish we were home. I thought we were supposed to be there by now," Sounder sniffled.

"Speaking of home, look at that. An old beaver lodge," Slivers cried.

"What makes you think it's old?" Challenger asked.

"See how dried and white all the sticks are, and all that grass growing on the mud mounds? And they have dug canals all around to carry their branches through the water and not drag them across dry land. They've been there awhile. Let's go pay them a visit."

"It might not be a good idea," warned Stasher, who was still feeling quite unsettled after Tristian's verbal lashing.

"They can give us a read on where we're at. We can get directions, at least."

"Yes, they might know how close we are to home," Sounder added.

The two wolves looked at each other and nodded at him. "You go. We'll wait here."

"I'll wave if it's safe," Slivers said, waddling quickly up to the pond, his flat tail dragging after him in a cumbersome fashion. Once in the water, the beaver transformed into a graceful new being, and with a slap of his tail disappeared from sight.

Soon Slivers and two other beavers stood at the other end waving to them. The dam itself covered the stream from end to end at its narrowest point. One could walk all the way across the stream on top if you needed to, though it was tricky weaving in and out of the branches. The mounds of earth and grass that had grown over the top helped to make a pathway on the dam, which the wolves and deer found to be advantageous as they picked their way across the roof.

Young beavers popped up from both sides of the dam to stare at the newcomers from the water. One by one they climbed onto the structure. "Who's the king?" one asked.

"What do kings do?" Trimmer wanted to know.

The animals didn't have a chance to answer as Slivers began introducing the two adults.

"Meet Knox and Feller."

"Avec les loups," Knox called out loudly over and over, making wolf sounds in between.

Seeing the animals look at him like he was crazy he said, "You don't know French, do you?"

They all shook their heads.

"No mind, no care. No one ever does."

The two wolves continued to look at him. "I keep speaking it to all new comers in the hopes of finding someone who does."

"What does it mean? What you said," Tristian asked.

"Avec les loups?" he asked and howled into the air. "Howl with the wolves."

"That's a bad imitation of a wolf," one of the younger beavers said as a few of his siblings began making wolf calls.

"Indeedy," Knox said looking at the younger beavers. "If that's what I sound like."

"Worse."

Knox looked at the wolves and asked, "Worse?"

Both wolves nodded and so did Teaser.

"No mind. No matter." He was standing in front of the group and looking them over. "So the little kings travel with the common animals. When Slivers here told me who he came with, I couldn't believe it."

"Yes, we all needed to see it," Feller said.

Tristian, taking affront to what Knox had said, proclaimed, "These animals are certainly not common. Stasher is a hero." The pup went on to tell the whole story of their journey and the Way.

"Far, far back in my memory is the knowledge of the Way of the wolf. Like it was put there or I knew it somehow," Knox said in a far off voice.

"Like hearing the story, you're hearing the truth. You remember that was the way things were, and are meant to be," Feller told them.

"You still mustn't trust the animals around here," Feller said, turning to his children. "The only reason these wolves are allowed here is because they are pups like you."

"And they didn't eat Slivers," Trimmer said.

"Indeedy," Knox said looking at the youngster. "How did the white wolf make a pact with all animals not to harm them?"

"Because they have the spirit of the Alpha in them," Tristian answered.

All the beavers reared back in fright.

"Do you?" Knox asked.

"Yes," Tristian said. "At least I think I do. I'm not sure." He watched the beavers move further back from him and the others.

"What's this spirit do?"

"What's it feel like?"

"What's it look like?"

"Does it hurt?"

The wolf cub felt a little alarmed himself. They sure were an inquisitive lot.

"I'm not sure. I was just learning about it. On a quest for it in my training when I was stolen away." He looked to Challenger for help.

"You can't see it or touch it, I know that," the other wolf said.

"That's not much help," Knox said.

"It helps you do good things to all animals."

"Like not eat them?" Trimmer asked again. Knox scowled at him and the little beaver said, "Well, it's on my mind, granddad."

"Yes. The Book teaches that all animals are equal. It makes you try to get along with them."

"Indeedy."

"There are no kinder, nobler wolves," Stasher testified.

"Indeedy. I never thought to see such a thing. Wolves who made friends and not meals of smaller animals."

He looked at the faces of the new arrivals. "Speaking of food. This old kindling box of mine needs stoking," Knox said, patting his stomach with his paws.

"There's fish and clams for the taking in this stream. You're welcome to help yourself," he continued and walked away. The other beavers followed his lead. Once he was in the water, he called, "We'll fish on the right side of the dam, you wanderers stay on the left."

A short time later the little beavers had climbed back onto the dam to see what all the clatter was. They saw the little raccoon throwing clams on to the shore and the deer stomping on them.

"Can we throw him some clams?"

"No, I don't want you that close to them," Knox said, still in the water.

"He's a deer. He can't eat us."

"He travels with wolves. It's not natural," Knox said, swimming closer to where his grandchildren were sitting. "And one claims to be vexed with a spirit. That's magic of some kind."

"But they're having such fun together," Trimmer sighed, and the six other young beavers agreed.

"All the better to draw you in. Stay away," Knox said, motioning to them to get back in the water.

His son swam up closer to them. "What do you make of the story of the black wolves stealing them?" Feller asked.

"Wise tales. If black wolves had gotten a hold of them, they would be dead."

The other beaver nodded in agreement. "It was black wolves who killed Old Lodger and his kin. Why have you let them stay?" Feller asked, peeping back over the dam.

"Looking for the boogeyman, I guess. I wanted to see with my own eyes. How does this magic work?"

"Go looking for the boogeyman, and you just might find him," Feller warned.

"Indeedy. That's what the wise tale says," answered Knox before diving down for another clam.

Back on shore the group had decided to make a campfire. They had full stomachs and wanted be warm as well.

"It sure is peaceful here," Teaser said, kneeling around the fire.

"It must be because we're close to home," Stasher answered.

"It doesn't feel that way to me. Our hosts aren't the friendliest types," Slivers said. "I sure didn't feel welcomed when I came a knock'in. And they sure didn't believe who I said my friends were. I think that's what finally brought old Obnoxious out."

"Don't make fun of our hosts."

"I'm not, Tristian. He told me," and the beaver stood up, puffed out his chest and mimicked the voice of the old beaver, "My given name was Obnoxious. Then for years it was Noxious, 'til I learned what it meant, and now it's just Knox. The older I get, the shorter my name becomes."

The other animals laughed and all turned their heads up and gave low, little howls.

Inside the beaver lodge they heard the howling and the women huddled together with the young ones. "This is Old Lodger's legend come to life," Merily, who was Knox' mate, chattered.

"They're not going to wage war on us. There's only two wolves and they're babes."

"First, comes the unexpected, and next you will be shown that what once was blackness will become white," Merily continued. "Isn't that what the wise tale says?"

"They're not really white wolves. They are white wolves…with blacks patches….on them." He spoke haltingly as it hit him that they may have once been black wolves and were now turning white.

"Indeedy. It's a slow magic that is working on them."

"See what you get for letting strangers in," his mate chastised him.

"And strangers with blue eyes besides. That should have told you both something. No animals have blue eyes," Fellers mate added. Silence fell on the crowd.

"Why not?" Trimmer wanted to know.

"Don't know. Never have seen one, though. Only thing I heard of was that man has blue eyes. And they spoke French. That's where Old Lodger learned it. From French trappers here about."

"Yes, and we all know about the evil of man."

"If French is evil, why do you speak it?" Trimmer asked.

"So we know when they come again. Old Lodger told us to watch for them. They nearly wiped us out the first time."

"Tell them to leave," commanded Merily.

"I will in the morning."

"No, now. I won't sleep all night."

Knox nodded. "Don't yell about us tracking up the lodge when we get back."

Feller followed at his heels, but once atop the dam they stopped in their tracks. They saw the travelers sitting around the fire light, and they shimmered and glowed.

"Golden lights rising in the air," Knox said, clearly awe struck.

"What kind of magic is it that dances and glows and makes the darkness light?

Knox shook his head. "Maybe the Great Wolf they told us about sent it."

"Or that spirit inside the one called Tristian."

"What does this brightness do?"

"I don't know, and I don't want to know. We have to leave at once. Take our wives and children and get far away."

"We've been here for generations since the Frenchmen left. Lodger's grandfather and father," Feller said looking at Knox. "You found your boogey man, and now you want to leave because of fear, father."

"I should have listened to the wise tales warning. I will from now on."

Inside the lodge the old beaver prepared his family to leave. "Remember stay under the water. Don't come up 'til we're a safe enough distance away. Do what I do," he said and dove into the water.

As Knox watched his children and mate enter the water, he spoke silently to the gods of nature. "Oh, river gods and wood gods get us safely away and I promise never to be curious about anything again. I won't look for trouble. I will let it lay where I find it. I won't as much as turn over a stone, even if I think there is a clam under it. I promise. Well, maybe not that far." A voice seemed to echo in his thoughts. 'There is more darkness where you go than what you leave behind.'

More darkness ahead? There couldn't be, could there? he asked himself. No, it was fear trying to make him stay. He knew the boogey man was behind them. It couldn't be ahead of them at the same time. He felt the water behind him ripple and turned in panic. It was Feller and his family. Good! Things would be just fine now.

The beavers swam until dawn and Knox left them in the stream as he went ashore to check things out. He shook himself off and noticed a big boulder to the right. He thought something dark flashed out from it, but before he could run, the smell of wolves entered his nostrils. He froze and felt the grip of teeth around his neck. *Somehow those wolves must have followed us along the banks and waited for us to come out of the water.* He caught site of the wolves paws as he swung from its jaws. Those feet were dark and they were big. It was not the white pups. *Wait. Maybe that was part of their magic. They grew as they ran and turned black. Yes, that must be how they do it. That was how their magic worked.*

Before he had time to wonder why he was still alive, the big wolf spit him onto the ground. He looked around and saw that he was surrounded by dozens of dark wolves.

"We want information. You tell us what we want to know, and we let you live," said Warrior.

Knox nodded, and the thought entered his head. *Here is the darkness Old Lodger warned me about last night when we started out. It must have been his voice telling me there was more danger ahead. Why didn't you just say there are more dark wolves ahead? You got to tell me straight out, Old Lodger. I'm not much of a guesser.*

"Have you seen any white wolves?"

Hmmm. Here it was again. White wolves.

"Big ones or little ones?"

"Big ones."

The beaver shook his head.

"They would have been through here a month or so ago. Coming from the fortress in the North. A hungry and mangy lot."

"No."

"He's lying. He lives right here."

"No, I don't live here."

"Your family is out in the stream."

"Kill him. He lies," Warrior barked.

"No. We just came from up stream. Our dam is up there. Twenty miles. Maybe more."

"Kill him."

"Check. You will see no dams out there. I do have information about white wolves, but little ones, not big ones like you asked. That's why we came here, to get away from them."

Warrior sent a wolf to scout the river bank.

"You ran away from little white wolves?" Warrior asked, which brought snickering from the rest of the pack.

"Now I know you are lying. White wolves are like little lambs. They harm no living creatures."

"They don't?" the beaver said, hanging his head down almost to the sand.

"No. White wolves swear an oath to the Great Wolf of the Way to help all animals."

Knox felt sick inside. These wolves seemed to know of the story he had been told.

"What is the golden light they have with them?"

"Golden light?"

"Yes, it breaks the darkness and makes you see around it."

"Ah, that's fire, you daft, wet rodent," Warrior said laughing and looking at his wolves.

"Fire? What does fire do?"

"Enough of this!" the dark wolf called. "We should kill you just because you're daft."

"Let him tell us what he knows of the little white wolves first," Snuffer said. "And what these little wolves did to frighten him away."

Knox told them of his meeting with the travelers.

"That's white wolves for you. They pair up with any animal that comes along."

"That's why I don't believe you've seen them. They are particularly fond of dumb, frightened ones like you."

"These wolves had blue eyes."

"There are dozens of white wolves with blue eyes."

"There are? These are magic wolves."

Knox's statement brought laughter and howls from the wolves. "They are weak wolves. Blue eyes are not good for hunting."

"The other animals said they were princes."

"Did these princes have names?" Snuffer scoffed.

"Challenger was one."

"And the other?"

"Tristian."

Snuffer looked at his brother, "Maybe the rodent is telling the truth."

"Can I go now?"

"No. You will lead us to them. Your family stays here," Warrior said, turning to some black wolves beside him. "Guard them until we send word." The wolves went to the banks and sat down.

"If you tell the truth, you live. Lead the way, rodent."

"I'm not much of a land traveler."

"Put him on my back, Snuf," Warrior said.

"I...I can't do this," the beaver said terrified.

"Sing him to sleep, Snuf."

The dark wolf trotted over and looked at Knox.

"Listen closely now," he snarled. "I'm going to sing you to sleep."

Snuffer cleared his throat and began his song:

"There was a beaver from Nolf,

Who rode on the back of a wolf.

He was told to be still

Or by heck or by will

By the end of the ride

He would wind up inside,

With the smile on the face of the wolf."

The beaver shuttered and shook and his little heart felt like it would burst. He didn't know how much longer he could take this. He stared at Snuffer with his teeth grinning at him and then a strange thing happened. The appearance of the dark wolf changed before his eyes. Instead of a dark foreboding face it became lighter toned and gentler. He wondered who this new face belonged to, and it answered him. 'I am the Watcher wolf. It will be alright.'

His next thought was, where have you come from? The face looked at him and bent forward touching him. 'I was sent by the Great Wolf. He protects all animals. No harm will come to you.' Just as the wolf touched him a great calmness came upon him and he slept.

It was dark when he woke and he was being taken off Warriors back. He decided to pretend to still be asleep as he was carried and put on the ground. He couldn't get over how unafraid he was. Even as the rope was put around his neck, he didn't open his eyes. His heart was beating in its regular rhythms. He was not afraid. He was sure he was going to be alright. He had been told that. They were securing him to a tree. "That should hold him," a dark wolf said. He listened as the wolves spoke.

"That's an uneducated idiot for you. Scared to death. Believing in fairy tales past down from other idiots."

"He's the first animal I know to be afraid of the white wolves, and pups at that."

"That's the kind of animal we want to breed in our new society. We should thank him. He can train all the rest to believe in his brand of stupidity."

"Be afraid of the white wolves. They bring golden lights that break the darkness," Warrior said laughing.

"Someday the white wolves will be expunged. Totally and forever," Snuffer said.

The beaver wasn't sure what expunged meant, but the word gave him a sinking feeling in his heart just like when he thought about the beaver being wiped out in Old Lodger's days.

Every now and then Knox let himself peek at the wolves. He saw them gather and carry drift wood from the shores of the stream and place it in a pile. Next, they rubbed two sticks together very quickly until lights came out from them. The lights grew larger and they blew on them and they continued to grow. Fire. They, too, had magic. No, not magic. Fire. This was fire. What did this fire do? How did they know of this and we beavers had never learned it?

"Ah, this feels good," Snuffer said. It's warming me right up."

So it felt good and it warmed you, thought the beaver. Maybe Old Lodger had been wrong in telling them to stay away from all other animals. They had not learned what these others knew.

These dark wolves had said beavers believed in old tales. Maybe it was true. That was all they knew. They had been taught to be afraid of all animals and stay to their own kind. Now he knew there was a good kind of animal, but how did one tell the difference?

The next day his questioned was answered. The wolves had come upon a group of otters riding the flow of a small waterfall. Five wolves waited for the family to get to the top of the waterfall together and then rushed them. Twenty or more wolves were at the bottom waiting as the otters slid over the cascading water to escape. It was slaughter. A couple of otters had managed to jump into the water against the current and fight their way up stream. Knox' heart lamented over the orphaned cubs. He quaked with terror at how quickly the black wolves had brought death, but mostly because the deed was done with such delight, even deliciousness.

After breakfast Warrior asked, "You're sure it's only a few miles now, rodent?"

"Yes, give or take."

"Put him on my back," Warrior said.

"Could I have some water first and breakfast?"

"Did we promise you water or food?" Warrior said, turning around to Knox and snapping his teeth.

"Tell him what he gets, Snuff."

"A song."

Snuffer and the wolves sang, "Oh there once was beaver from Nolf."

So he was to be eaten at the end of his journey. If only he was in his lodge. There at least was a back door by which to escape. He would be underwater where the black wolves could not go. The beaver tried to escape in his mind, but his wishing did not change the reality of his situation. The sun beat down on Knox. Even the fur of the dark wolf was hot. He wanted to go for a cool dip. He needed food and water. He felt the wolf stop, and he looked up and saw Old Lodger's dam directly ahead of him.

Warrior ordered his wolves into attack mode, spreading them out in a wide circle. The little animals were resting quietly on the banks. Suddenly Knox realized there was no one was left to guard him. When the wolves rushed, he began to shout at the top of his lungs, "Avec les loups," over and over and howled. He swayed his body to and fro on the back of the black wolf and then sunk his teeth into his neck deeply. He was a big beaver and all forty pounds of him leaned into the dark wolf's hide.

Warrior twisted his head and upper torso instantly to attack the beaver. He spun with such force that the beaver was thrown to the ground. He turned quickly to pursue his fallen attacker, but he saw the animal raise up on his hind legs and yell, "Avec les loups." Howls of terror came from him. The beaver stood facing him, eyes wild and fixed. Foam ran down the sides of his mouth.

"Rabid rodent," the dark wolf said in a cursing manner, but he didn't go after him.

Knox sensed the wolf was fearful of him, and in that second he broke to the left and scurried into the water, howling like a mad, wounded animal all the way.

From downstream Knox smelled something and turned upon his back to swim so he could see what was behind him. Great yellow fingers reached into the sky. Fire. It was the lodge. He continued floating on his back; watching as the lodge burned and the dark wolves closed in on the little travelers. *What had he done?*

CHAPTER 13
GLIMPSING THE FOREST FOR THE TREES

Pieces and the wild bunch were delivering the last little survivor, Fighter the wolverine, to his parents in Fen when the black wolves marched into the streets.

"Quick! Inside," Slasher said. "Don't let them see you."

"They haven't been back for a few weeks. We had hoped they were gone for good."

"Yes, we were just starting to get out a bit," Miss Kiss said.

"That's a funny name for a wolverine," Serious ventured, remembering her name from their brief introduction outside.

"That's because her bites are so soft. She's not much of a fighter," Slasher said turning to her.

Since Washer was nearest the entrance he peaked out to see what was going on. The dark wolves were unloading bundles of wires from carts. What he saw next horrified him. A long line of beavers were tied together and being led into a building that was once was used as a schoolhouse.

Washer motioned for the others to come and look, and as he did, the two wolves pranced forward and called, "All animals to the school now. We have news for you. The white wolves will not steal your children any more. We have come to protect you from the white wolves. We are going to put wire fences around your town to keep the white wolves out."

Animals from all over the Fen came out into the streets and rejoiced.

"He lies," Washer whispered. "It is because of the white wolves you have Fighter back."

"You come from the white wolves?" Slasher gasped. His family drew back as far as they could in the tight enclosure.

"Yes."

"How is it that you are still alive?"

"Why do you ask us that?"

"Get out," said Slasher.

"Papa, no. He tells the truth. It was the black wolves who stole me. The white ones freed me. These animals were with the white wolves, and many other kinds of animals lived among them as well."

"Even our kings, Khoa and Tor, had their sons stolen," the raccoon said.

"It's true, papa. I was there. Tor was wounded and near death when the white warriors freed us."

"My brain feels foggy. This doesn't make sense. Why would they try to protect us from the white wolves then?"

"They lie," Washer said. "That is all I can tell you."

"Why didn't the white wolves come themselves instead of sending you?" Slasher asked.

"They prepare and train for war. We were chosen by the white wolves to return your children." Each time the raccoon spoke, Fighter nodded.

"Believe him Papa, the wolves were good to me and all the others."

The wolverine scratched his head. "I don't know what to do. I can't make sense of any of this. Something's not right, but I need to get to the meeting house. I'm late already," he said and looked nervously at his mate and brood.

"We will leave now so your family will be safe if that's what you are worried about. All the wolves are in the meeting house so it's a good time for us to escape," Washer said, looking at the rest of his group.

With a flick of his tail, Washer dashed into the sunshine and the others followed him.

Slasher watched the animals until they vanished into the forest and ran as quickly as he could to the meeting house. As he pushed against the door to open it, he met resistance. A dark wolf was standing on the other side, but he finally opened the door when he saw it was a wolverine.

"Well, well. Why are you late?"

"My wife is taking care of our sick cubs," he puffed out of breath.

"Come up here," the black wolf said. He was a formidable wolf with a rakish smile named Dropper, and he grew larger with every step Slasher took.

Without a word the black wolf struck Slasher across his snout with the stick he held in his paw.

"Short rations for this one for a week."

When the wolverine started away, the wolf caught him by the tail and said, "Stay here where you are in my reach." The wolf yanked on his tail again and Slasher sat down.

Dropper turned back to the crowd and continued addressing them. "You need to see this fence as a positive event. The fence is to protect you from the outside world, not keep you in. You're looking at it from a negative point of view. No intruders will be allowed to get in. Your children will be safe."

A great roar of approval rose up from the animals, but some had questions.

"How will we feed ourselves if we can't hunt in the woods?"

"Ah, there's the best part. There will be no need to hunt your selves. We will provide food for you. You will no longer have to face the danger of the woods to provide for your families."

Joyous shouts and chants came from the throng of animals. "Black wolf good, white wolf bad." Could it really be that simple? the wolverine wondered.

Once Dropper released him, Slasher went straight home. There was a lot to talk and think about. Kiss immediately attended to the blood on his nose and asked what happened.

He told them all about the meeting and the building of the fence.

"A fence, why?"

"They say it is to protect us from the white wolves."

"But how will we hunt and teach our young to hunt? What will we do all day?"

The wolverine just shook his head and Kiss asked, "What did the others say?"

"Same as usual. They think it is a great idea. Though, I noticed that there were some who didn't cheer."

"Yesterday I would have believed them. Today I am not sure."

"What are we going to do? We are losing our way of life."

"I feel the same."

"What can we do?" asked Kiss again.

"We should have left with Washer and the others. We should have gone back with them to the forest of Fienix and on to the Wilds," Fighter cried out.

"Be still," Slasher said to him.

They could hear voices coming nearer and then a sharp rap at the door. They froze where they stood until they recognized the voice of Cushions, the porcupine, at the door. "We have been told Fighter has been returned. Let's meet the hero's."

Slasher went to the door and stood quietly looking at the porcupine. "They have gone."

Dozens of animals crowded behind Cushions. "It is true then, Fighter's home," everyone cheered.

"Did they bring others?" It was the black squirrel who spoke. "Did they bring Chaser?"

Slasher kept shaking his head and then turned to look at his son with a scowl. Miss Kiss shook her head at her husband. "It is not his fault. Gabs came over for some soup while you were at the meeting and she saw him."

"Bring him out. Let's see Fighter. Who brought him home? Why didn't they stay?" The questions made him dizzy in his head and stomach.

"Let us throw a picnic," Cushions said.

Slasher stood and looked at them silently, but Miss Kiss brushed past him. "That is a marvelous idea, Cushy. Let us all prepare a munch, munch and meet at the stream at the suns three quarter arc."

"Let's see Fighter."

"He's dirty and needs to clean up," Miss Kiss said. "I prefer him clean," she tried to laugh.

Most of the animals in town stared at her. When she saw they were not moving, she said, "Please, let us get ready. We will see you all soon." She watched from the door as the crowd reluctantly began to leave.

"You're acting queer, Miss Kiss. I've known you all your life," Fluff, the black squirrel, said.

The wolverine shook her head in denial, but she was about to cry. "It's just been a shock. We're in shock. Let us get our paws underneath us," she said motioning with her head at Slasher's bandaged nose.

"Who?" asked Fluff.

"The black wolves. At the meeting. Because he was late," Kiss said between sobs.

"Hmmm. There is something underneath those wolves I don't trust. I can't say why, but it is a feeling that comes on me."

Fluff looked up at her friend. "Don't fix a munch, munch to bring. I will make two. You get ready, Kiss, and take care of your family."

Inside the wolverines huddled closely. "There's no way we can get out of this," Miss Kiss said.

Slasher looked at them both. "Not one word about the white wolves. Let me do the talking. Say only what I say."

The evening shadows had lengthened by the time Slasher and his family made their way through the town square and down towards the creek. The noise of falling trees and the working beavers were heard all around them as they walked. In front of them they could see a crowd had formed for some reason on the path that led to the creek.

"Why are they stopped there?" Miss Kiss asked Slasher.

"Stay here," he advised, and ran towards the crowd.

"You can't pass the perimeter of where the fence is going up," Dropper was saying.

"You'll have to turn back and have your picnic in a new place."

"We always have it by the creek," Cushions answered.

"How will we get water if we can't get to the creek?"

"Why don't you include the stream inside your fence?"

"Yes," the crowd roared at Dropper. "Extend your fence to include the creek."

"You can't leave us without water."

"You're trying my patience," the black wolf snarled, and raised his stick into the air. Within seconds, a full unit of wolves stood in front of the crowd snapping their teeth, and straining forward with eagerness.

"We're protecting you. This fence is what protects you from the white wolves. Now move back, or we will move you."

"You can't shut us off from water."

"You will be given water. Did you think we would leave you without water? We give you everything."

"We want to talk to the head wolf," Cushions said.

"Yes, and you shall. He will be here within the week."

The wolves lunged forward a step or two and the crowd of animals dispersed. They started back up the path carrying their food and taking their young with them.

"Slasher. There you are," Cushions said walking towards him. "Hiding in the back, are we? Can we picnic at your end of town? You are farthest away from here and closest to the forest."

The wolverine gave a nonchalant shrug. "Which question do you want me to answer?"

Cushions, as usual, ignored the wolverine and called out, "Slashers place."

All the animals marched in a close pack.

"They've taken the creek from us."

"We must do something," Cushions said.

"I say we fight." It was Tango, one of the mixed wolves left among them.

"That's a little rash, don't you think?" the porcupine retorted with a half snort. "If it wasn't for your kind we wouldn't be in this mess in the first place."

"What do you mean, 'your kind'?"

"It was the white wolves who stole our children and brought fear into this place, wasn't it? Maybe you'll turn on us, too. You're a wolf aren't you?" Cushions yelled.

"Look to the black wolves. They are the ones doing everything to you, but you keep saying they are helping us. Well, they've helped you right out of our creek," Tango said, trotting over to his wife and cubs. The women were just beginning to put the food down and he picked up the munch, munch his wife had prepared and handed it back to her. He corralled his cubs and headed off.

The rest of the wolves began to pick up their mates and children as well.

"Fighting among ourselves is not going to help," one of the wolves called back.

"I don't trust them anymore, so I'm glad they left," a badger said half way under his breath.

A few of the animals nodded in agreement.

"I say it is time to banish all wolves, white or not."

"And the black wolves?" Cushions asked.

The badger hesitated and looked around. "Well, they can stay. They are good," he said nodding his head and seeking approval from the rest.

"There are no more white wolves in our midst, and as far as I can see it didn't help our town, it hurt it," the porcupine said, waddling back and forth in front of them.

"It's because they stole our children that all this is happening."

"Yes, and the black wolves took all the white wolves away. Now that they are gone, why do we need fences?" Cushions asked, stopping by Slasher.

No one could answer the porcupine and the badger tried to change the topic of conversation. "Well, we've forgot that we came to honor Fighter."

"Let's hear all about your trials with the white wolves," the males cried out. Some of them came up to him and patted him. "Your name fits you. You are a fighter."

Fighter looked pleadingly at his father. "It wasn't white wolves who took me."

Loud gasps came and then silence followed. Slasher came up next to his son. "He hasn't been in his right mind since he came home."

"I have been. I am more in my right mind than I have ever been. I won't lie."

Slasher took his son aside. "Would they believe you?" he asked. "Look at them. You heard what they said about the wolves. They mistrust them all. If they thought you stand with the white wolves, what do you think they will do to you? To all of us?"

The wolverine didn't wait for his son to answer. "I'm sorry," he said, turning to the crowd. "I need to get him home. He needs rest."

Ignoring the reactions from the animals, he called loudly, "Kiss, Fighter needs you again. Come take him home." The little wolverine was crying uncontrollably as his mother lead him away.

Five or six black wolves had just come upon the group to investigate. "What's up around here?" the black wolf asked.

"We're celebrating the return of one of our own," Cushions replied.

"Whose return?" the sergeant wanted to know.

"Slasher's son was returned today," Cushions told him.

"Yes, he was stolen by the white wolves, but escaped," another voice rang out.

The dark wolf padded up close to the wolverine and looked him over. "You again. Let's see this son of yours. I want to talk to him."

"He's not in his right mind. You can see," he said, pointing to his wife and cub in the distance. He saw Fluff running beside them.

"When did he return?"

"Just a few short hours ago."

The dark wolf looked up. The sun was almost down. "It's dark now and late. We will come for him the first thing in the morning. See that he's ready."

The wolverine immediately departed, relieved to get away and didn't look back. Behind him he heard the wolf say, "Time to head home. Take your families and leave." When the animals didn't budge one way or the other he shouted, "Now."

When Slasher entered his home, he saw Fluff sitting by his wife and Fighter was telling them about the carts and the animals that got away. "I don't know about Chaser, but there were wolves from Fen, white ones, who got away."

Slasher had seen that look on his mates face before. Her heart was too kind, and she was going to let Fluff in on the truth. She was asking for his approval in that look, and he just said, "No."

"Slasher, she's been my friend forever. Chaser is gone. She has no one else."

"You know I don't click and clack to anyone around here. I don't throw my nuts just to see them land."

The wolverine hung his head and then lifted it to look at the women. There wasn't time to waste. "You won't have a chance to throw any nuts. We're leaving tonight, and you're going with us."

"What's going on to make you say that?" Kiss asked with fear in her voice.

"Cushions and some of the others let slip that Fighter had been returned. The black wolves are going to question him in the morning."

Miss Kiss rose from her spot immediately. She knew what that meant. "I'll get some things together."

"No, there isn't time. We leave now." He looked at the squirrel. "I'm sorry, Fluff, but a door of escape has been granted us for whatever purpose, and you're going through it with us. Like it or not."

"This hasn't been my home since Nutter and my children were killed. I'm sure it was the black wolves. Hopefully, Chaser is somewhere out there. I will consider this my chance to find him."

Kiss looked around at the things that made up her home.

Slasher noticed the look of sadness leaving her home and belongings brought to her face.

"I'm sorry we can't take your keep sakes with us, Kiss," he said.

"Where will we go?"

"To where Fighter has been."

"It's a better place?" his mother asked.

"Yes. It's wonderful, mother. It's like Fen use to be."

"Let's go. Let's just go, then," Kiss said putting her arms around Fluff and Fighter.

The darkness had settled completely around the forest when the four animals stepped out. It was maddeningly quiet. No birds or locusts or crickets stirred. The sounds of life in their forest were gone. Down towards the creek, the campfires of the black wolves lit up the new fence. They sat on the outside of the fence they were putting up to close the rest of them in. "Do you remember the way, Fighter?" the wolverine asked. His son nodded and they dashed into the brush to avoid being detected.

CHAPTER 14
THE LOST SHEEP AND THE WILD BUNCH

It was a few days later when Slasher and the others came to the outskirts of Fienix Forest. Slasher had insisted that they watch from a distance to judge if it was safe. Scout and Winter were training the white wolves, but there was little other activity in the town.

"I see mostly white wolves about. Where are the others?" Slasher asked.

"Gone to the Wilds to be protected, I'll bet," Fighter answered.

Although Fighter had told them all about his encounters with the white wolves, they were all hesitant to meet these wolves. There were hundreds of white wolves training for war in the town square and they were only five unarmed and untrained animals.

"Even after all we have heard about them from Fighter, it is frightening to be among them," his mother said.

"I know them. I will show you," he said, darting from the forest.

"Winter! Winter! It is me, Fighter. My family is here. We have fled the dark wolves."

The white wolf turned in the wolverine's direction and said to Scout, "Take over."

Slasher and the others watched helplessly as the great wolf ran to meet Fighter.

"Fighter, you're back. Pieces and the others told us the black wolves had come."

"I'm glad they made it back safely."

"Yes, they arrived about ten hours ahead of you. I will take you to them."

"My family is with me," the wolverine said, and turned back and waved them forward, but not one of them were there. "They must have run back into the forest. They are afraid of wolves since the black wolves came."

Winter nodded understandingly. "You go to them. I will send Pieces out to you with some food."

Fighter returned to the edge of the forest. "See I am safe. Winter is sending Pieces out to us with food."

Within minutes they saw two raccoons and two rabbits coming towards them. Before they could speak, fish and vegetables were set in front of them. Washer came up and gave Fighter a hug.

"Been so long I hardly remember what you looked like," Washer teased the little wolverine.

"This is very generous of you," Miss Kiss said.

"We need very little reason to call a feast," Pieces answered.

"Is this all of you that escaped?" Serious asked.

"For Pete Sakes, let them get a bite," Pieces said.

"We are all that believed it was necessary to leave," Slasher said, and told them of the wire fence and how it would cut the town off from the creek.

"But worst of all they had learned of Fighter's return and were coming for him this very morning. They know we are gone now."

"They won't get him here. Not without a fight," said Pieces.

"Speaking of water, would you like to settle in by the stream? Most of the others animals have set up camp there," Washer said.

"There are others besides the wolves?"

Pieces saw them look at each other warily.

"Yeppers. Not as many as there were when Fighter was first here, but some stayed to aid the warriors with logistics."

From the tree tops the osprey began to signal to Winter. "Flyers coming in."

Within minutes a dozen or so birds set down where Winter was training the warriors. "Khoa and the warriors are coming back. A cadre of beavers, too," Lunger reported.

"I've never seen a king," Miss Kiss said.

"You'll see two kings now. Tor lies in the school house recovering from wounds of the black wolves," Serious said and ran off. Washer followed right behind him.

"Two Kings?"

"Come with us," Pieces said. "We will explain it all."

Climber still sensed their hesitation. "Come meet my wife and other children at least. You can stay with us, if you choose."

Slasher nodded. "I am beginning to see what has happened." He motioned to his family and they followed after the raccoon.

The animals of Fienix knew as soon as they saw the warrior's that there was not good news. As Khoa dismissed his wolves, they disbanded quietly and those who had family went to them. It was a few steps into the headquarters, but it felt like a mountain to the young king.

Inside, Tor was having the healers help him up. Since it was his rear flank that was injured, he had a hard time standing by himself. He limped towards his brother. "Judging by your slowness, Khoa, you are no better off than me, but it is your heart and not your body that troubles you."

Khoa nodded, greeting his brother by touching his nose.

"You have bad news." Tor searched his brother's eyes for a clue, but he saw none. "Tell me straight."

"We buried four white cubs. There was no way to tell who they were."

"You sound angry, Khoa."

Khoa did not move towards his brother, but he could tell from his voice that he was grieving. "I feel old, tired. News like this brings no peace, no closure about our sons or anyone's. The Book is wrong. It doesn't warn by its patterns. It tricks us into believing there are answers to problems when there's not."

"You sound like you still expect to find answers by seeing a portent in nature or dreams. I thought you had given that up. The Book doesn't promise that, Khoa. It doesn't give you a picture of the future for you to stop it, change it, or move anything off its intended course."

"Then why let us see these omens, if we can't change anything? What good are they?" All of a sudden he saw himself as a pup with Tristian. He hadn't grown up or learned much since then, he thought.

"It prepares you to understand who sent it. Good or bad, it all comes from the same source that controls all things. He tells you so you can prepare your heart for what is coming, not for you to change it, but for you to accept it."

"I shared this mystery of the patterns with you on an evening and you divine its truth."

"You make it sound like that takes something away."

"Not from you, Tor, from me. I can see it through your eyes. Why couldn't I see it for myself? I chased myself in circles."

"I have had many hours to contemplate in this room alone. The Great Wolf tells you the design so you can give it back into his hand when it becomes too much. Give it back to him, Khoa."

"I want to make sense of all that has happened. I want so badly for it all to make sense, Tor."

"You want to change it, so you don't have to accept it. You think you should have the power to change it, to have somehow stopped it. It's not for mortal wolves, Khoa," Tor said coming closer to his brother.

"I guess I am mortal, king or not," Khoa half laughed. "I'm not so sure about you, though."

"Ask my left flank. It'll tell you just how much flesh and blood I am," Tor said. "You see the truth then?"

Before Khoa could speak there was knock at the door.

"Come in," said Tor.

It was Winter, Pieces, and the group.

When Winter saw the two brothers standing together he said, "We can come back."

"No, you need to hear this as well," Khoa said, waving the group over to them.

"They have built up another great fortress in the east. A lake sits in front of it so there is no way to attack it head on and a mountain protects its left side. They have used the animals they have taken as labor and now murder them as they wish when they judge them to be of no more use."

"Scoundrels!" Serious cried.

"The longer I live, the more I can't believe how evil the black wolves are," the old rabbit said shaking his head.

"Now we must plan. We know they have at least two fortresses. Did you calculate the numbers in the fort?" said Tor.

"Over five hundred, closer to six," Khoa answered.

"That's a thousand plus with the fort in the Blackstone's."

"That's nothing new. They always out number us," Serious said. Washer gave him a push from behind. "What?" the younger rabbit asked, looking behind at his friends.

"At least the Venger's done for," Pieces reminded them.

"These new black wolves have replaced him," the younger rabbit said. "They are the new spirit of the new Venger."

"They are? How can they just do that?" The rabbit was quite ashen and his words sounded hollow.

"They come from other wolves, rabbit."

"They do?"

"Have you lost your reason completely?"

Pieces remained dumbfounded and Serious said, "Where do rabbits keep coming from?'

"Why, other rabbits, of course."

"Well, that's the same way, the Venger keeps coming. The same wolves that brought him have passed him along."

"How many Vengers are there?"

"How would I know? How many wolves are there?"

Khoa stepped up to the rabbits. "We've got business to attend to, Serious. If you need to discuss things further, take it outside."

Neither one of the rabbits said anything further so Winter spoke. "Serious, tell them about the news from Fen."

"Keep it pertinent, Serious. We don't need any more of your jibber jabber just now," Khoa said in a sharp, curt tone.

The rabbit looked at the king. He had never heard Khoa speak in that manner before, and he answered in a subdued voice. "A wolverine family has run away. Young Fighter's."

"I remember him." Khoa said.

The wolves listened as the group told them all Slasher and his family had said about the new wire fencing, and the beavers who were tied together and forced to work.

"We saw that wire fence, too, on top of the fortress in the east," Khoa said.

"Yeppers, pronged wire that they are telling the animals of Fen will protect them from the white wolf," Pieces said in his quick patter.

"Let's head out and get something to eat," Tor said in a loud voice. "I feel like a little stretch of the legs."

"Can you?"

"I have orders," Tor said, glancing at the healer wolf. "The cold water does wonders, though."

"The town needs to be told what's going on," said Khoa. "And I could use something to eat myself."

At the stream the animals listened quietly while the king talked. By the time Khoa had told them everything, they had grown so quiet that even the wind could be heard rustling through the trees above.

"No wonder he snapped at me," Serious said. "The cubs are dead."

"Might be. No one knows," Washer reminded him.

Slasher, his family, and the black squirrel were sitting on the other side of them. "Even the white wolves have had their cubs stolen and killed by the black wolves," Fluff said and cried and cried. Luella put an arm around her. The little squirrel tried to smile at her. "I'm sorry, but it seems everyone is suffering so much, not just us."

Luella looked at her. "You have a heart just like mine. I feel the same way. We will get along nicely."

One of the ospreys that had been listening in the tree above the little group swooped down. It was obvious to all that he was focusing on the black squirrel. "I saw a little black squirrel traveling with white wolves. Riding on his back, he was, and sitting with a raccoon," he said, turning to the raccoons.

"Do Khoa and Tor know this?" Pieces asked.

The bird shook his head. "I have only flew in. I am going to tell him when he is finished here."

"This can't wait," Pieces shouted and sprung up running.

"Khoa, Tor, good news from the birds. White wolves seen, and squirrels, and raccoons."

Before Khoa or Tor could say anything, cheers rose up and everyone looked at the osprey who was hopping behind Pieces on the ground.

"When was this?" Khoa asked, padding over to the bird.

"About a week ago."

"In what group did you fly?"

"The northern most group. Straight up from the new log bridge," Lunger answered.

Khoa turned to his brother. "It could be. The cubs I buried were in the east and they died long before that. These have to be different cubs."

"Were there other animals with them?"

Lunger turned to his right. "Skimmer, read the list."

"Two white wolf cubs, one raccoon cub, one black squirrel, one beaver, one deer, and a badger spotted coming out of the forest in the north and crossing the meadow heading west."

"It could be," said Khoa.

"A raccoon and a squirrel rode on one cub. A beaver rode on the other cub's back, and a badger sat on the deer. They were friends to be sure," Skimmer added.

"They have to be some of those that escaped from the prisoner caravan that day," shouted Washer.

"It's them. I feel it," said Pieces. "Head'in west for the Wilds."

"How far north?" Tor questioned Lunger.

"Near on to three hundred miles or so," Lunger said, and stretched his wings. "The big river doesn't go up that far. There's eight or ten smaller streams from the mountains that run into it about two hundred miles above the point where the tree bridge is."

"And I judge it was a hundred or more miles to the fortress," Khoa thought out loud. "But that was deep into the forest so they didn't head inwards towards the fort. That's how they missed being caught by patrols."

"They must have followed the forest edge until they thought they were safe and then started west," Winter said. "That's straight out of the tactics training we teach."

"I knew it. They're our boys. Smart as whips them cubs," Pieces bragged.

Khoa looked around at the parents, whose voices rose in excited waves around him. "Don't get your hopes up," he said sternly.

"Khoa, you're wrong," Pieces said, touching his leg. "That's what everyone needs, hope." The rabbit motioned for the wolf to bend down and he whispered, "It's that feeling we talked about on the ridge that day. It's whispering stuff. It tells me to believe, Khoa."

The white wolf gave a half nod, but didn't say anything.

"Do we leave tomorrow?" Serious asked.

"Search and rescue team ready," Washer said. "My nephew is waiting."

"None of you is listening. Washer, we don't know for sure that it's Stasher, or any of our sons from the Wilds or Fienix out there. It will take some time and planning. Please let those of us in the army do our job," Khoa said, and walked away.

"Khoa's right. We need to have a plan of attack. Like how many towns are held by the black wolves, where they are, and how many of these towns are on our side of the river. Sit tight," Tor added, and followed his brother.

After limping away a few paces, Tor turned back around to face the crowd. "Give him time," he pleaded, and then turned to speak to the bird. "Lunger, bring your notes to the war room first thing in the morning."

The bird nodded at the wolf and then looked back at the little group. "I'm sorry if I got your hopes up," he said to the squirrel, "but there aren't many black squirrels in this part of the world."

"He is the only one besides me that's left. My mate and my other babies were found dead outside of Fen."

"There's some black squirrels in the Wilds," Pieces told her.

"I would like to meet them," Fluff said.

"We're not going back to the Wilds," Washer said looking around. "At least I'm not."

"What makes you so sure that it is Stasher and the king's sons that were spotted?" Climber asked.

"The fact that those little ones were riding on the back of those cubs. That's how we came to the Wilds ourselves."

"I'm not making the connection," Climber said.

"They knew those stories, don't you see? They were doing what they had learned from all the stories we told them."

"I think you've got something there, Washer," Serious agreed.

"There's a short cut that leads north from here to the Spider Leg Lakes Lunger was talking about," Climber added. "Better yet, that route would take us around Fen and all the trouble."

"I remember," Washer said. "We went up there when we were young."

"That's where we were born, up in the lake country," Climber added proudly.

"Hey we're veterans like Tor told us. We can do this," Serious laughed.

"What's to finding lost sheep? We aren't going to fight, are we?" Pieces added.

"Those dark wolves aren't looking for a few strays like us. We can stay hidden well enough," Washer said.

"Yeppers, we didn't have a bit of trouble taking all those youngsters home," Pieces said.

"We'll leave a note and say we've gone back to the Wilds," Serious suggested.

"Perfect. They won't worry about us and we won't have to worry about them coming after us," Washer said.

"That could be good and that could be bad. Suppose something does happen?" Pieces asked.

"Nothing's ever set with you, rabbit. You're always toss'in stuff back and forth in that little mind of yours. Let it alone."

"Take things as they happen," Serious joined in.

"That's what I'm wanting to avoid."

"You can't do anything until it happens, can you? How can you plan for a thing, if you don't even know what it is?" the younger rabbit came back.

"Well, the warriors practice for if things don't happen just right."

"That's for in the heat of battle, Pieces. When you can't think so straight. We're finding lost sheep," the raccoon said, but then stared at him a little longer. "Are you trying to tell us that you don't want to go?" Washer asked.

The elder rabbit shook his head. "No, what I'm saying is…," here he paused and looked at them all. "Remember when we came to the great cliff, the chasm?" he asked.

"Of course," Washer answered for himself and Serious.

"Well, not having good plans makes me feel like I'm standing on that cliff," Pieces declared.

"How so, old rabbit?"

"Well, I don't want to experience jumping if I don't have to."

"Now, why would you jump? Why would anyone jump? That's a life or death decision. That's ridiculous. No one would choose to jump. That would be certain death," Serious fumed.

"That's the kind of decision I'm talking about. The life or death kind," Pieces said sitting down.

The younger rabbit looked at him with some irritation, "There's no cliffs where we're going." After he spoke, he looked over to Climber. "Is there?"

The raccoon shook his head. "Not that I know about."

He turned back to the rabbit. "See? No cliffs. You make the decision not to jump before you go. You know you would never jump. There are certain things that you just know you would never do," Serious said excitedly. He walked over to his friend. "You would never jump would you?"

The old rabbit was shaking his head in his hands.

"See? You've already made the decision not to jump, so what's the problem?"

Pieces still sat with his head in his paws shaking his head, and then looked up at the younger rabbit. "Something's got lost in the translation. I'm just not sure where it turned off," he continued, looking at the others.

"Boy, you're telling me. You go from talking about plans to jumping off a cliff. You're lucky to have animals like us who are patient enough to talk you through it."

Washer came up to Pieces. "Don't you mean where the idea got dropped off, instead of where it turned off?" he whispered and both of them burst into laughter.

"What's so funny you two?"

"Nothing, drop it," Washer said as he and the rabbit rolled and tumbled over each other in the grass.

"I'm going to bed on that note," Serious announced.

"Drop it," Pieces said and jumped on the raccoon, who was on his back laughing so hard he couldn't move. He lay with his back legs kicking in the air and holding his stomach.

"You two have lost it," the younger rabbit said.

"But we don't know where," the elder rabbit uttered between bouts of laughter.

"Stop, Pieces. Don't say anymore. I can't laugh anymore. My side hurts," Washer begged.

"Yeppers, I'll drop it if you want me to," Pieces said, which made the raccoon roll over holding his stomach.

Just before the sun rose and light barely made the path to the school house visible, Climber was on his way to his meeting with Khoa and Tor, map in hand. Slasher was with him. A few of the other animals made their way along the path as well. Mist rose from the ground and hung in the trees around them. Lunger and Sure Claw were sitting on the roof waiting, and flew in when the door was opened.

A giant map had been drawn on the chalk board and the wolves stood by it. The two vast compounds of the black wolves were easily locatable; one in the east, and the other to the north, and both were marked by a red circle around it. A region of mountains, labeled Blackstone's, separated the two. Streams and rivers were visible as was the kingdom of the Wilds in the west. The names of towns where the young had been snatched from were written in red.

"Climber," Khoa said looking at the new arrivals. "You can start filling in towns and landmarks you know which aren't on here." Khoa looked at the osprey perched on the backs of the chairs. "Lunger and Sure Claw, help us extend the map of the areas you have flown over and where you saw the young ones."

Next, the white wolf turned his attention to the wolverine. "Can you tell us what you know about Fen?" Slasher looked closely at the white wolf. There was a handsomeness in his face that put the wolverine at ease, and his eyes were blue and gentle which seemed to draw him in. By looks, one would judge him to be a king, he thought, but by actions, one would not.

The wolverine told Khoa and Tor all that had happened in Fen as the others listened.

"Where are the white wolves that lived among you now?" Khoa asked.

Slasher shrugged. "Gone. I don't know where. I'm ashamed at how I let the dark wolves turn me and the town against them. They were our neighbors once. We should have trusted them more than the new wolves. Why didn't we see it before it was too late?" the wolverine lamented.

"You didn't think you were being lied to. You had no reason to."

"You are all very gracious not to hate me. Now I know what I should have known to do in the first place. Ask why a group is doing what they are doing. Everyone has their own motives."

Scout called out, "Lunger's making his mark."

When the wolves turned around they could see that the map on the black board was taking shape with the names of more towns and streams. The place where he placed his circle was in the center of the Spider Lakes region, and in a meadow just outside and west of Vale Forest.

"I'll mark where the cubs are buried," Khoa said, and went up to the chalk board, and placed a red circle southeast from the black circle made by the osprey, and directly in the Forest of Vale. "How far away are the streams from the point they were seen?" he asked, turning to Climber.

"Fifty miles give or take between each of the Spider Leg streams that cover the area."

Khoa drew the mountains above, and it was clear to see that the only path not on high ground between the two fortresses was the one the youngsters had taken.

"Whether the young ones keep on a path due west or head south, they will meet the dark wolves at some point. They are surrounded. To the south and west are the towns the black wolves have entrenched themselves in, and to the north and east are the fortresses. We won't be able to go after them until we take back all these towns."

"Unless you send animals other than wolves in to find them," Climber said, standing on his back legs.

"Like raccoons?" asked Khoa.

"And rabbits," Climber added.

Khoa thought for a moment. "We could coordinate the attacks on the towns. The warriors could go in and take back a town which would allow you and the others to go on to the next town on the list. If caught, you can tell the black wolves you have fled from the white wolves."

"Yes, good thinking. We can tell each town we enter that the last town was recaptured by the white wolves. That does make a convincing cover," the raccoon said.

"We will be right behind you to prove it's true," Khoa answered. "And rescue you if need be."

"We will start at Charter Oaks, then Fen, then…" As Khoa read off the names of the towns, Climber wrote them down in his book.

"You had planned this anyway, didn't you?" Tor said.

"This is much safer, and I'm sure Old Pieces will be relieved to have a backup plan. Our other plan lacked some things."

"Yes, we've seen the kind of plans this bunch have put into action before," Khoa said, looking at the other wolves.

"Tell Washer and his wild bunch I want to see them. Bring them in tomorrow for the briefing." Khoa paused and then said, "Tell them I'm against sending you all in, but there isn't much choice."

The birds sat flapping their wings. Khoa turned to them and asked, "Will one of you act as a guide for the wild bunch?"

Lunger stretched his wings out. "I will be glad to help find the young ones. When I saw them crossing the meadow, I had a heart for them straight off."

"When they are found, no one say or do anything," he said to Climber. "Let Lunger report back to me. Then wait. Just before we attack I will send three birds to circle over the town. That will be your cue to take the youngsters and head towards us in the midst of the assault. You'll need to prepare them for the chaos of the attack as best you can."

"OK, Khoa. See you at dawn," Climber said.

"Add a wolverine to your list of the wild bunch," Slasher said.

CHAPTER 15
READING THE STARS

When the black wolves had attacked the little travelers, Slivers had gotten away by jumping into the water, but Teaser had sprung off through the meadow. Several wolves had pursued the deer. From the shoreline Tristian and Challenger saw him brought down in the high grasses. One wolf had caught him by the flank and started to drag him down, then another wolf caught him by the neck, and then two more wolves had added their strength in bringing him down. There was a brief struggle before the wolves surrounded the body.

"Care to make a run for it?" Warrior laughed, looking at the rest of them.

No one moved. They were all looking past him and at the action in the meadow.

"How is it that two small, white wolves are here all alone with a raccoon and a tiny black squirrel?"

Not one of the group answered, and Snuffer came forward with a leap and snatched Sounder up in his teeth and shook him.

"Talk, or Snuff here will eat your friend in a gulp."

"Let Sounder go first." It was Tristian who spoke. Warrior came over and swatted him with his great paw and he fell sprawling. "You'll give me no orders."

The young wolf came to his feet, head down, and stalking forward with low growls.

Snuffer bit down harder until a sharp squeal came from the squirrel. Challenger called out, "Tristian, no." The little wolf stopped his advance.

"Tristian?" Warrior gasped, and turned to looked at his brother. "Well, Snuff, we have someone famous here, I think. Someone descended of royalty. We will have to treat him specially."

The dark wolf came up to the cub and hovered over him. "Who are your parents that they gave you that name?" The white wolf sat looking at him. Warrior turned to his brother. "Eat the squirrel."

"No, please. I'll tell you what you want to know," Tristian pleaded. Warrior turned to his brother and nodded. Snuffer spit Sounder out on the ground and then stepped on the squirrel with his paw to hold him down.

"Don't mess with me, cub."

"I am Tristian, son of," but Challenger jumped in front of him and said, "Son of Tor, and I am his brother, Challenger." Tristian looked at him questioningly, but remained silent.

"Tor, brother of Khoa of the Way?"

"The same."

"We have little princes in our midst. Tristian's name sake," Snuffer said.

"You're not heirs of the king now. Tor lies dead." Warrior laughed.

"You lie," Challenger said coming towards him. "How would you know?"

Warrior slapped at the pup with his paw and knocked him to the ground.

"Because it was I that killed him," Warrior said standing over the pup. "Do you want me to show you how?"

Tristian came to help Challenger to his feet. "Don't believe him. I don't," he whispered. "Just get up and stay quiet."

When the two pups were on their feet Warrior said, "Now tell us how you come to be here alone."

"We were taken from the Wilds by black wolves," answered Tristian.

"That part is true for I sent them. You start with the truth. Where are your captors now?"

"Drowned," Challenger answered.

"Not all of them," came the strained voice of Sounder.

"Let the little squeaker up," Warrior said.

Snuffer took his paw off the squirrel. "Drowned by who?"

The squirrel shrugged. "The big river we were crossing."

"How is it that the river didn't drown you?"

Sounder turned to point at the raccoon. "Stasher here saved us. He untied the bags we were in before the carts sank in the river."

"The river was overflowing and the current strong, but some of the wolves who had taken us tried to cross it and were swept away," Challenger said.

"Did any of these wolves have names?"

"Stoner and Strider," Tristian said.

"Our sons," Warrior said turning towards his brother. "You're telling me they drowned?"

"No, they didn't drown. They were on the other side of the river," the cub continued.

"After they saw what happened to us, they didn't try to cross."

"You're sure of that?"

"Yes," the squirrel answered quickly.

"And how did you get here?"

"We walked."

"That's over two hundred miles."

"You came through the forest and met with no black wolves?"

They all shook their heads.

"How is it that they could travel that far on the Black Ribbon Road and meet no one?" Warrior asked his brother.

"Someone's not doing their job," Snuffer said getting up on his hind legs, dancing in circles, and shaking his right paw in the air. "Batter. Batter. Mad as a hatter," he sang repeatedly until Warrior knocked him back down on all fours.

This brought laughter from the little ones.

"Drunk as a skunk, you mean," Warrior said. "He's a wolf that's past reigning in. We head to the Lake Embattlement. Now."

"Fall in behind me white wolves and friends," Warrior instructed, and then yelled out to his army, "Fall in."

The dark wolves, who held torches in their hands and stood watching as Knox' dam burned, immediately tossed their torches into the heap of flaming sticks and loped up to the them. Tristian could see the other wolves ahead of them where Teaser had fallen. These wolves raised their heads to look back towards their leader, and then came running.

Seeing the feeding wolves ahead of them, Snuffer asked, "What about these two?" pointing at Stasher and the squirrel. "Part of our lunch is already gone."

"That squirrel's only one bite and the raccoon two," scoffed Warrior.

After the dark wolf spoke, the two animals quickly jumped up on the back of the white wolves.

"You're right. There will be bigger prey ahead."

As the dark wolves started away, Tristian looked back to the stream and the dam. He could see nothing in the water. *Slivers must be miles away by now,* he thought. A thin black trail of smoke swirled up into the blue sky until it disappeared. He turned around just as they came to the spot where Teaser had been taken down. He told himself not to look, but he couldn't not look. The deer was his friend. It was almost like he had a duty to honor him. What he saw startled him and he threw up. Luckily not much was in his stomach. Teaser lay on his side in the grass, his face clearly visible. Just looking at his face, his eyes closed, he seemed to be sleeping. His face looked serene, calm, Tristian thought, but he had seen all of the deer. There was no meat or fur on the body itself and the bones were exposed in some places. The thin legs looked frail. The front ones lay in a running stance, and the back legs looked disjointed like they had been broken. Flies swarmed in spots making the open flesh appear to move. He looked at Challenger. He was staring at Teaser, too.

Just then his cousin noticed he was staring at him, and turned to look fully at him. Tristian recognized the hallow stare on Challenger's face. It was what he felt in his heart. He heard the soft weeping from the black squirrel on his back, and felt as Sounder nestled his head deeper into the nape of his neck. He noticed Stasher was staring at him from atop his cousin's back, but the raccoon had turned away when their eyes met.

The wolves had been traveling for hours. Tristian looked above at the blueness of the sky. The sun was out and it was perfectly blue. Not a cloud anywhere. Even a slight breeze blew wafts of the sweet meadow flowers into his nostrils at times and cooled the sweat on his fur. *What right did the world have to such a beautiful day?* he wondered.

'Most things live. Only a few have fallen today. Ones close to your heart.' It was a voice in his head. It seemed to be answering him. Where had it come from. He didn't recognize it as his own. Just then he saw what he thought was a wolf standing at the crest of the hill ahead of them. It wasn't a black wolf, but had a tawny appearance to its coat. As he stared at the wolf, it vanished. He blinked his eyes and looked again. It was gone, and he quickly jerked his head to look at the black wolves and Challenger. They trotted on as normal. They had not seen the brownish toned wolf in the distance. 'Most things live and so will you,' the voice said to him. 'There will be another day where the sky is as blue and it will be yours.'

Tristian grew perplexed. *The voice seemed to be giving him promises, but how could it?*

'They are promises, Tristian. They are promises to wolves who walk in the Way,' the voice answered him. Just as he heard the voice say that he remembered the day he had been in training and searching for the spirit that is inside all animals. He had heard that voice before. It had spoken to him when he had looked at the sky and gave it the name, Alphas' blue. It had said, 'Remember that color. You will need it.'

He looked over head again. Yes, it was the same wondrous hue that he had seen that day, but what did it mean? He studied the heavens. This blue was deep and light at the same time. It was that blue that you could look through and reach all the way to tomorrow. 'Not just tomorrow,' the voice said. 'Forever.'

Suddenly Tristian felt a sharp pain across the bridge of his muzzle. He saw Snuffer next to him holding a branch.

"Looking for the sky to fall?"

Tristian growled.

"The little king want to fight?" Snuffer asked waving the stick at him.

Tristian caught a slight movement on top of the hill ahead and he turned to look. The tawny wolf looked down on him. As he looked at the wolf, it just vanished. As he turned back towards Snuffer, he realized that he was no longer growling. Seeing the wolf had calmed him.

Without warning Snuffer attacked Tristian and seized him at the juggler, knocking Sounder off the cubs back.

"Drop him Snuff," Warrior called out. When the dark wolf didn't respond, Warrior was on him in an instant and had him clamped between his jaws.

Snuffer shook Tristian a tad and Warrior clamped down harder. Feeling his brother's teeth break flesh, Snuffer let the cub drop from his jaws. Small rivulets of blood were visible around the young wolfs neck where the fur had been torn away. Challenger rushed to his aid.

"Touch him, and I'll snap your neck like a stick, cub," Snuffer said rushing towards him. Challenger stumbled backwards tripping over his own paws.

Snuffer laughed. "All white wolves are cowards."

"Enough. We will see them fight in the matches. Maybe they will die there," Warrior declared. Turning to Tristian he said, "Get up, little king."

The cub struggled slowly to his feet. He saw the squirrel looking at him and watched as Sounder went over to Challenger and climbed up along his front paws. Even Sounder was ashamed of him.

"There's a weakness in all you animals of the Way, or have you've given it up?" Warrior taunted his captives.

"I walk in no way but the way of the raccoon. Of my fathers and their fathers," Stasher said.

"Oh, you deny being of the Way then?"

"I deny nothing. I have heard stories from my Uncle Washer. He walks in the Way. My father was not a convert. I am my father's son."

"He has a foxes' tongue," Warrior announced loudly, which brought jeers from the ranks.

"Sly words or no, being among the white wolves makes you guilty by association."

As they traveled on, Tristian thought about what Stasher had said about his family's beliefs. His father had told him what Old Tristian had said, "You must know in your heart that you can die for what you believe. In truth is strength." *Is this what he was being forced to face?* What once were mere words, took on a new reality to the cub. There was power in those words. The power of life and death.

A few days later they reached the green sloping hills where the badgers lived. Warrior made camp by the stream where they had camped some weeks before. Tristian and the others kept looking at one another. Just over the rise and down the other side were the holes of Old Grumps, his kin, and their friend, Bodger.

Why weren't the black wolves picking up their scent? Tristian turned to look up the hill. He feared that the family would suddenly appear on the rise and come down to the stream for a drink. In an instant an animal appeared on the rise. Now, instead of seeing the badgers, he saw the tannish colored wolf standing in full view. It was small and compact. It was not a dark wolf. It stared down at him and looked him eye to eye. He drew Challengers attention and motioned for him to look towards the hill.

"Who is it?"

Tristian shrugged and whispered, "I've seen him several times. He appears and then is gone."

Stasher said, "I see him, too."

From a distance away, Snuffer noticed the four animals staring together at the hill top.

"What's up there that you are so fixed on?" Snuffer asked, coming up behind them.

"Don't you see it?" Challenger asked.

"See what?"

"The wolf," the cub answered cautiously since he could see Snuffer looking exactly where the wolf stood.

"You don't see it?" Tristian asked unbelievingly. The wolf was clearly there. It stood stone still. It looked straight at him.

"What's going on? What are you up to?"

"Nothing. I need water. I guess the heat is getting to me." Why didn't the wolf move? Maybe he was seeing things, he thought, and shook his head to clear it.

"Crosshairs, bring some water up here," ordered Snuffer.

As the dark wolf drew near, the animals could smell the water and their thirst was enticed. The wolf's fur was tangled and sprung up wildly in all directions like bristles on a brush. His name certainly fit him, thought Tristian.

Standing on his hind legs Snuffer took the small pail from Crosshairs and threw it on Tristian.

"Whatever notions you got, get over them," he said, and walked away laughing with his companion. The water which he had waited for was lost to the ground. Luckily the captives were on large stones by the shore and the water pooled into small troughs worn and rounded in the rocks by time and water. Seeing Challenger begin to lap at the rocks, the others followed him.

They moved from tiny puddle to tiny puddle lapping quickly. The water was warm and bits of sand lay at the bottom and coated their tongues as they drank. The heat from the rocks rose in their nostrils and the hot stone burned their tongues. The sun had beaten down on the rocks all day, and its heat dried the water off quickly. Soon the only wet spots visible on the rocks were from their tongues and they gave up searching.

In their frenzy to get water they had forgotten about the wolf. It was Tristian that looked back towards the hill. "He's gone," the little cub whispered to the others.

"So you really believe you saw a wolf?" Challenger asked.

"Indeedy," Stasher said, and scratched his chin to mimic Knox.

"Then why didn't Snuff' n 'Guff?"

They all looked blank. "Maybe he's going blind," Stasher offered. "I'm still so thirsty. I don't care about him right now. Where's all the rain when you need it?"

A low steady grumbling echoed from above the mountains in the distance and the animals turned towards it. Clouds blackened the heavens, erasing the line between the mountains and the sky itself. Day became night in the distance and the thunderheads flashed lightning. The billowing clouds grew as they tumbled and spread across the sky. Even from a distance they could make out the wall of water that fell over the mountains from the dark clusters of clouds.

"There's your rain, Stasher," the squirrel said.

"My rain? I never asked for that. I meant a gentle rain that would bring us a drink. I've never seen a sky like that."

"Maybe it won't reach us here," Sounder exclaimed. "It's so far away up in those mountains, it might just end before it gets down into the valley."

"Look," advised Tristian, "They're pulling up stakes." The wolves were rushing around and putting out fires. Fish bones were being thrown away. Crosshairs was moving towards them at the gallop. He yanked their tether from the sand and pulled them forward with him. The two wolf cubs could barely keep up with the wolf and the ropes grew taut around their necks.

Behind them the raccoon and squirrel bounced and tumbled through the grasses unable to keep pace down the hill. *They're going to die,* the cub thought. Tristian looked to the right at where the holes of the badgers should be, but there was nothing there except a solid wall of earth. No sign existed that badgers had ever been there. *Maybe this wasn't the right spot, but what about the tan wolf? Where was he?* Tristian wondered. *He wasn't on the rise or anywhere either.* A sudden sharp tug on the rope brought him down. He rolled a time or two and then came to an abrupt stop.

He put his paws up to loosen the rope from around his neck. Suddenly he was aware that everyone had stopped.

Crosshairs was coming back towards him, but stopped half the way there. He bent over and tried to untangle the rope from some branches of a fallen log. So that's what had caused them to stop. The rope had gotten caught up on some branches. Tristian looked back. He could see movement in the grass and soon he saw Sounder and Stasher moving towards him on the other end of the rope. "Hurry. Jump on board."

It took a few more minutes for Crosshairs to free the tangles from the branches. While the dark wolf fumbled with the rope, the animals were able to catch their breath. Challenger was way in front of them before where the rope was snared. When Sounder and Stasher climbed up, Tristian whispered, "Hang on tight. I might take another tumble." The rope jerked and they were on their way again. To Tristian's surprise, he found it easier to run the second time. His muscles felt loose and ready. He could run forever. In back of them came the rumble of thunder. The wind had picked up. It blew from the north and pushed behind them in tremendous gusts that nearly knocked them off their feet.

When they were near the entrance to the forest, they could see the wolves huddled in the trees. With the sun blocked by the approaching clouds, the sky took on a yellowish green appearance which tinted everything. Quick flashes of lightning gave an eerie appearance to the faces of the dark wolves as they peered out from behind the trees. The dark clouds rushed forward with the momentum of an attacking army which could not be stopped. "Look," said Tristian, "Those clouds look like charging horses."

"Yes, powerful ones. They are coming for us. I know it." Challenger said.

"The horses? Why would horses want us?" Sounder asked.

"Not real horses. Those horses are really wolves. Our wolves. White wolves."

"Hey, stop that chattering." It was Crosshairs.

The animals looked towards the dark wolves and could see that Warrior was looking at something on the ground. One of the other wolves picked it up and folded it.

"Off to the right there's an old mining town. We'll find shelter there," Warrior announced.

They started off again, but this time at a walking pace for there was no path and the trees were thick. The branches thrashed wildly above them in the rushing wind which drowned out every other sound. In between the gusts of wind it was silent. No birds sang, no animals moved. It was as if nothing lived here. Soon they reached the place of shelters. There were many of these shelters and they were built on both sides of a wide path. They were constructed of wood and stood almost as tall as the trees. "A canyon of wood shelters," said Challenger looking upwards.

"Crosshairs, you take those prisoners and go in here. Quirk, go with him." Warrior stood by the open door and waited for the troupe to pass in.

Once inside, the animals could smell the mustiness of the old wood. "Whew! What's that?" Stasher said.

"Don't like it?" It was Quirk who spoke. "That's man. He'll kill you quicker than we will," he said clicking his teeth at them. Quirk was a strange looking wolf even by black wolf standards. He had a rounded back that kept him from standing straight. His head was always down, almost to the ground, and he shifted his eyes from side to side and up and down to see what was going on. This habit of moving his eyes in a circular fashion made it uncomfortable for others to talk to him because they never knew what he was looking at. In that half crouched position in which he moved, he always looked ready to attack, and that made him menacing. He was a lone wolf.

Tristian thought of the stories that he and Challenger had been told about man. An old woman had nursed Khoa and Tor as pups. His own mother, Ani, had been helped by man when she had been found in the jaws of the iron dog. As the hunched wolf busied himself with chores, the rain pelted against the side of the wooden shelter and against the windows and sounded louder when gusts of wind drove it in torrents into the glass.

"What are you staring at white wolf?" Quirk asked, slapping at Challenger with his paw. Without waiting for the cub to answer he continued. "Think I'm ugly, don't you? Well, I am ugly. Ugly and mean."

"No, sir. I wasn't looking at you. I was looking at the holes in the shelter. I can see the rain, but it isn't coming in. Why?"

The humped wolf turned to look behind him at the window. "You never seen a window? That's glass. Man stuff."

"Can I look out?"

Quirk nodded and Challenger trotted over to the window and stood on his hind legs to look out. Turning back to the others he said, "Smart. You can see out, but the outside can't get in. See! I'm dry."

"Come away from there now," Quirk ordered.

"I'm going to have one of those windows one day," the white wolf announced.

The dark wolf threw him a sideways glance. "That's likely to be the only window you'll ever see."

"Why?"

Quirk turned away. The look in the pup's eyes had reminded him of his own family, his own son. He thought back to his life before his injury and before his mate had left him.

"Oh," the white wolf said, catching the meaning of the wolf. The black wolfs head was down and turned, but Challenger saw him peek his way for an instant out of the corner of his eye. Quirk felt a twinge of something he hadn't felt in a while. This pup had awakened something in him. He looked again at the wolf cub who knew he was going to die soon. Quirk thought back too, to the sight of Tor's death. These cubs were orphans. He knew what that felt like and what it meant for them in life. They would have no chance now. Well, they didn't anyway, he told himself. Warrior would kill them soon enough.

"Those old pans should be more than filled with water by now," the hunched wolf said and went to open the door.

When he returned, he had a pan in his teeth. He set it down and began to drink. Crosshairs came and lapped up the rest. The cubs watched as he picked up the empty pan and went out again.

He returned with another full pan. He brought it over to the little band and set it down and motioned towards them with his head to drink. He walked away and checked the security of the ropes by tugging on them and went over to where Crosshairs was already asleep and lay down, too. With his eyes closed he heard each one of the animals say, "Thank you, Quirk.'

The animals waited until they were sure the wolves were asleep before talking again.

"I don't know how they can sleep in this storm," Stasher said, turning to the cabin door which rattled violently. For a moment all the animals listened as the wind shook everything, creating howling sounds as it swept into the cabin.

"What's that?" Sounder asked, coming closer to Tristian.

"It's the wind."

"Why is it making that whistling sound? I don't like it."

"It's like it's trying to speak," Stasher said.

"Well, it can stop. I don't want to hear it," the squirrel said, curling on top of the white wolfs' paws.

"We'll talk so you won't hear it? How's that?" Tristian asked, and looked down at the squirrel scrunched tightly into him. The black squirrel nodded.

Suddenly he shot up from Tristian's feet and said, "Say, Challenger how did you know today that the horse clouds were really white wolves?" Stasher blurted out. Instantly Tristian leapt to his feet as well until he realized what was happening. "You scared me, Sounder."

"Sorry. I'm nervous."

When the two had settled back down, Challenger said, "The story of the Alpha is in the sky. He wrote all over it." The raccoon looked at Tristian, who nodded his agreement. "Even if we don't have the Book, we can read his stories in the stars.

The Great Wolf said, 'paint the signals in the sky and let them be a path. Make them into stars and light the sojourners' way.'

"How do you read a star?" Stasher wanted to know.

"They are pictures that tell a story."

"What kind of stories?"

"The stories of the Great Wolf and us. Like the Lupus Constellation which shows the Great Wolf slain, but that is in the southern sky, which we can't see from here. It witnesses his great love for all animals and how he came to die."

"That's a sad story," the raccoon said.

"But it has a good ending. In our part of the world, the northern sky, we can see Sirius, the Dog Star, where the Great Wolf is on his feet again and protected by Orion, the shepherd of all wolves."

"Do you think that can happen in real life?" Stasher asked. "Do you believe the wolf will come back to life?"

Everyone knew what the raccoon was asking and it took a long time before Tristian said, "Yes, the Great Wolf was slain in the southern sky, but rises in the northern sky as the brightest star. It will happen as it is in the sky."

"Why?"

"To show that he overcame all. It is the sign he left to remind us that he is coming back and that he watches over us until that day. He is Orion, the Hunter some say, but those who walk in the Way call him the Shepherd who goes before and leads the way."

"I never heard that stars formed pictures," the squirrel said. "I'm sorry about your father, but I'm glad he's in the sky."

"That's not him in the sky."

"It could be," said Sounder.

"When the clouds go away and the stars come out, I will show you where to find them."

As he finished speaking, Challenger noticed Quirk looking at them.

"If it's possible," he added in a subdued voice, still mindful of the dark wolf's warning. He wondered how much time they had left. He was nearly five months old. He had not even seen all the seasons come and go yet.

"Did the Great Alpha only put wolves in the sky?" asked Sounder.

"No, every animal that walks the earth is there."

"Even squirrels?"

"Yes, a squirrel named Ratatosk from the Norse tribes runs up and down a tree relating words to the great eagle above him and the dragon in the earth below."

"He does?"

Challenger nodded. "Just like you did that day and warned the badger."

"Where is he in the sky? I want to see him."

"If you follow the last star on the bottom of the Big Dipper almost straight over to the left you will see Ratatosk."

"I bet there's' no raccoon," Stasher said.

"Yes. Procyon. The genus name for raccoon. In Canis Minor."

"Who's he by?"

"If you find Sirius, the brightest star, and go left a little and north you will see Procyon. He is the companion of the Dog Star."

"Sounds like it's a little crowded up there," Stasher said. "Are we all that close together?"

"I never thought of it, but yes, we are grouped closely with one another."

"That explains why we are together here, then. It is painted in the sky," the raccoon said excitedly.

"You promise to show us?"

"Yes, when the weather clears."

"What's the one we can't see?" asked the squirrel

"Lupus. There's another one that you would like Sounder, but we can't see him from here, either.

"It's called Equo-sciuridae."

"Eco, sci dae? What?"

"Just call it the horse and squirrel. The other name is his name in Latin."

"Horses? What's the deal with horses today?" Sounder questioned.

"This squirrel is riding a horse. He is a warrior and brandishes a sword over his head."

"You are cat teasing me now."

"No, for truth. We saw a picture of him in a book, didn't we, Tris?"

"Indeedy," his cousin replied.

"How do you know all this?" Sounder asked, coming closer.

"I loved these stories and asked my father to tell me over and over. Every night in the Wilds the animals would come to our cave and stories were told and retold."

"Why can't we see the wolf and squirrel warrior again?"

"It's in a different part of the world."

"Isn't the whole world above us?"

"You can only see the half you're in."

"Why?"

"Well, it's like the sun. It comes up over there, east right?" the wolf said, pointing to the side of him. "Then it travels all day and goes down in the west. You don't see it when it's on the other side of the earth, do you?"

Sounder and the raccoon nodded. "Say you're right. I never thought about it," Sounder said. "I never even thought about there being another side of the earth or sky, but there must be. The sun goes somewhere, like you said."

"And you know it's there because it comes up each morning and travels across the sky until it reaches the west and hides itself again."

"How far is it?"

"As far as the east is from the west. You can't see it. It's forever," Challenger said.

"That's how far away home seems right now," the squirrel said.

Everyone grew silent until a gust of wind rattled at the door loudly.

"Talk some more, Challenger," Sounder said.

"East and west never meet," the wolf added. "It has something to do with the roundness of the earth."

"Can I go to school with you, Challenger? I want to learn all this."

"We learned it at home under the stars during story time, not at school."

"That's even better."

From the corner of the cabin Quirk said, "You animals get some sleep."

CHAPTER 16
THE THERAPY OF THE QUIRK

It was the middle of the night when the storm hit full force. The thunder roared down on them shaking the contents of the cabin. Now and then flashes of light lit up the blackness about them. In the next instant, an ear splitting crack of thunder came as a bolt of lightning brightened the room for a second, and then the sound of splitting wood reached their ears.

Their two captors were on their feet and staring out the window. "Fire down the line and across the street," Quirk shouted.

"It's in the trees, too," Crosshairs said.

The army of black wolves had come out into the streets. They pulled the barrels of water that had collected next to the buildings out into the streets and used mining pans to dip water out and throw onto the fire.

"You stay here, Quirk. I'm going out to help."

By now the scent of the fire had reached their noses and the smoke began to sting in their nostrils. The group stood up and went to the window on their side of the cabin to see.

"Sit down," Quirk roared as loud as the thunder had cracked.

They sat still for a while, and then Challenger asked, "Why did our going to the window make you so angry?"

"It wasn't you're going to the window that made me so angry," Quirk taunted back at the cub and wobbled his head back and forth in a sarcastic manner. Challenger noticed that when the wolf was talking to him his eyes were steadily fixed on him. They weren't roving around. Come to think of it, Quirk had stared straight at him a couple of times from across the room that night.

"Then you didn't like being left behind with us," the white wolf said.

"I'm always left behind to do the things other wolfs don't want to do. I'm the ugly one."

"You're not ugly."

"Don't try to grease me up. I know what I am."

"Well, you make circles with your eyes and you don't have to," the little cub ventured.

The dark wolf shot him a glaring stare, but Challenger continued. "I've seen you look straight at me when you want to. You're staring straight at me right now."

"Yes, I can see them," Stasher said. "They are straight as an arrow."

"I have to look around. Watch what's coming. I can't trust no body to help me."

"Why not?"

"Cause that's the way things are among these wolves."

"You're looking at me straight right now. It makes you look much more likable when you keep your eyes focused."

"It does?"

"Yeah, not so scary," Stasher agreed.

"I need to be scary. Keeps the wolves away. I won't live long if I'm not."

They were all quiet. "Besides," Quirk continued. "Even if I held my eyes straight, I still have this humped back."

"How did it happen?"

"In battle. How else?" he said in a sharp tone. "I just lay there in pain for months and when I tried to get up I was like this. Crooked."

"No one helped you?" Tristian asked.

"No one was around. I just lay on the battlefield. Even if they had found me, they would have killed me."

"Why would they have killed you?" This time it was Stasher who asked.

"That's the way our creed is. It is merciful to kill and not leave a wolf crippled."

"How did you eat and drink if you couldn't move?"

The dark wolf didn't answer for a long time. "There were these birds. They brought me water and food."

"See someone helped you. You were meant to live," Challenger shouted.

"So I could do what? Be made fun of by the pack? Derided every day?"

"Why don't you try helping yourself?" Challenger said angrily. The others looked at him, and Tristian shook his head in warning at his cousin.

"Maybe I don't want to live. I wish a lot of the times those birds hadn't helped me and just left me to die."

"They didn't need to. You're dead already," the pup said. As Challenger continued to speak, the other animals kept backing up. They waited for Quirk to come at the cub, but instead of pouncing on him, the dark wolf turned away, went to the door, and walked out without saying a word.

Rain spilled in torrents into the room as the door blew back against the side of the wooden walls and banged back and forth. The wolf didn't shut the door and the animals went to do it. Since they were tethered to the wall they couldn't quite reach the door to get a hold of it, but they could see the wolf standing on the porch drenched in rain staring out into the darkness at the others.

Morning came gray and wet with rain. Mist rose from the ground and spread eerily through the trees making it difficult to see more than a few feet ahead. What sky was visible was as white and thick as the mist.

It was Sounder who woke first, shivering. He tried to burrow further under the body of Tristian and woke him. Noticing that the door was still open and no one else was around the wolf said, "Let's go see what we can see."

Quirk was lying on the porch, but he didn't stir. Beyond where he lay, there was lots of activity. The black wolves still worked steadily to contain the fire. Smoke rose steadily from where the fire still smoldered. Small hissing sounds came from the embers as droplets of rain fell on to them. Most of the shelters had burned during the night. There were only a few buildings left standing. Part of the forest was blackened, too; at least what little they could see from where they stood.

Suddenly the black wolf turned to look at them, and they scampered away from the door. As their claws clicked across the wet floor boards, Challenger and Stasher awoke and sat up immediately. Before anyone could say anything, Quirk entered the room. He took the pan, filled it, and set it before them. "Hurry up before anyone sees you," he said and walked back outside. While the others were drinking, Challenger stepped to the door. "Quirk, I'm sorry for what I said last night."

Without turning around to look at the white cub he said, "Don't call me that. My real name, the one my mother gave me, was Trapper."

"That has a better sound to it."

"Doesn't it though? When I heard someone say Trapper, it made me feel real. Quirk is just a label for my injury, not me as a wolf."

The dark wolf did an about face and looked at Challenger. "Do you think you could help me?"

"I will try. What do you want me to do?"

"Fix me."

"How?" he asked, looking away from Trapper. Just as Challenger was thinking he had gotten himself into a mire of mud he would never be able to get out of, his friends appeared.

"I've got an idea," Stasher said. "We unrust him."

"That doesn't work on live things, Stasher."

"Well, that's probably not the word, but my older brother, CJ, broke his paw this spring and Papa brought a healer wolf in to put a splint and bandage on it. They made him wear it a good long time and said not to use his front paw at all. When Papa took the wrappings off, CJ said he couldn't move it from its place. He said it was stuck."

"Can he use it now?" Challenger asked.

Stasher nodded, saying, "Too good, if you ask me. There ain't nothing he can't do."

"How'd they unstick his paw?"

"By tear-py. I don't think that's the right word. I don't remember."

"Do you remember how it works?"

"Slowly, is what my brother told me."

"How did they do it?"

"Papa had him move his paw a little bit at a time. He just kept on until his whole paw was unstuck."

"You think that's what's wrong with me?" Trapper asked.

"I don't know, but we can also humble ourselves before the Great Wolf and ask him to help you," Challenger said.

"Can a dark wolf come to the Great wolf?"

"Dark wolves most of all."

"It's going to hurt at first," Stasher warned. "CJ screamed a lot."

"Hey, your eyes aren't shifting around like wheels," Sounder exclaimed. "You're getting better already."

There was a long, low rumble of thunder, and then the rain started up again. From around the left side of the front porch, Warrior leaped up. "Well, well. The magic of the white wolves holds. The whole town and part of the forest burns down and here you sit untouched."

All eyes fixed on the two pups sitting on the floor. They moved their front paws up and down anxiously in nervous anticipation. Before anything could happen, a wild crack of thunder broke right over head and the rain poured down like a waterfall unleashed.

Warrior looked outside at the rain coming down and then said, "We're taking over this building, Quirk. Find another one. Move."

Quirk immediately set about untying the main lead rope from the post in the middle of the room and yanked gruffly on it to pull the animals away. As soon as he stepped from under the overhang of the porch, the rain let up and they crossed the street and entered another building that had not been burned. This building was more lavishly furnished. It had a chair whose stuffing was coming out, and all sorts of bottles lined the shelves. "Jackpot," exclaimed Trapper. "An old general store and stocked with goodies," he said spying the old glass canning jars. There was food still visible in them.

He tied the animals back up to a post. "Food. Now if we can find a way to open them," he said looking around. He took the bottle down and began trying to open it with his teeth.

"There's food in them bottles?" Stasher asked.

Trapper nodded.

"I can open it. That's my specialty," the raccoon said, waving his little front paws in the air and moving his fingers. He took the jar and twisted the top. "Whoa, this is really on there."

He turned to Challenger. "Hold the bottle with your paws so I can get a better grip on it." After a few tries and some groaning sounds, the lid began to move and soon Stasher sat with it in his paws. Another barrier remained as he looked at the second lid on the jar. "There's another lid. Someone went to an awful lot of work to keep us out of here," he said.

After looking at the flat lid, he decided to pull up on it and it gave way with a loud pop, which made the raccoon jump back from the bottle. He looked at the jar and when no more sounds came from it, he walked back over to it and smelled the contents. "It smells wonderful. Heavenly," he declared to the rest as he looked at the yellowish orange peaches.

"What is it?"

"Yellow things floating in water. Sweet water," he said breathing in the aroma.

"Give me one," Trapper said, and the little raccoon dipped his small paw in and fished out a piece to toss to the wolf. Everyone watched as the wolf gulped it down. "Hand'em out," he said, and Stasher put his hand in the jar again and brought out another piece and tossed it to Sounder, who put it on the ground and began nibbling on it.

So it went, the raccoon dipping his paws into the jar, eating, and tossing the slices of peaches to everyone until the jar was empty and only the sweet water remained. Trapper went to find a pan and had the raccoon pour the juice out in it and they all drank. Stasher climbed up on to the shelves and began looking into each of the three bottles that were left. "No more yellow stuff, but there's two green and a purple."

So the animals continued with their dining experience and ate the green beans and beets and curled up to rest. Stasher went about looking for more jars, but could find none. He noticed the others looking at him and he rubbed his stomach and said, "I haven't found the bottom yet. It's still empty." The others were content and curled up to sleep.

After a while, the raccoon gave up searching and came down from the shelves. He sat thinking so hard that the dark wolf was curious. "Piece of food for your thoughts."

"It's stupid. You won't want to hear it."

"No, tell me."

"Well, I was thinking that people eat like raccoons."

Hearing this, the wolf let out a baying laugh.

Stasher frowned, but continued explaining, "They put their food in water so it's washed just like us. I might like them."

"Why do raccoons wash their food?" Trapper asked, putting an emphasis on the word, do.

Stasher shook his head and asked, "Why do people?"

When the wolf didn't answer, Stasher said, "People have done good things for animals."

When the wolf challenged his claim, the raccoon went over by him and asked, "Would you like me to tell you some stories of them and the white wolves?"

Even though Quirk hadn't said he wanted to hear his stories, Stasher began to tell the wolf the tales he had been told by Challenger and Tristian until they both fell off to sleep.

It was sometime later that Stasher awoke and poked the dark wolf. "We should start your tear-py."

"Maybe we should just forget it."

"Then how would you ever know if you would have gotten better?"

"Hmm," was all the wolf said.

The raccoon scrambled to where the wolf was sitting. "OK, get up," he ordered.

After the wolf stood up, the raccoon was now underneath his head. "I can't reach you from here. I need something tall to stand on so I can see your neck and your back," he said searching around the room for something that would work. "There," he said when his eyes spotted the chair. "Come over to that thing."

"It's a chair."

Stasher quickly climbed on to it. "I like it. It's soft," he said, kneading his front paws into it over and over. "I could sleep here."

"Let's get things rolling," Trapper snapped.

Stasher positioned the wolf by the arm of the chair where he sat.

"You're sure you know what you're doing?"

"I watched the healer wolf work with my brother."

"Healer wolf?"

"Yes, the white wolves have healers that help hurt animals, but the real healer is the Great Wolf."

"I have heard of them, but never knew they really existed."

"Okay, now is this as far as your neck goes?"

Trapped nodded.

"So now move it upwards a smidgen."

"Ouch. I can't."

"Keep trying 'til you can."

"Some help you are."

"I am only telling you what the healer told CJ. Now, keep trying."

The dark wolf kept trying to lift his head. In between the cries, they two of them talked.

"Why do the white wolves have healers?"

"Because life is sacred."

"Why?"

"Because it is given by the Great Wolf."

Finally the intermittent cries of the wolf woke the others. Noticing the others stirring and looking at him, Stasher proclaimed proudly, "We started his tear-py."

"You better lay off before you have the other wolves down on us," Challenger said.

"Yeah, my neck really hurts," Trapper said.

"Good. That means we're ready for step two."

"Step two? I don't think I can…" but the raccoon cut him off and patted his head. "Relax. The next step is the one my brother liked," he said, jumping down and going to the windows where the curtains hung. With a quick yank Stasher brought the curtains down on his head. Once he had unwrapped himself, he brought the curtains over to Tristian and said, "Take hold and pull." The pup pulled and the raccoon held on to the other side of the cloth until they heard it rip and both fell to the floor. Challenger joined in and so did the squirrel. The animals played and teased each other running as far as they could on the rope with the curtain section in their mouths.

"This cloth is supposed to be clean. There's not supposed to be spit or dirt from a floor on it," Stasher yelled.

The animals saw a stove that had ashes in it. They collected some old pieces of wood that were scattered about and lit a fire. They put a pan of water on to heat. They placed the curtain pieces into the boiling water. After it had boiled for a few minutes, Stasher took the pieces out with a stick and put them in a bucket of cold water. "We'll do the cold water pack first. It should be icy water, but this will have to do," the raccoon said as he took the cloth out, wrung it, and placed it on the neck of the wolf. "Challenger, bring me the rest. Leave them kind of wet so more of the cold water is in them," he directed.

"There's a stream out back," Trapper offered.

"Hey, that would be perfect. Take these rags off and you can just lay in the water for a while."

"We'll all have to go," the dark wolf glared.

Trapper lay in the cold water up to his neck. It was only a foot or so deep and the group drank freely from its coldness. "There's a trout," Tristian shouted. "He's coming your way, Stasher. Get him." The raccoon looked up and saw the fish. He reached out from the rock he was standing on and managed to snag it. "Help."

In an instant Challenger was by his side and took the fish in his mouth and trotted with it to shore. He laid it where Trapper could eat it.

"You're giving it to me?"

"There's more where that came from."

"Yes, let's catch some more," Stasher said.

As the two friends walked away, they could hear Trapper sniffling quietly.

Stasher walked back to the wolf. "Are you in pain?" he asked. "Maybe you've had enough tear-py for the first go around."

"Yes," the wolf answered. "Maybe it's enough for today," he said, and came out of the water.

Stasher watched the fish flopping on its side rigorously and pushed it back towards the paws of the wolf. "You better eat him before he gets away."

"I want you all to share it with me."

"You won't have to ask twice," the raccoon said, biting off a piece of fish and taking it to the stream to dunk it in. "Hey, guys. He's sharing," he called to the others.

Sounder watched his friend dipping his fish in the stream and looked up at the falling rain. "Don't you feel the rain, Stasher? Doesn't that count for washing your food? Besides that, it's fish. It came out of the water."

"Habit," the raccoon answered, coming back for another piece. "Want me to wash yours?"

Sounder shook his head. "Like I said, it's wet already."

Instead of tearing off another piece of the fish, the raccoon stared at the wolf. "It still hurts?" he asked.

The dark wolf shook his head.

"If it doesn't hurt, why are you crying?"

"Kindness," the wolf said.

Without warning the rain began to fall harder again, and the troupe picked up their food and took it back to the shelter. After they had eaten, Stasher said, "I feel like a nap in the chair," and hopped up into it. Instantly he noticed there were places where he could put his hands down into and around the cushion, and he busied himself poking deeper and deeper into it until he managed to push the cushion out of the chair itself, which sent him climbing onto the arm to save himself. "It comes apart," he said, looking at the padding on the ground. "Try it out. I've never felt anything so soft."

"I didn't know you were such a busy little guy," the dark wolf said.

"I got food. I feel great again. I was near dead before."

When he said the last sentence a loud silence fell on the room. "Ouuggghhh. I shouldn't have said that."

"Why aren't we traveling in the rain?" Challenger asked.

"Warrior doesn't like it. He don't like anything that makes him cold, wet, or uncomfortable."

"I hope it rains forever then," Sounder commented.

Laughs came all around.

"I think he is afraid of it," Trapper said.

A rushing wind was heard that rapped at the door and blew it open suddenly.

Trapper got up to shut the door. As he looked at the stream he saw something in his low field of vision. "Your friend's here again," he said staring.

"What friend?" Challenger asked, looking around at the others questioningly and they all rose to go to the door. There on the other side of the stream was the tan wolf staring back at them expectantly as if waiting for them to come to him.

"You see the wolf?" Tristian asked amazed.

Trapper nodded and said, "I seen him the other day when Warrior and them didn't."

As they stared across the stream, the wolf vanished. A voice said, 'You need to believe to see.' Tristian turned to look at his companions. They hadn't heard the voice. "He must have stepped back into the mist," he said quietly, but didn't tell the others what the voice had whispered to him.

"Speaking of animals disappearing, do you know of a family of badgers that use to live around here, Trapper?" As soon as the words were out of his mouth, Tristian wished he hadn't asked the question. It had just popped out before he could stop it. He could see the startled look on the faces of his friends. As they held their breath, the dark wolf answered calmly, "No, there are no animals along the Black Lake road."

Stasher was still looking towards the back stream. "I always feel like there's nothing in the world I could want that would make me feel any better than when I see that wolf. Isn't that strange? He fills my heart."

"You don't know who that wolf is?" Trapper asked. "I feel it watches over you."

"We had never seen it before the other day. I thought it was one of your sentries," Challenger said.

"It's a tan wolf. Two toned. Almost like he was all the colors of every wolf. We have no wolves that color among our packs."

"None?" the wolf cub asked.

"Not for years. They have all been…," he looked at Challenger. "Erased. Just like all the animals along the Black Lake Road. Haven't you noticed there are no birds singing in the trees, no other small animals?"

"There was a few weeks ago when we came."

"Then they weren't real. Any more real than that tan wolf seems to be."

He turned to them and said very solemnly, "It's the magic of the white wolves, isn't it? The magic that Warrior is afraid of."

"There is no magic. There is only the Great Alpha," Tristian said.

"And the Watcher Wolf," added Challenger.

"Watcher wolf?" Trapped questioned.

"The wolf who guides all animals. The one who shows the way," Challenger said.

"The tan wolf," Trapper said in an awed voice, and looked towards the back door.

"Yes, it has to be. It has to be," Tristian leaped up. "She is a tawny colored wolf."

"Didn't you know?" Trapper asked the others.

"We have never seen the Watcher. We have only heard stories of her," Challenger old him.

"Yes, a she wolf. So that is why I feel like I am in my mother's paws, content as a cub when I see her," the dark wolf said.

"Why is Trapper the only one that can see her besides us? What keeps the others from seeing her?" Stasher asked

"The coldness of the heart," Tristian whispered. "It keeps them from believing."

"What do you mean?" asked Sounder.

"Maybe we should tell them the stories we have heard about the two spirits that travel in the world," suggested Challenger to his cousin.

Tristian nodded, and the two white wolf cubs took turns telling them the stories of how the Watcher had helped Khoa at the waterfall and trained him in the Way.

"It still sounds like magic to me," the dark wolf commented.

"Not magic. Promises. The Great Wolf is the provider, the path maker, beginning and the end. He is everything. If you believe, he provides. He makes a path," Challenger said.

"So what is this Alpha wolf going to do for you?"

The cubs shook their heads. "We will just follow and see."

"What if it's a trick? Why has this Great Wolf put you into the hands of us dark wolves, then? I don't understand."

"Only the Great Wolf has the answers."

"How can you trust when you don't even know why he does what he does? When only this Great Wolf has answers he won't share?"

"That is the great mystery you learn."

"You only have stories of how others were helped. What if he doesn't help you? Why doesn't this watcher just come and get you?"

"You have many questions, dark wolf. You are walking in the right way."

"I'm more confused now than I was before. How can I be going in the right way? This is a most baffling belief you animals hold."

Outside the rain came harder and almost beat the roof apart. Small holes formed and the water came in. Trapper moved pans under the falling water.

"See? Fresh water," the squirrel shouted, running over to drink.

"That's not magic," the wolf answered.

"But it is providing," Challenger said smiling. "See the difference?"

"It's a riddle. One that seems to be backwards in its logic," Trapper mused.

"Hey, it's almost dark," the raccoon said, looking up from his chair. "Time for your tear-py."

CHAPTER 17
ALL PATHS ARE CHOSEN PATHS

The rain came down for another five days and the group fished, talked of old times, and helped Trapper with his therapy three times a day. They were careful to go to the creek only after the other dark wolves had fished, and were glad that they didn't even look in on them once. Neither Warrior nor Snuffer ventured out once. Each day they looked for the Watcher to return, but she did not come.

Today the sun was out and the sky was pure blue without a cloud in it. Its rays filtered through the trees and made the green leaves appear to shine with a brightness of a newly formed world. Sounds of the dark wolves moving outside reached the animals. A sharp rap came at the door.

"We're moving out. Fall in at the end of the line, Quirk." Trapper and the cubs waited until the last black fighter had passed them before joining the procession. The earth was still wet and the trunks of the trees soaked to a deeper brown. The scent of damp earth and wet bark was pervasive and pungent, but the smell of fresh greens from the low growing bushes and herbs was released from their leaves as the marching wolves pressed them into the ground under their feet. A thin scent of mint, cat's paw, and laurel mingled together and made the air sweet.

In the afternoon they reached a plateau on the mountain. A path of loose rocks wound down to a canyon where there was an old river bed.

"How is it that the river is dry with so much rain?" Challenger asked Trapper while they descended. "The dam which stands and surrounds Black Lake Fort holds the water back from the canyon."

Soon Trapper and the others could see the wolves with Warrior and Snuffer cross the dry wash of the river bed and climb up on the other side. It saved a good three days travel around the rim of the canyon by damming the stream. The path was narrow, and only two wolves could traverse it at a time, so the line in front of them was long. As they descended, the rock walls seemed to press in on them. There was only one way in or out of the canyon and that was by the path they were on. The walls were too steep for an animal to climb, Challenger thought, as he looked upwards. On the other side of the wash, and at the top of the plateau, he spotted the Watcher. She was by the edge of the rim and turned to the left and looked behind her. "The Watcher," he whispered to Trapper.

Since the dark wolf could not lift his head up to see her he asked, "Where?"

Stasher was riding atop his back and answered, "On the top of the far cliff."

"She keeps looking in back of her," Challenger added.

"That's where the dam is," Trapper said.

As the wolf spoke, a great trembling was felt in the earth. Soon the sound of rushing waters reached their ears, and in seconds a moving wall of water filled the canyon. Giant rocks and logs tumbled in front of the waters and swept the dark wolves crossing the dry bed away with the other debris. Even some of the wolves who had been on the banks above the river bed were caught up as the water spread itself out and rose higher. In a wink, a breath, the army had been cut in half. With a single stroke more than two hundred warriors were felled by the striking hand of the water. Its abruptness left them without words, and with no way to answer the attack. Nature's authority was final and resolute.

Almost two hundred had made it to safety on the other side along with Warrior and his brother before the torrent had been unleased. Only twenty wolves were left on this side with Trapper and his prisoners. The dark wolves in front of them had rushed past them in their attempt to get up and away from the raging waters. They could see the wolves running up the steep incline. Some kept racing and disappeared over the hill, but some wolves stopped when they felt safe and looked back on them tethered together. By now the water had spilled itself out and calmed into a steady flowing stream. Two wolves trotted back down and began shoving the prisoners roughly back up the hill. Musty saw Warrior waving and shouting at them to take the path to the left around the canyon rim. He waved back. Musty saw the slit throat sign that Warrior also gave and nodded.

"What did he say?" Trapper asked walking up the slope. They had come to the wider part of the path again. The wolf shrugged and stopped. "Something about hunting down the cowards who bolted." He was looking at Stasher sitting on top of Tristian's back, and swatted the raccoon off with his paw as he passed by. Sounder, seeing this, clung more tightly to Challenger's neck. Musty broke into laughter. "You're going to die anyway, squirrel. Maybe tonight for supper," he said walking away. "We'll be picking our teeth with your bones."

"Warrior will have your head if you kill them," Trapper said. "He wants to kill them himself."

"Shut up, Quirk, or we'll kill you with them. Warrior would never be the wiser," Musty said, but he didn't look back at them. Once at the top, he looked down and called, "Hurry. We'll not wait on you."

When they reached the summit, Trapper asked Challenger what was going on. Challenger told Trapper he could see the wolves who had deserted running to the right and that Musty and the other wolves were headed left.

"Musty, those deserters are heading back the way we came. We best go after them," Trapper called out. The hunched wolf stood with his head down in its usual fixed position so he didn't see Musty galloping back towards him. Challenger warned him and Trapper called out, "Stop where you are, Musty."

There was a surprised look on the face of the wolf, but he stopped, and then began walking slowly up to him. "You are a sorry excuse for a wolf, Quirk. You can't fight or even defend yourself," he said and spit at the wolf, which landed on his nose. Trapper lowered his head further and wiped his nose off in a clump of scrub grass. The others had come up behind Musty. "Quirk's right. It'll be our heads if we don't find them," one of them said. "Besides there's that meadow and that nice stream a few hours back. We can lie there a few days."

When Musty didn't answer, another wolf asked, "What are you thinking?"

"We should join up with them," Musty said, and he threw a quick glance behind him and then looked at Quirks lowered head. "C'mon, big, bad wolf," he said, swatting Quirk on the nose. "Get your babies moving."

Just as night fell they reached the meadow and the holes where the badgers had lived. As they passed by, Tristian searched over the hill. Brown dirt still covered the cliff like slope where part of the hill had fallen away, but there were no visible holes, no telltale signs that any creatures had ever lived here. They were gone. But where?

The wolves made camp and lit fires, but when Trapper and the animals came to sit by them, Musty said, "You stay down wind, Quirk, or we might get hungry."

The dark wolf led his prisoners up stream.

"We'll help you gather wood for a fire, Trapper," Tristian said. Once the fire was going, they began to fish in the stream. By the time they finished eating and drinking it was completely dark.

The squirrel was on his back looking up. "Why are there so many stars? We'll never find ours," Sounder said.

"It's easy, "said Challenger. "Look for the brightest star. Sirius, the Dog Star."

"I don't even know where to start."

"There to the right," the cub said pointing.

"Yes, there it is. I can see it," the squirrel said excitedly. "It is brighter than the rest."

"Now go over to the right and you'll see the bottom of the Big Dipper."

Tristian brought a stick over and drew a picture of the dipper with its curving handle in the sand by the fire. "Remember when your dad drew them out for us?" he asked Challenger.

Tristian gave the stick to his cousin. "Yes. Great idea," Challenger said, and picked up a rock and placed it to the left of the pan shape, saying, "This rock is the Dog Star, the brightest star."

Stasher and Sounder looked at the picture in the dirt, and then up into the sky. "I found it already. It's easy to find when you know what you're looking for."

Tristian lay down with his head on his paws. This reminded him of home and his heart reached out into the darkness to grasp hold of the warmth and memories that stirred in the night stars. Their bright eyes only twinkled back with cold indifference. In the back ground he could hear Challenger. "Now from the bottom of the Dipper go left and you will find Ratatosk." He drew the squirrel to the left of the bottom star in the Big Dipper.

"I am in the sky," the squirrel shouted.

"Now, find the Dog Star again, and go in a straight line upward, and to the left. There is Procyon. It's Canis Minor, the little dog star."

"I thought you said it was the raccoon star," Stasher reminded him.

Procyon means raccoon. That's its genus name in the ancient language. He is the companion to Sirius." Challenger eyed the raccoon straining to look upward where his paw directed him.

"Now look to the right of the Dog Star and follow it up to the three little stars in a row. That is Orion's Belt."

"He's the shepherd right?"

"Hey, it does look like we are following after him," Stasher exclaimed.

"Some call him the hunter because of his bow, but we know him as the shepherd who goes before."

Tristian let the conversation of the others drift off in his mind. He wanted to be home now more than ever. "It's strange," he said out loud, "We can see these stars over us in the sky just the way we did at home, but we're not at home."

Just then Challenger said, "Look, a falling star." All turned to watch it arc and then fall with its tail streaking after it briefly.

"That was fast. What happened? How can a star just fall out of the sky?" Stasher wanted to know.

"That's how stars die," Challenger answered.

"It means something is about to happen," Tristian said.

"It must mean something terrible," Sounder said.

"No, not terrible, just that something will change and that things will not remain as they are."

"What do you mean, Challenger?"

"One star has died so the sky has changed, but there are thousands of stars left. Life goes on. Other stars are born to take its place, but the sky has changed forever. No star will fill that space in exactly the same way again or be like that star."

"Just like here on earth. My mother still talks about the old tree we had in Fen before the great storm came and I was born. She said it had great swaying branches all the way to the ground and you could jump clear to the top on them. She said it had a big knothole with lots of room inside. The new tree we had was crowded, she told my dad, and didn't smell just right. She kept looking at the new trees and wondering if one of them would grow into the old one, but my dad kept telling her it was one of a kind and not for her to count on seeing its likes again. Is that what you mean, Challenger?"

"Yes."

"We have seen things die and change, but nothing has replaced them," Stasher said in a less than accepting tone. "The white wolf cubs who were killed. Teaser. All the others who were drowned. There's just four of us now. I feel empty when I think about them."

"Each death lessens us all."

"Even the black wolves who drowned today?" Trapper asked. "I would think that you would be glad your enemies had fallen. Especially since they killed your father."

"Then it's true. My father is really dead."

"Yes. I saw him fall."

"How?"

"You should not know that."

"Tell me. I have a right. I need to carry the story. It is something greater than this time."

"You speak of things beyond your years, Challenger."

"Was it in battle?"

The hunched wolf looked away a moment and then said, "He fell by the sword."

Before the white wolf could press him any further, he held his paw up. "That is all I will tell you tonight." He looked at the young cub. "Do you hate the black wolves now?"

"The Great Wolf created us all. He tells us all animals are equal under him."

"Then why do we dark wolves hate white wolves?"

"I was thinking that you should be able to answer that," Challenger said through tears.

"We try to kill you because you try to kill us," Trapper said matter of factly. "It has always been that way."

"Why did you send in Stoner and Striker to steal us? And what about the other animals? What did they do to you?" Tristian said, taking up the fight.

"We are taught from a young age that the white wolf will poison us with their thinking."

"With the Way of the wolf?" Tristian asked.

Trapper nodded.

"What are you taught about the Way that makes you so afraid?"

"That you will come in and change the way we live."

"How?"

"By telling us how we should live and that we must accept the Great Wolf only and cannot commune with the gods of the river, the woods, and the meadows."

"There is only one who rules over all of nature. The Alpha who created all," Tristian said.

"What have the raccoon and the squirrel done to you? You eat us when you find us," Stasher commented.

"The gods of the hunt tell us that we can. They give us the power to overcome you."

"But look at you. You are much larger than we."

"The gods of the hunt give us the power and the Great Wolf cannot stop us."

"He does not stop you. He lets you choose whether you will kill."

"Yes, it is each of us making a choice that creates good and evil in nature, not the Alpha."

"There are few laws the Alpha gave us to follow. Love all. Hate evil."

"Doesn't the Great Wolf say that black wolves are evil?"

"No, he says the choices they make are not his way, his law. And we should not follow the black wolves' way or we would become like them."

"If I wanted to follow the Way, the Great Wolf would let me?"

"Yes, but you can no longer kill at your own choosing. The Great Wolf gives life and takes it."

"And what happens if you do kill?"

"You can ask him to pardon you and come back to the Way or go back to your old ways, but at the end of life you will not be taken into the great gathering."

"And?"

"You go to where you are hunted day and night. You feel pain, but are never given death."

"Yes, we black wolves have heard of the place of endless night and the endless hunt, but we do not believe in it really."

"It's because you do not believe in the One True Wolf."

"Why would the Great Wolf permit such a place where wolves and animals run forever, sweating with fear and can't even find a drink for their thirst? What kind of god would send animals to such a place?"

"He does not send you there, you choose it yourself."

"Why would I choose to go there?"

"You don't come out and say,' I want to go to the place of endless night, but you make the choice by not following the ways of the Great Wolf. You kill and hurt what the Alpha says not to."

"Yes, you go there by choosing your way and not his."

"Why doesn't he stop us from going against him?"

"He does not force you to choose him. He doesn't want those who don't want him."

"Hmmm," the dark wolf muttered. "Like Warrior whipping us or killing us to make us obey his laws. A lot of wolves hate him and some run away when they can, like those we are after."

"Yes, some animals believe you can make others do what you want by fear alone. Animals come to the Way because they have chosen to."

"He is a most wise wolf," Trapper said.

"We haven't done your tear-py all day."

"Hey, my neck does feel really stiff."

"Then you need it."

It was barely light when Musty and a couple of others dashed among them saying, "We've decided that you should stay here with the prisoners, Quirk. You'll only slow us up."

"You can handle babes alone, can't you?" another wolf said laughing. "Beware the white wolves magic," the wolf called back as they galloped away.

The animals got up and watched until the dark wolves had disappeared in the distance and then went to fish breakfast and do Trappers therapy in the stream. The dark wolf saw the two white cubs keep looking behind them on the hill. "Waiting for your friend to show up?"

The wolves nodded. "Why is it so quiet, and where are the birds and other animals?"

"Nothing lives along the Black Lake Road. I told you that."

"There was all sorts of animals when we were first came through here."

"Then patrols of black wolf hunters came through and killed them."

Challenger looked at Trapper. "Even the birds?"

Trapper looked over and up at them. "It is fall for the birds. They have headed south."

"Hey, Trapper. You looked at us. Your head moved sideways to look at us."

"It did?" he said standing very still.

"Try it again," Challenger shouted.

"I'm afraid to."

"Look, over there. A giant bear," Stasher screamed and pointed in the opposite direction.

Trapper swung his head around and looked.

"You can move your head from side to side," Stasher cried. "Now try up."

The dark wolf tried, but it did not move as easily upwards.

"I think it goes a touch further up, but it swings fully from side to side," the dark wolf said. "It doesn't even hurt. It moves like it's part of me again."

Trapper lapped at the water. "Yes, the water is further away now. I can tell my head moves from here to here," he said, showing the group how far down his head use to be and where it was now.

"It's sprung free to the sides. I wonder why that happened first? I can turn to see all around me now. Look at the forest. Look at all the leaves changing colors. It's beautiful. I had forgotten what things looked like seeing the ground all the time." The dark wolf kept moving his head in every direction. "I can see a lot more than I use to. Thank you, Stasher."

"It is not me or the tear-py. It's the Great Wolf."

"You believe that, don't you?"

"The Watcher has been nearby, who else could it be? The Great Wolf gave the wisdom for the tear-py, didn't he?"

"Yes. Yes, he did, didn't he?" Trapper danced around in circles and splashed in the water. "I can see the trees, part of the sky. It's so wonderful."

Of a sudden Trapper stopped his splashing, and said, "After years of being stuck, I have been made half free in weeks. Thank you, Alpha, the wise one," he howled over and over. He noticed his friends stretched out on the ground with their paws in front of them.

"What are you doing?" he asked them.

"Honoring and thanking the Great Wolf," Challenger said.

"There is a way to do that?"

Trapper came onto the shore by them and Challenger showed him how to give thanks and talk to the Alpha.

After sometime the dark wolf exclaimed, "I feel fresh and new inside."

"The Great Wolf has touched you, Trapper. You have been chosen." It was a new voice that none of the animals had ever heard and they all looked up at once to see the tan wolf standing in their midst.

"Don't be frightened."

Stasher stood up and went over to the Watcher. "I want to touch you to see if you're real."

The wolf laughed as the raccoon's little paws patted her all over. "I am Jen, the Watcher Wolf, and I am just as real as you, Stasher."

The raccoon touched her from the bottom of her feet all the way up to her mouth, and turning back to his friends said, "She's solid as a rock."

"Are you the Watcher that led our fathers to the Wilds? That saved Khoa from the snakes, and healed him from his injury over the water fall?" they all cried out to her. She nodded at each question. "Your friends, the badgers, are safe and well. The beavers, too."

"Where are they? Can we see them? Take us to them."

"There will be another time, another season, but now is the time of darkness. You must trust in your faith. It is the only thing you have."

She walked over to Tristian and touched the top of his head. "You are Khoas' Tristian. Keep sight of the Alphas' blue."

"How did you know about my name for the sky?" he asked, but she had already vanished.

"Why is it important?" he said looking about, and his voice trailing off.

"Why did she come just to leave us again?" Stasher asked.

"I don't think she's left us," Challenger said.

"What do you mean? I can't see her."

"She's the spirit of wolves. The Watcher. The one that talks to us inside. How else would she know your thoughts, Tristian?"

"I think I see, but I don't."

"How does she fit inside?" Tristian said, looking down at his heart.

"How did she become invisible, and then not?"

"That's part of the mystery, the journey we are all on."

"That's like forever," Stasher said.

"Yes, maybe, but what a mystery it is," Challenger shouted with his paws in the air.

"Just what is the mystery we are trying to solve?" Sounder whispered.

"Why and how the Alpha has done all that he has done," Challenger yelled, chasing his tail. He stopped running in circles when he saw all of the animals staring at him and said straight out, "His heart of course. He wants us to know his heart."

"Why doesn't he just come out and say it?" Stasher wanted to know. "Why make it a mystery?"

"Because he is a wise wolf. He unfolds things in steps when we are ready. Not before."

"Why?"

"So we continue with the journey. He leads us on to tell us one mystery at a time."

"Ahhh! That's how he gets us to follow him, but I think it would be easier if he just told us," the raccoon replied.

"Would you believe then? It's not a telling thing, it's an experience thing. You have to experience it to get it into your heart, so you know its's true beyond all doubts."

"How do you know all this?"

"I didn't know it until now. It came in a thought. From where I don't know, but my heart heard it, too."

"The revelation," Tristian said.

"It's like listening to all the stories our fathers told us about the black wolves. They weren't real until we had experienced being among them. We could be free to believe this part of the story or that part, but now we know what the truth is about the black wolves and what is not."

A sigh of understanding went through them and then a silence.

Challenger moved over to where Trapper was seated. "You are one of us now. The Watcher said you had been chosen."

"I feel freer than I have ever felt. Even with my head stuck towards the ground. How can that be?"

"Your heart has been changed."

"Let's waste no more time," the dark wolf said as he began to untie the animals from one another. "Freedom for all," he shouted. "Move," he waved at the animals. "Squirrel, raccoon, jump on your mounts. There's no time to waste. I have been given something wonderful, and my heart has become generous. I give what I can and that is freedom," the wolf shouted.

"Where are we going?" Challenger asked.

"To your kingdom, where else?" the wolf said, standing back and waving his paw to let the cub come forward. "Lead the way."

"We will take a new way this time and follow the stream to the big river. They will go after us the way they knew we took before."

"Out foxing the foxes," Stasher said. "I like it."

"We will be losing the natural cover of the forest by going this way. We will be out in the open," Trapper advised.

Challenger had just heard an inner voice warn him of the same thing. Or had it merely been the echo of what Trapper had just said? Without bothering to sort it out in his mind, he shrugged it off. *'Nothing will ever be the same,'* the voice inside him said. He chose to ignore its warning again because it did not make sense to him, and he thought it was speaking only of this current dilemma. He was confident he could overcome this single obstacle of the dark wolves chasing them. They would find cover when they needed to.

CHAPTER 18
THE IRONY OF THE BLACK WOLF'S TRUTH

In a few days Warrior and Snuffer had reached the Black Lake Fort and found that Stoner and Strider had not made their way home; that no one from the caravan had ever been seen. Warrior gathered some wolves together and set out with Batter to the crossing where the white wolf cubs had said the carts had been swept away. When they reached the spot, they saw the huge tree that now lay as a bridge across the span of the river. The waters had receded and the tree sat in shallow water. They noticed the tree bridge had been secured to standing trees to keep it from being swept away in the current.

"Why didn't you tell me of this?" he said, slapping Batter across the muzzle. "Someone's come across, and it wasn't my sons."

"No one's come across this tree. No one," Batter said. "We killed four white cubs. That's all we've seen."

"This was not made by four white cubs."

"Not by cubs, Warrior. By your sons and the others. They may have gone across and are searching for the ones who got away."

"We found six animals, who got completely away, who strolled through this forest like they were on some picnic. Do you know where we found them?"

Batter was visibly shaken and fell to Warriors feet.

"To the north and west. They trotted down the Black Lake Road. I should take your head," the dark commander said, pulling his sword and laying it across his neck. He let the sword rest there and said, "Because I lost over two hundred wolves in the canyon wash just days ago, I will let you live."

Batter let out his breath and stood up, but Warrior pushed him back down with his sword.

"There is a condition under which you live. Find my sons, or I will finish what I started today."

"What if they're already dead?"

"Then your life is shorter than you expected."

Warrior put away his sword, waved his paw to motion his army forward, and started across the bridge.

Once across the stream, they looked at the forest and how many trees had been thinned and cut down. "All beaver marks," Batter said.

"Yes, an army of beavers. So many beavers that even a blind and stupid wolf should have tripped over them," Warrior said trotting over to the road. The dark wolves fell in close behind him.

It was sometime later that Warrior called out to his fighters. "Wagon ruts. They seem to be leaving the road and heading into the forest."

They were the only marks on the road that could be seen. The dark wolf looked behind him. "They must have been coming back from the river, and now head north, but why?" A few large birds circled overhead, and Warrior looked at them for an instant, but they flew off to the north just as Batter spoke.

"Maybe they got tired of waiting for the water to go down and headed for the nearest town to get out of the rains," Batter offered, and got out his map.

"What town is near?" Warrior asked.

"Fen. It's one of the towns that you ordered wired in."

It was night when the wolves reached the little town, but immediately Warrior sensed something was wrong. Posts had been put up to string the wire on, but no wire surrounded the town. To the far side of the town he saw tangled masses of wire strewn about. They lay free and unbundled as if they had been used. "Batter, take a unit and see what's going on," Warrior said, motioning towards the wire. "That wire has been put up and taken down."

The dark wolf had his unit spread out in a wide circle and they moved in quickly. Nothing stirred except a lone bird, who hovered above them. Just as he spied the bird, animals attacked them like a swarm. As Batter recovered from the shock, he could see that they were wolves. White wolves. They were outnumbered and his black wolves fell on every side. Behind him he could hear Warrior give the order to retreat. He was going to be left there. His commander was not going to come to his aid.

Batter decided there was only one thing to do and that was surrender. He would not fight or give allegiance to the dark king who had promised to take his head. Having no flag of retreat, Batter rolled on his back and showed his belly. It was the universal sign of surrender between animals. No animal would fail to honor it. No words were needed. It had been passed down as body language before animals could speak.

The battle was over. Batter and the few wolves left alive were gathered together and herded to the meeting house.

Inside they found five other dark wolves tied to the rafters. Soon they were tied with them.

"There's the brave wolf who surrendered," Dropper said. "We saw you through the window."

"Warrior called retreat and left us. I will not give my life for one who will not give his for me."

"The king was here?"

"We were only a small patrol," Batter said.

"That explains it. He will be back," Dropper announced with confidence to the others.

"And just how did you come to be caught?"

Dropper smiled wryly and let it go. This new wolf had guts.

Within the week Warrior had arranged a parley with the white wolves. He wanted an exchange for his sons, Stoner and Strider, and he would bring two white wolf cubs, Tristian and Challenger.

"There's your great hero," Batter told his companion when the news of the bargain reached them. "He bargains only for his sons and not his fighters."

"Well, I heard that the Great King, Khoa of the West, is coming to meet with him. He is breaking off his campaign of liberating the towns to come back here."

"So you were taken, vanquished by Khoa here? There are not many of you left," Batter said.

"He fights with a zeal I have never seen in a wolf. His whole army sweeps like a vapor into your bones, and dries them up," Dropper said.

Batter looked away at this point. He had experienced a similar feeling when he had surrendered. His very bones had felt drained to the marrow.

"You fear the white wolves?" he asked Dropper.

Dropper nodded and said, "Surprised? They are not the weak wolves of legend which Warrior and Snuffer speak of. I can see how they defeated the black wolves in the last war. They are a bold lot."

A moment later Dropper walked to the window. "Look, here comes Warrior with four wolves, but I don't see any white wolf cubs with him."

"There are no white wolf cubs," Batter announced. "He came into the Eastern fort empty handed. He lost half of his army in the canyon when the dam broke and washed them away like so much sand." The other wolves looked at him, but he could see tell from their faces that fear gripped them.

As Warrior walked across the compound with his wolves, he was thinking of the last time he had seen Khoa. Over five years had passed. Would he recognize him as Deuces' son? The door opened and out stepped two wolves, but they weren't white wolves. A sharp whistle brought twenty wolves from the compound into formation behind them.

The dark wolf realized the white wolf he wanted to see wasn't there. "Where is Khoa?"

"I stand in for him."

Warrior kept looking at the mixed wolf. He was familiar, but the wolf could not place him.

"Who are you?"

"I am Scout."

Yes, thought Warrior, one of the wolves from his own Liar who had betrayed them in the last war of the Blackstone's.

"You are not a true white wolf."

"Nor am I," the other reddish wolf said.

As soon as the second wolf spoke, Warrior knew who it was. He tried to hide the fact that he was startled, but knew it showed. He looked at the wolf more closely now, sizing him up. Retread was more muscular and stouter than when he had seen him last. He looked sure and confident now. That's why he hadn't recognized him at first.

"Life among the white wolves has grown you into a fit looking wolf, brother."

"You did not come to see me, did you, Warrior? What do you want?"

"I came to speak with the King and they give me my own pack members. They have spit on me."

"Goodbye then," Scout said, and the two wolves turned. "Escort them out," he said to the warriors.

"Wait," Warrior shouted.

Scout put up his paw and the wolves halted.

Warrior said, "I have reason to believe that you have my sons. I came to find out if that was true. I came to say that I have sons of the king, of Tor." When he said the king's name he searched their faces to see if they knew of his death. They did not react and he felt safer.

"And who do you say you have?"

"Tristian and Challenger."

Scout looked at Fisher.

"What are your son's names? I'm not aware that we have anyone who belongs to you. We have captured only wolves from the camps and towns," Fisher said.

"No, they would not have been among the towns fighting. They were in a caravan of carts."

"The thieves you sent among us to steal our young?"

"Do you have them, yes or no?"

"Bring us proof that the white cubs are alive and we will talk," Scout offered.

"I need incentive to barter as well, mixed wolf. Why should I go to all that trouble if Stoner and Strider are no longer living?"

Scout looked at Fisher again, who nodded. "They are alive."

"We know that four white wolf cubs were found dead. Bring proof that Khoa and Tor's sons live."

So they had been the ones to place the tree bridge there, Warrior decided when he heard the word of the dead cubs. White wolves had been in their territory and had not been seen or noticed. Batter was a crazy wolf, one who loved to kill, and that's why he had left him in charge. He was sure that Batter's wantonness to kill would keep him patrolling the woods and protect the fortress. He had been wrong. Batter's craziness was also his downfall because it made him careless in the bargain.

"I want to see Stoner and Strider," he demanded.

"They are not here."

Warrior stared at the two white wolves. He tried to keep his anger under control. Seeing Retread have the upper hand against him was proving to be a hard test. He was just about to step forward and challenge him, make him back down like he had in the past when he remembered that Scout had said,' Khoa's son.'

"You said one of the white cubs was Khoa's?"

"You didn't know that?" Scout asked.

"Of course, but they wouldn't tell us which one was which," he stammered. Now that he knew one of the cubs was definitely Khoa's. It must be the one named Tristian. He should have guessed by the name alone. He was angry at himself for letting his tongue wag by itself without his consent. *What had made him speak?* Ever since he had been in camp, he had not felt like he had been in control of his faculties, or at the very least, not quite sure of himself. He should have planned things more fully before approaching them. At least Khoa had not been there to witness it. His enemies were looking at him, waiting for him to react. *Why was he not in control? Was this the magic of the white wolves that kept him silent when he wished to speak, and made him speak words when he didn't want to?*

"Bring the cubs to the river crossing where the great tree has fallen. Be there in ten days. We will be on this side of the water with your sons," Scout said.

"Ten days," Warrior found himself saying.

Scout motioned for his wolves to move and they escorted Warrior and his party out of the city limits of Fen, through the forest, and all the way to the river crossing. The dark wolves waiting in the forest were astonished when they saw the escort of white wolves behind Warrior.

"Make no move against them," Warrior called loud enough for them to hear. "We make an exchange for our sons."

Once they had crossed the river by way of the tree, the dark wolf stood and watched. The wolves who had escorted them stayed on the other side and set up camp. "They know the direction of our attack now," one of the dark wolves, who stood beside Warrior, remarked. The leader drew his sword and struck the wolf's paw. Then he and his fighter wolves moved into the forest; leaving the fallen wolf.

The groans of the wolf reached the other side of the river.

"What has happened?" Drew called out to the dark wolf.

"My paw is gone. My paw is gone."

"Cross over and we will help you."

Gripper continued to lay there and groan, afraid to cross over to the wolves, but soon the pain became so unbearable that he crossed the log despite his fear of the enemy. As he hobbled and stumbled over the trunk of the tree, the white wolves could see his paw hanging from as if by a thread and the blood pour from it.

Ossie, Ani's brother, who had been trained as a healer wolf, ran forward to help him. "Prepare the herbs," he called back. "His paw is still attached."

Once they reached the other side, Gripper dropped. "We're going to give you some herbs to help you sleep."

"I don't want any herb to make me sleep."

"It'll take the pain away."

"Are you sure?" The dark wolves' eyes searched Ossie's. He was a young wolf.

Ossie nodded. "You want us to try and save your leg don't you? You have a long life ahead of you."

"Why are you helping me? I'm the enemy."

"Have you done anything to me?"

Gripper shook his head.

"Then how can we be enemies?"

JoJo brought the herbs in a pan of water. "Drink this mixture," he directed the hurt wolf. "I know the fear of the dark wolves against their leaders. I was raised among the black wolves when I was a pup. With the same wolf that tried to cut your paw off."

"Whose line are you?"

"We are sons of Scout and Sara who were taken into captivity by Deuce after the Great War."

"I have heard of him."

"Good things, I trust?" Ossie said with a tight smile.

"Not so," the dark wolf answered with a smirk.

Ossie pushed the pan with the herb water in it closer to the wolf and he lapped it up.

"I noticed that you are not full white wolves. It was your father who left with Khoa from the Lair and established the kingdom of the white wolves. It was him that talked to Warrior at Fen."

Ossie nodded. "What's your name?"

"Gripper. Whew, I'm feeling really sleepy."

"Let go, Gripper. You will be a new wolf when you wake up."

Ossie watched as the dark wolf closed his eyes. "Get the paw cleaned. It was sliced through the bone, but clean, and it hangs on by a thread. I think we can sew it on and set a splint. The bone may knit itself back together."

"Lucky swipe. It missed all the joints," JoJo said.

When word reached Khoa about the trade, he was in Black Loop, just forty miles from the Black Ribbon Road, which tied the two fortresses together. His plan was to take all the towns on this side of the Spider River and then all settlements to the north and west. Next he would take the main fort of Blackstone itself where Tor and Winter had been held. This would cut off the flanking maneuver of the black wolves and force them all back towards the east to the big water fort.

"Things are going so well I wonder if this is a ploy to halt our retaking of the western edge of the realm," Khoa told his sergeant. "We've done it so quickly."

The sergeant didn't say anything as Khoa stared off into the distance. Soon Khoa turned towards him. "Could you continue with the warriors?"

"I was hoping you would ask that, Khoa. We've got the momentum and surprise. Why stop?"

"Agreed. I will travel back with the runner alone."

"Take the time you need. The towns aren't well defended. Only a handful of guards and a few wolves to keep order."

"It is a better day now than when the sun came up," Khoa said, looking up at the sky.

Word had traveled through the ranks quickly and the warriors cheered and waved as Khoa and the runner passed by them, calling out the names of Tristian and Challenger.

Tor was there to greet Khoa when he arrived back at Fienix. He was walking better, but still limped noticeably.

"I can't seem to keep the stiffness out of it," he said to Khoa, but his voice was strong and full of promise. There was happiness in his eyes.

"The cold and dampness of the season won't help any."

The time was well into fall and the forest was turning from green to amber hues of orange, brown, and yellow. The leaves had become dry and brittle. Their life sap having been cut off, they surrendered to the winds hands and fell to earth. The days were shorter now and cold. The forest held a stillness that was not felt in the summer season. It was as if the leaves demanded reverence at their falling, and warned the earth itself that all things fade and are no more. Nature spoke in this way to all creatures, reminding them how brief life was.

The two wolves walked in silence along the path until Tor asked, "Do you believe it is our cubs? That both of them survived?"

"To a certain point I am permitting myself to, but I am not letting it run away with me."

"Wise."

"It is you that has made me wise, Tor. I have thought about what you said, and I have a question for you. One from the spirit in me. One I should have asked you long before. I was raised by Tristian and taught of the Book and the Alpha, but you had no one to teach or guide you, yet you have a deeper reverence."

"You're wondering how that can be? I did have a teacher, Khoa. I did have someone who raised me. The same one our lost sons have now."

Khoa looked quizzically at him.

"The Great Wolf himself." Tor said. "That is how I know they are in better hands than ourselves."

"You do not think our sons have been raised by the black wolves, been influenced by them?"

"I see the Great Wolf's paw all over them, brother. Just as I see it on you."

"Clearly you had the better teacher."

"Not better. It is harder to argue with the Great Wolf than with mortal wolfs."

Khoa laughed. "Yes. I'm sure old Tristian was worn weary at times with me.

"Come, I want to talk to this black wolf who had his paw nearly chopped off. I waited for you to come so we could meet with him together."

As they walked to the building which was serving as the healing place, Tor filled his brother in on the story of the black wolf Ossie and JoJo had helped.

"The boys think that he could be a convert," Tor said just before they entered the room.

Gripper eyed the wolves as they approached him. They were larger wolves than he thought they would be. Powerful and sure. The color of their blue eyes drew him in. He noticed that one of the wolves walked with a limp in his back flank.

When the wolves reached him Tor said, "I see you're on the mend."

"I see you are, too," Gripper answered.

"Yes, wounded from the same source, I understand."

Gripper did not fully understand what Tor had said, but took it to mean that he had been wounded by a sword also, and said, "There is much magic among the white wolves." He struggled to his feet by rolling on to his right side, and using his right paw and back legs to stand on. The dark wolf did not put any weight on his injured paw and held it curled above the ground.

"It's not magic, but knowledge," Tor corrected him.

Standing face to face with the white wolves, Gripper asked, "Why do you heal the black wolves, or any of these wolves? We black wolves believe it is merciful to let an animal die and kill him if necessary."

"How do you feel having had your paw saved? Having been given a life that you may run again, hunt, and not die?" Khoa asked him.

"Grateful. Close to the heart of my enemy."

"That's the way the Great Wolf meant it. Return the same kindness to another when it is needed."

"I have seen what the white wolves are like and it is very different from the way we live."

"Better or worse?" Khoa laughed.

"If you chose life, then better. It is without strife among yourselves."

"Let's go where we can talk," Tor said.

The two white wolves turned and went out, and Gripper followed them to a tree near the old prayer building. Gripper told them he had been born a year after the Blackstone War five years ago. His father had been killed and he had been put into training as a pup. He had not seen his mother since. "They told us that although it hurt not to see your parents, it hurt worse if you did see them," Gripper said looking down. He looked up suddenly and changed the subject. "What can I do to repay you?" His voice was now more direct.

"Tell us what you know about our sons."

"I will, but I'm afraid I don't know much. I was not of high office or rank."

There was silence between them for a while before Gripper spoke again in a low, slow voice.

"I do not think they have your sons."

"What makes you say that?" asked Tor.

Gripper fixed his gaze firmly on the wolf's blue eyes. "When Warrior returned to the Eastern Fort from the Blackstone's, he had no prisoners with him. Since Strider and Stoner had not returned from stealing the young ones, we set out to look for them. 'Course there was talk of prisoners, but not who or how many, and certainly no talk of kings' sons. Some way or another, Warrior found out that his sons were in your hands. Probably from the prisoners he had. We don't usually take prisoners, so if the patrol had run across them they would have put an end to them after they got the information they wanted."

"Yes, I found four dead white wolves halfway between the crossing and the fort," Khoa said.

"That would be Batter's handy work. Talk to him. You've got him prisoner."

"That's good to know. Thank you for what you were able to tell us," Tor said.

Gripper looked at them and then away for a moment. "Let me say again, I seen no pups. I heard no plans of a ransom for Kings' sons until I stood here in this camp."

"Tomorrow we will know for certain," Khoa said.

"One more thing. The Blackstone Fortress has been abandoned, I think. Tribald, the eastern king has fled. When he came to take possession of it, and was told of what happened when the white king was killed, he broke off his alliance I heard, but do not know for sure."

Justice led Gripper back to his sick ward and Khoa said, "I wonder what they would say seeing you in the flesh, Tor."

"It would be a matter of great delight," he answered.

It was during the night that Fisher and Scout returned from the Wilds with Stoner and Strider and brought them to the school where Khoa had set up headquarters. This time Khoa looked the dark wolves over more closely. Yes, there were some family resemblances now that he watched the wolves move so warily about; always on their guard. Stoner seemed to be the less nervous of the two, and Khoa elected to talk with him. He put Strider in a building alone. There was no need to alert the other dark wolves that the sons of Warrior were now in their camp.

"Welcome Stoner, son of Warrior," Khoa said as he approached the wolf. The wolf faltered and halted in his tracks and answered, "So that is why you moved us. You know who we are and have brought us here to kill us."

"We have a proposition for you," Tor said moving closer.

The dark wolf backed up.

"No need for fear."

"You make me feel like a shadow when you stand close to me."

Tor circled the wolf. He was frail of frame and thin. Clearly neither he nor his brother were of fighter status. Warrior had not raised his sons to take over, he thought.

"I want to know who the white wolves and the animals that got away that day were."

"I don't know. They ran away on the other side of the river."

"You want to live, don't you?" Tor could see the wolf's eyes light up with interest. "I take you to a trade with your father if our sons live," he said, and let his voice trail off before raising it again. "Or I ask your brother and give him the opportunity."

"Who got away that day?" the white wolf asked in a forceful tone.

"You're really going to set me free?"

"Talk."

"Step back and give me room to breathe."

Tor moved back a few steps, and Stoner told him the story of the raccoon untying the bags and how the animals ran away. "There were four white wolves that ran into the forest before the others. Two or three white wolves headed south with a group of animals, and two went off with the raccoon that had untied the bags." That was all he told the white wolves, he did not want them to know he had anything to do with them along the journey. They might take it out on him.

"There were three separate groups of white wolves who fled that day?"

Stoner nodded. "Yes, three groups that left from the shore."

Tor looked at his brother and then turned to Fisher, "Tie him inside here. Keep them separated."

"How about some food," Stoner said as the brothers walked away.

"I'll give you the leftovers from our breakfast," Fisher teased. "From what I hear, that's better than you gave those you held prisoners."

"It's possible that they may be alive," Tor said when the door closed. "From what he said there are maybe four or five white cubs still left out there and more than a dozen or so other animals."

"Yes, at least he spoke the truth. We have heard all that before."

He looked over at the training ground and yelled for the sergeant.

"Send two units ahead and have them wait in the forest where they can't be seen. They will be our reserves if Warrior decides to do anything. Have a runner tell Ossie the warriors are there to back him up and to fall back to their line in case of trouble."

"Yes, he'll be glad to know that he isn't being left to manage things by himself," the sergeant said.

"Have Sure Claw fly back here when they have seen the cubs to let us know the trade is on. Then we'll move out with Stoner and leave Striker behind until we have exchanged the first cub."

"Yes, sir," the sergeant said and turned to leave.

"There's nothing to do but wait now," Tor said to his brother.

"That's the hardest part," Khoa answered.

"Let's take a turn around the compound to keep you settled, Khoa."

It was almost light when the wolves stepped onto the parade grounds. No animals stirred except the white wolves who were preparing to move out. The population was still leery of the new wolves and did not believe that their freedoms had been restored. Up to now they had only ventured out in groups to drink water from the creek. Khoa couldn't blame them. Their town lay in ruins and they were near starvation. He had ordered that a feast be organized to bring all of them together. The first feast was to be held tonight. He saw some of the arrangements had already been set up.

When the sun came up, its light was dulled behind a wall of gray that promised rain. The air was thick and heavy; coating everything with its dampness, holding the leaves to the ground where they had fallen. The musty smell of the leaves and the wet earth filled their nostrils. A faint trace of pine needles helped lighten the heavy scent of the decaying leaves. A taste of snow was in the air.

It was past noon when Sure Claw was spotted overhead. The sun was visible as a small ball behind the clouds; its glare barely lighter than the sky around it. Khoa and Tor headed for their headquarters and arrived just as Sure landed on the railings of the porch.

"War. It's war," he exclaimed, flapping his wings to help him balance on the rail.

"The cubs?" Khoa asked as they went inside.

Sure shook his head.

"Warrior and Snuffer met with Ossie. They told him that the cubs had escaped from the unit left behind after the dam had burst in the canyon. A unit of black wolves had been ordered to catch the deserters and Tristian and Challenger were with them. When another unit was sent to find the unit who did not return, they were told that a hunched back wolf named Quirk had disappeared with the prisoners."

"How did war start from that?" asked Tor.

Sure was still shaking his head. "The four wolves were on the log crossing and all of a sudden JoJo falls into the water off the log with a yelp, and Ossie is pulling him up and saying to the dark wolves, ' "Go home. We have nothing for you." ' Then Warrior raised his paw and dark wolves started pouring over the log."

"Ossie and JoJo?"

"Our side ran forward to meet the charge. Some wolves got them to the safety of the trees, but they'll need reinforcements."

Tor grabbed the oryx and blew three short blasts which brought the white wolves on to the parade ground. Khoa was at the front and they moved out at the gallop. As Tor and Sure watched the troops, the wolf turned to the osprey. "Gather the warriors Khoa left behind to free the other settlements. Bring them back here." Tor watched Sure's dark shape against the white sky until it disappeared.

"Lieutenant," he called. "Put this one in with his brother."

"White wolves are liars. You go back on your deal," Stoner cried out.

Tor limped slowly to the creek and stepped in. He stood letting the icy coldness relieve the pain in his back flank. If only it was as easy to quell the pain in his heart, he thought. The cubs would not be coming home. He should have expected the outcome given the history of the black wolves. Still it was a great defeat.

Before Khoa and his warriors came around the bend in the road to the log bridge, they could smell the blood, but there were no sounds of battle. As they turned the corner onto the straight part of the road, they saw the carnage in front of them. Hundreds of bodies of both black and white wolves lay entangled together. He saw Ossie tending the wounded and dropped out to talk with him, sending his warriors on to help with the cleanup. Clearly the battle was over. There was no sign of the black wolves on the other side. It would do no good to set chase to them now.

JoJo had been struck with a rock from a sling shot in the chest which had thrown him off balance and into the river, but he was fine. Apparently Warrior had been angry when he found out that his sons had not been brought to the river. He had wanted to see if it was true, and had sent a few wolves over the tree to find them. Things got out of hand and led to the battle.

"When he found out that his sons were really not here, he broke and ran," Ossie said. "I guess he thought we lied to him after he informed us he didn't have Tristian or Challenger to trade with."

Khoa left his friends side and went to the shore of the river. Across its waters lay the path to the eastern fort, and he wondered if the cubs were alive, or if it was them which lay buried under the half fish sign carved into the tree. If they were alive, Warrior would have brought them. The more he thought about it, the more convinced he was that Tor and Challenger were dead.

He turned from the river and looked on the aftermath of the battle. As he walked among the dead, a cold rain began to fall. Even nature was weeping, he thought. Near by a pit had been dug and both black and white wolves were thrown into it together. Their bodies lay side by side now and quiet. Death had made peace possible between them. How could life make it possible? The white wolves believed in the Great Wolf who would one day bring justice to the earth. It was not in the hands of mortal wolves do to so. The black wolves put themselves above the Great Wolf, and said it was they who would bring justice to all creatures on the earth. Peace between them would not be possible. Their ways of thinking were different. The dark wolves saw ridding themselves from the laws of the Great Wolf as freedom, yet enslaved themselves to the rulers of the black wolf. They had merely exchanged what they considered enslavement to the Great Wolf for enslavement to the black wolves, and in the process had lost their freedom and their wolfhood. Why couldn't they see that?

By nightfall of the next day, Warrior had made it back to the Lake Fortress and was cursing the deserters and the wolves who had captured them. "How could you have let a hunchbacked old wolf outwit you?" His voice was full of derision. "You have killed my sons and started a war that I fear is one in which much more sacrifice is required than I wish to make."

Musty looked at the king. "Stoner and Striker are dead?"

"I don't know, but why would they let them live now when they think we have deceived them? How can this be? I give them the truth and it turns into war."

"You told them the truth?"

"Yes, isn't it a joke?" Warrior asked pounding his fist on the table.

At exactly that moment, a guard at the door was saying, "King Tribald. You can't go into the court just now."

"I will do what I will, or my Captains will have your head," Tribald screamed, pushing the guard aside.

"Guard, take these deserters to the holding cells," he whispered, and then turned towards the on rushing wolf and his retinue.

"Tribald! I see you have urgent business."

"No business. Just an announcement. I have seen your fort. I have seen your army and I am withdrawing to my land."

Warrior stood silent as Tribald's wolves threw the sacks of money onto the floor and all walked away.

"King Tribald, surely we can work this out. If it's more money you need, I will..."

"Hold your tongue, black wolf," Tribald called back without looking, "or I will think you play me for a fool and you start a war right here. Right now."

"I don't understand," Warrior yelled.

"You have wakened sleeping dragons. I leave them to you."

When Tribald had left, Warrior sought an explanation from his own aid. He was told that an edict had been issued by Snuffer to attack the Wilds while they were trading for their sons at Fienix. There had not been many wolves to fight, only females and the young. Tribald had taken it as an affront to him and his army that he was sent to fight against she wolves and their young, and as treachery that they were being used by Snuffer for his own ends of getting your sons."

"Were Strider and Stoner gotten to?"

"No, they were not in the Wilds. It seems they had been taken out to trade for their own cubs at Lone Oak Crossing."

"They weren't there either! What are these devil dogs up to?"

"Do you wish me to continue?"

Warrior nodded.

"Tribald stopped the battle right after it started and vowed to end his alliance with us," Bern, Warrior's advisor, reported.

"It is said that after the battle he was given over to dreaming dreams and visions. Dreams of dragons and great death."

"If mere dreams frightened him, then he is a coward. I'm better to be done with him."

"He said the dream was a warning of prophecy. He was caught in the middle on the earth between the two planes of unseen forces from the heavens above and the pits below."

"Unseen is right."

"He said that when the unseen forces reached the earth they became visible. The great dragon turned on him from the bowels of the earth, the third realm, and then heaven reached down with its own hand and the stars fell from their places like rain. Then the place of thunder, the first realm, was moved against him, too. He was caught in the middle between them."

Warrior gave him a furrowed look of contempt.

"There are three planes of existence. The first and third realms above and below us are unseen. It is the middle plane of the earth, the second realm, where all is seen."

Warrior gave the advisor wolf a stern look. "I understood from your first explanation. I order you not to believe in this. You sound as if you did. Do not repeat this to anyone. Not even my brother."

"It is a prophecy from the white wolves Book concerning the three realms. I'm afraid it is common knowledge among the wolves who traveled with us back from the Blackstone's."

"Order them not to speak of this stupidity. Where is their common sense? Tell them the wolf that dares even breathe a word about realms and dragons will be executed."

The advisor departed with the words, "As you order, Warrior. No stupidity. Common sense must prevail or death."

"You mock me?"

"No, Warrior. It is just that the web has begun to untangle. Tribald has had counsel with your brother. The death of Snuffer's sons has been talked about. Tribald is no fool. That is one of the reason's he has departed. Treachery in the king's court."

"Who saw you kill anyone?"

"No one these past five years, but coincidence is a poor excuse in these times. Walls have ears. It is four sons now that have met with death. Even Snuffer is getting wise."

"Now you tell me that walls have mouths also." He came closer to Bern. "Is Gambler dead?" Bern shook his head.

At the time Warrior was deciding what to do about his deserters, the loss of his allies, and the beginning suspicions of Snuffer, Khoa had made it back to Fen. Tor was sitting outside with a few other wolves. They had just been informed that the Wilds had been attacked by Tribald's army. It was a short battle and the dark wolves had left abruptly without destroying the Wilds.

The leftovers from the feast were brought out. Khoa, Ossie, and JoJo were given special attention by Scout and Fisher. They ate mostly in silence. Tor came down from the porch and sat beside Khoa. He gave his brother a pat on his back. "Time to go home," he said loud enough for all to hear. The warriors nodded in agreement.

"Time to prepare for killing dragons," Khoa added in a tone that made his brother flinch, but Tor kept his thoughts to himself. Khoa, too, was deep in thought. The dark wolves had invaded the Wilds. The force of protection that had surrounded them had been breached. He sensed it. The Great Wolf had moved his hand from them.

'No, Khoa. It is you that have left Him,' the voice said clearly. He ignored it, and in that moment his heart hardened.

"Why do you put it that way?" Tor asked.

"I have been dreaming of dragons since you left last spring."

"The Book speaks of dragons," Tor said. "Remember what it says?"

"I must have forgotten. Tell me." Again the voice came. 'You have forgotten many things. He who sets up kings, also releases dragons.'

Khoa could hear Tor reciting from memory over his thoughts, "Reality and eternity of the three planes lies in the first realm above and the third realm below. The third realm is where the great dragons wait chained. In the middle, on the earth, it is all shadow. In the end the dragons will come and none can stop them. They come onto the earth and are made real for a time and half a time."

"We'll stop them," Khoa said. "We have to."

"I'm confused," said Scout. "How is the earth shadow and real at the same time?"

"We see earth as real, but the Book warns us that it is illusion to believe in it, to absorb it into us as real. It is heaven and the pit which are the only true realities. It tells us this so we know this plane is not our destiny. So we don't count in anything or anyone that is in the second realm because it is without substance."

"You are given discernment among wolves, Tor."

"No, experience. I was there and passed through the planes in my time of sleeping. That is how I came to understand it."

Khoa looked around at his men. "To killing dragons."

The warriors lifted their voices in agreement. The pact that bonded them to each other and the future had been made.

"I almost have no heart to go on and fight," Scout said.

"We all feel the same," Tor said.

"Then how do we? What makes us go on?"

"Without something great for us to come together for like the war, or destroying the black wolves, the bond between us would not exist," Tor said. "Without this common foe our hearts would not be entwined."

"Those are noble words, Tor," Fisher said. "Truth."

"It is one of those twisted logic enigmas that the Book speaks of. We die, fight and kill, but out of it we find freedom and life," Tor said. Silence prevailed over the small group of warriors.

"Never forget, redemption lives outside of ourselves. It comes in spite of ourselves," Tor said.

Not one wolf spoke. Finally, Tor leaned over and whispered, "Let's go home, Khoa.

There was longing in his brother's voice, Khoa thought, but his last words carried a resignation that he was unwilling to accept. Khoa pushed his thoughts aside, and sent a runner to Meadows Edge to tell Pieces and the rest of the animals that they were going home to the Wilds because they had been attacked. It was time for them to journey home as well. They would keep a small training garrison in Fienix if anyone needed closer help. Climber's wife and children, and the other animals from Fen would journey with them. They would leave in the morning. It was dark when the runner set out to find the wild bunch. A cold rain misted on everything.

Two days later the morning sky was sullen and gray. The sun was completely hidden behind the thickness of clouds. The grass lay stiff beneath their feet. All color had vanished from the earth, and a thin layer of frost coated everything in white.

Part of the army got under way first, and then the families started out with their carts and donkeys. Khoa, Tor, and the rest of the warriors fell in at the tail end of the procession. They had waited for Pieces and the wild bunch for an extra day, but they had not come.

"I should go after them with a unit or so," Khoa said.

"They know the way," Tor answered.

It was not the time to run away, Khoa thought. It was the time to fight like they had never fought before, but everything spoke to him of defeat as he watched the long, slow movement of animals ahead of him round the first turn in the path.

"The cubs are gone to us, aren't they?" he asked.

"It was a short season," Tor said.

The retreating line of his army, and the rag tag band of civilians had barely made it into the trees when Khoa noticed the first snows of winter fall.

Also Available By Joan Walsh

The Wolf, the Watcher, and the Oryx
(The beast tale scrolls Book 1)